Murder in Geneva

A THIRD-CULTURE KID MYSTERY

MURDER IN GENEVA

D-L NELSON

FIVE STAR
A part of Gale, Cengage Learning

GALE
CENGAGE Learning®

Detroit • New York • San Francisco • New Haven, Conn • Waterville, Maine • London

GALE
CENGAGE Learning®

LIBRARY OF CONGRESS CATALOGING-IN-PUBLICATION DATA

Nelson, D. L., 1942–
    Murder in Geneva : a third-culture kid mystery / D-L Nelson.
    — 1st ed.
        p. cm.
    ISBN 978-1-4328-2616-1 (hardcover) — ISBN 1-4328-2616-6
(hardcover)
    1. Women authors—Fiction. 2. Murder—Investigation—Fic-
tion. I. Title.
PS3614.E4455M88 2012
813'.6—dc23   2012017581

First Edition. First Printing: October 2012.
Published in conjunction with Tekno Books and Ed Gorman.
Find us on Facebook– https://www.facebook.com/FiveStarCengage
Visit our website– http://www.gale.cengage.com/fivestar/
Contact Five Star™ Publishing at FiveStar@cengage.com

Printed in Mexico
1 2 3 4 5 6 7 16 15 14 13 12

To Mary and our absolutely ridiculous adventures

ACKNOWLEDGMENTS

Although I've lived in Geneva for almost two decades, this book had much help including Ariel Pierre Haemmerlé for his wonderful knowledge of old and new Geneva. Julia, of the twenty pages and three-plus decades living in Geneva, added information that only experiences different from mine could give. Certain books were great references: *Histoire de Genève* by P. Guichonnet (third edition, 1974, published by Edouard Privat) and a very limited and half-destroyed 1953 edition of *La Vie Dans Les Temps de Calvin,* written by a UN diplomat and found in a *marché aux puces* became my bible for information such as which streets existed in the 1500s, how medicine was practiced and other small details from the period. Personnel at the Reformation Museum, Tavel House and the Cathédrale de Saint Pierre filled in holes in my knowledge. And there are people without whom my life as a writer and as a human would be less rich: Susan Tiberghien, TCK Jennifer McDermott, TCK Scott Schmitz-Leuffen, Sylvia Petter and Llara Nelson, mostly for being who they are and understanding. And my editor Gordon Aalborg for his carrot-and-stick approach. For my Genevan friends, there is no new police station but most of the geography is correct.

CHAPTER 1

Geneva, Switzerland
October 27, 1553

The smell of burning wood and wool floated through the air. Then the odor of human flesh cooking wafted into the mixture. It reminded Elizabeth of feast days and meat turning on a spit. She shuddered: knowing a man was about to die in agony, the sixteen-year-old couldn't stop herself from wanting to see. She stood on tiptoe to peer over the heads of the crowd.

The wood crackled and the flames rose higher and higher as the huge stack of wood caught and shot yellow spikes against the gray sky. Everything but the fire was gray: the clothing of the witnesses, the frosted ground, the sky, gravel and stones as well as the leafless trees.

The babble of the crowd stopped the second the faggots were lit. Elizabeth had expected to hear cries, but the victim, Michel Servetus, was as silent as the crowd.

She should not be here. If her uncle caught her she would be punished, but she risked his temper to see the man who had dared to challenge Calvin on the Trinity.

When the subject of Servetus came up at the dinner table, Elizabeth had to hold her tongue. She had too many heretical ideas herself. Much of religion did not make sense to her, but she would never say it. Expressing doubts was far too dangerous. Too often what God wanted seemed to match what the people in power wanted, another thought best kept to herself.

What made someone feel so strongly that they would sacrifice their life for it? There was nothing she believed in so much that she would be willing to die. What was he feeling? How much could flames hurt before he would pass out, pass away?

Because she was shorter than the people standing in the six rows in front of her, she couldn't see. She pushed, twisted and moved through the crowd heading up the knoll without looking at any of the faces she passed. She was disgusted that they wanted to see the gore and mad at herself for being like them.

"Elizabeth, what are you doing here?" It was Jean-Michel, the young man who lived next door to the house of her aunt and uncle. Elizabeth had been forced to move in with them after her mother and brother died this past January: her father had disappeared last year. Her aunt and uncle raged on that it was improper for a young woman to live on her own.

Jean-Michel's hands were discolored by the inks that he used as he learned the printing trade, the trade that would eventually give them a good life together if he had his way.

She pulled the hood of her cape closer over her face—half to protect herself from the chilly October air and half to not be recognized. She really didn't want Aunt Mathilde and Uncle Jacques to discover she had been here. They disapproved of everything about her, from her posture during prayers, to the spelling of her name with z instead of s—given by her English mother—to the half-English blood running in her veins. She never was as good or as obedient as their children—her cousins. From seven births and seven miscarriages, which followed too closely one after another, three boys and two girls had survived. Her aunt seemed to never know a nonpregnant year.

"Wild child," they called her, even though at sixteen she was more woman than child. They employed other terms: Satan's offspring, clumsy, hopeless, disobedient were those most often dropping from their lips.

"Don't tell my aunt and uncle you saw me," she said.

"It's our secret." Jean-Michel followed her further up the hill where they had a better view of the burning. He bent over and kissed her on the cheek.

"Don't," she said. "If anyone sees us . . ."

He nodded. "If you would let me talk to your uncle about marrying . . ."

"Not yet." Her eyes were riveted on the scene below. The flames were so thick, it was impossible to see what or whom they were burning. She did not know how to tell him that she did not want to marry, which made her completely out of step with every other young woman living in Geneva. She knew her childhood had made her different from others. No matter how hard she tried, she could not think the way her aunt, uncle and neighbors did. Although she was able to hide her ideas and mimic their behaviors, too often she was caught out and earned a lashing either with her aunt's tongue or a broomstick.

She felt nothing but love for Jean-Michel. Looking at his face made her eyes, soul and heart happy. The problem was marriage itself. Although her parents had been wonderful together, most couples that she knew, not just her aunt and uncle, grew sourer as their years together increased. She would rather be without Jean-Michel than have *that* happen.

When she was little she loved to listen to her father tell her how he had met and married her mother while he was on a mission to England as an *avocat* for the new Swiss watch industry. Her childhood had been strange by city standards, having been raised just outside the city walls near Plainpalais. Instead of having to be as circumspect as her aunt thought all young girls should be, she had been allowed to run through the fields and the nearby forest.

In summer she would be tanned and her black hair would get tangled because she hated wearing a bonnet. Her mother tried to comb out the knots, which hurt. Tired of the battle, her mother gave her a choice: do it herself or cut them out. She had chosen to cut them, so she was the only little girl with short hair, shocking her aunt almost into unusual speechlessness when the family had visited one Sunday.

All that ended when her father never returned from his last trip to England. A letter, which arrived two months after his departure, only showed that he had gotten off the boat and bought a horse to ride to London. And that he had asked someone to write and send the letter for him, which was strange, because usually when he went on a trip, he wrote her mother at least once a week himself.

Her mother suspected that he had been robbed, for he had been carrying dozens of watches, samples for British jewelers to take to court, fulfilling contracts he had negotiated on earlier trips. Had Calvin not forbidden jewelry, and the jewelers thus forced to find new products, her father would never have left the country but would have continued solving the small legal battles that he and her uncle undertook for the local burghers.

But, then, he would never have met her mother, and Elizabeth would never have been born, and as hard as her life was now, she never even thought about that possibility, because she was still able to snatch moments of joy when her aunt and uncle weren't looking.

What made her the happiest was drawing. Her mother had encouraged her and on many a winter night the two of them would sit by the fire and draw. Sometimes the sketch would be of a pot or pan, another time of the dog curled up in a ball. Sometimes they made up designs.

This was a pastime to be hidden, lest her aunt once again lecture her on the state of her soul. Sometimes she smuggled her work over to Jean-Michel or to Antoine, the shoemaker, keeping the papers under her clothes. Sometimes she stashed the uncompleted work between the mattress of her bed and the ropes supporting it.

Bless Antoine. Two months ago he had offered her his room above his shop as a place where she could draw whenever she could escape chores.

She knew something was wrong with her. Why couldn't she accept that a person's fate, including where they would go in the afterlife, was decided at birth and there was nothing one could do about it? If she were damned why should she deny herself the pleasures that were possible and if she were not damned and nothing would change why deny the pleasures that were possible? She knew better than to ever voice these thoughts, even to Jean-Michel.

A light mist began to fall and the crowd seemed restless as if they were afraid it would put out the fire and destroy the spectacle of the heretic's death. In listening to her aunt and uncle talk about Servetus, she didn't understand the antipathy. That he was so well-travelled, a doctor and multilingual should have given his opinion more weight instead of his knowledge being used to destroy him.

Not that she was included in the conversations when clergy, lawyers and the city fathers were at her uncle's table. But, from the kitchen below, she could listen to the conversation through a fault in the narrow house that made it possible—if one were very, very still—to hear dining-room talk.

When her father and her mother were alive and the family was forced to go into Geneva for dinner between Sunday services, her father and uncle often argued about religion. Her father told her mother that the only reason that he spoke to his brother at all was that their legal practice had been so success-ful—supposedly a sign of God's blessing—that splitting it in two would hurt their finances. Her father and uncle did agree on one thing: her father should be sent to this or that land to negotiate contracts for watches as it reduced their chances of an argument over religion, one that could not be healed. At the same time his trips increased their profits.

Her father was as much of an anomaly as was her mother. Neither was religious. Her mother said that the way religion changed at the mere whim of a monarch made her doubt a participatory God. She had had an unorthodox childhood as the daughter of an Oxford scholar who ended up a church historian and teacher at Saint George's Church in Beckenham when Henry VIII had changed England's religion. She thought the back and forth between Protestantism and Catholicism was an example of the stupidity of man. Her viewpoints, according to her father, were what had attracted him. If ever there was a *coup de foudre*, love at first sight, it was their couple. He'd teased her mother that her "twisted" religious views made her all the more of a catch for him, but "please, please don't aggravate my brother by talking about them."

Thus Elizabeth had grown up to music and discussions of art and literature, with a bit of animal husbandry thrown in. When they had visitors from other parts of the world, people who were free thinkers not bound by the limits of time and place, the conversation would become animated and often last the entire night, with the guests falling asleep as dawn broke.

Elizabeth's younger brother had died of a *grippe* last winter. Her mother, struck by the same illness, followed shortly afterwards. Elizabeth had watched her mother's spirits fade with the surmised death of her husband and the real passing of the son that she adored.

Sometimes Elizabeth felt that she had not been enough to make her mother want to live. Her mother's last words, as she slipped from life to death: "At least your father didn't have to suffer through our boy's death." There wasn't a final word for Elizabeth, although during Anne Smythe's life she had been a loving mother, full of hugs, smiles and praise falling from her lips for her firstborn and only daughter on a daily basis.

At her parents' death the chains had been tightened, and she tried to be grateful to her aunt and uncle for taking her in, no matter how they emphasized the burdens she caused.

Her aunt lost no time in introducing Elizabeth to the household arts. Her free time, considered a tool of the devil, was so curtailed that she could do little of what she wanted. Had she not been sent to the butcher at Place du Molard and given other errands, she would never have been able to come to the burning.

The wind picked up, not the *Bise,* the wind that could cause trees to uproot and water to fly from Lac Léman when it was at its strongest, but just a normal wind. And the mist turned to drizzle.

"Maybe God does not think Servetus should die?" Jean-Michel said in a whisper although no one was near enough to hear. The crowd was still straining to see the burning. Elizabeth tried to seal the images in her mind to put down on paper. She would have a long wait, because she was out of paper.

"Do you need more paper?" Jean-Michel asked. He supplied her as often as he could, usually from scraps that the press had torn or wrinkled. He also gave her makeshift pencils—lead wrapped in string. Every now and then he would have her try his latest experiment with beeswax and various pigments that he molded into squares until she suggested making them into cylinders. When she has these she could add color to her drawings.

"I always need paper."

The crowd started to disperse as the force of the rain increased. She could see that Servetus's remains had slumped on top of the charred beams. The rope that had held him to the stake must have burned through and unless someone looked closely he looked no different than a charred piece of wood.

CHAPTER 2

Geneva, Switzerland

Annie Young punched her birth year and the letter A into the code box outside the apartment building.

Nothing.

She tried B and her birth year.

Damn.

She punched in the four numbers of the building and an A as the taxi's rear lights disappeared down the road.

They must have changed the code, which had been so easy to remember. Unlike some of the other buildings in the complex this one had no intercom. She was not going to knock on the windows of any of the ground-floor residents. Even the concierge would be long asleep at this hour. She should have been here hours ago, but the train from Argelès had been late due to yet another strike, albeit one that only lasted three hours and was only in the south: she missed her connection in Lyon, and the train to Geneva from Lyon had left after 11 P.M. Her feelings on the strikes were mixed: she admired people who would not accept less than optimum working conditions and salaries, but was annoyed when it inconvenienced her.

Only one taxi had been parked outside the train station. She had grabbed it with a silent thank-you to whatever fate had encouraged the driver to stay. The area was spooky that late at night. Even the kids who hung out in hopes of scoring drugs had gone home or to whatever squat they were occupying.

Although she had walked the distance from the train station to this building many, many times when she had once lived there, she had a large suitcase and her laptop. Pulling them up the Route de Ferney hill hadn't been something she had wanted to do.

She tried another combination.

Still there was no click. Hoping she had just not heard the click, she pushed against the glass. Nothing budged.

At least it wasn't raining, but it was foggy and cold, not surprising for Geneva in October. Geneva, Genf, Genève, *gray, grau, gris* . . . all G words for the same place and the same thing. This was not the time to be poetic.

Pulling out her cell phone she dialed Mireille, the woman subletting her old flat six floors above. The condition of the sublet was that Annie could stay when necessary. In Geneva where fifty applicants could show up for one vacant apartment, Mireille, who had been Annie's friend at the University of Geneva and her coworker at their first job after graduation at Carsonwell Auctioneers, had thought it a wonderful solution especially since Annie stayed so seldom.

When she was in Geneva, Annie normally went to her parents in Corsier Port on the other side of the city. But the senior Youngs had been in Caleb's Landing for the summer and fall and weren't expected back until December 1. Not that Annie couldn't have crashed there without them being home, but the place had been let on a short-term rental to an executive from one of the multinationals moving into the city until the house the company was building for the family could be completed.

No answer. She had e-mailed Mireille that she was coming in and had left a message on the answering machine earlier that her train was delayed.

She could always go to the Intercontinental Hotel down the street but she did not fancy lugging her suitcase and laptop downhill any more than she wanted to do it uphill. She could call a cab, but the cab fare from the station had taken all her Swiss francs.

"Vous-êtes chez Mireille. Je ne peux pas répondre, mais laissez un message. Je vous rappelerai."

"Pick up Mireille. Are you there? Pick up, pick up."

"Annie, is that you?"

She whirled around to face a teenage boy with brown hair and eyes. In the light that illuminated the area by the front door she could see the grin that she had known from the time he was missing his front teeth in his first year of school. But that was eleven years ago and his teeth were now perfect. Despite his thinness, the handsome man he would become was hiding under the pimply skin.

"Marc!"

"It had to be you. Who else has uncontrollable red curls halfway down her back?"

She resisted saying "you've grown," because he had told her often enough he hated people telling him that. However, the last time he had been with her at least three years ago, he had measured himself against her and they had been level. Now he was a good six inches taller and instead of being pudgy, he had slimmed down and toned up as far as she could tell from his open jacket. "I can't get in."

"The code is 7272B now. They just changed it last week, again. If Mireille isn't home how will you get into the flat?"

"I've the key unless she's changed the locks."

The lobby with its banks of mailboxes on each side felt welcoming warm. As usual, it was spot-free, thanks to the concierge who considered a speck of dirt a personal affront. Two plants, bigger than the last time she was there, neither of which Annie could identify, broke the monotony of the paneled walls.

Two elevators, one small and one large, were on each side of the stairwell. Annie had no intention of walking up six flights and automatically headed to the smaller one. Her flat was on that side of the building.

"What are you doing here?" Marc pressed the button calling the elevator.

"I've a short-term job at Carsonwell's. They've a catalog they want translated from French to English, German and Dutch. Some prince needs money and he's selling paintings, furniture, probably his wife too."

"But I thought you only did tech writing and translations."

"I worked for Conrad, he's the owner, when I was first out of university. Don't you remember?" she asked as Marc pushed button six, the floor where they both lived.

Marc had befriended Annie when he could only reach button four and had to walk up two flights from the fourth floor to his own flat. He often turned up at her apartment after dinner to tell her about his school, his problems, and to show her the latest adventure *bande dessinée* that he had just acquired.

In the elevator where more than three people turned into sardines, she smelled alcohol. "You've been drinking."

"I was at a friend's with some *copains.*"

"And your parents will kill you."

"My mother is at some meeting in New York till tomorrow, and I don't know where my father is. He took off a couple of days ago for work and hasn't come back."

Annie did not care for either of Marc's parents. His mother was from Uruguay, his father from the Swiss Canton of Schwyz. Herr Professor Dr. Urs Stoller never mentioned where he came from without reminding any foreigner that it was one of the original three cantons that banded together to form the country in 1291. Some people, especially those who were meeting him for the first time, forgave him the conceit because of the smile that made the receiver feel as if they were the only person on earth. Annie, like many others, had found him charming at first, but he grew less so, the more she got to know him. He had been her art-history professor.

One of the reasons Marc and Annie had become friends when he was little was that he'd wanted to improve his French. Having spoken mainly German or Spanish at home he had known at some six-year-old level that school would get easier if he could open his mouth with the certainty that what he said would be understood. Thus, many nights they would chatter away in French. Later he wanted to speak English with her and that had become their language.

As a little boy he had loved hearing how she had spent her first eight years in the US. Then when her father had been transferred to Nijmegen, The Netherlands, she'd found herself in a language soup only to emerge when a click went off in her head many months later and she found she could not only understand but could make herself understood. After that her father had moved the family to Stuttgart, Germany, and finally to Geneva. Her stories of her removal of a vowel from many Dutch words and the problems she had getting her tongue around certain French sounds had left them both laughing.

On the ride up in the elevator she asked, "Do you know there's a special name for people like us?"

"Half-breeds?" he asked.

"That too. No, we're called Third Culture Kids. We're not totally of our parents' culture, but we aren't totally of any other one either. We even have an online support network."

"It doesn't bother me like it used to," he said. "Remember how I hated to have people over because my parents were always speaking in German or Spanish?"

Annie didn't say fighting in German or Spanish, nor did she remind him of the number of times he had fled to her apartment. His parents had the knack of fighting when she was in the middle of writing a paper or studying for an exam. She just nodded.

The elevator arrived at the sixth floor, and the doors opened to solid darkness.

"The lights must be out."

Marc's hand moved next to the elevator, pressed a button and the narrow corridor was awash in light showing the seven apartment doors. "Nope, we've just gone eco. They stay on for three minutes and there's a switch by each door in case you can't find your key. Get your key out before they go off."

Annie did. She bid the boy good night. His flat, the one three-bedroom on the floor, was at the other end of the hall. In between were four two-bedroom apartments. At her end were two one-bedrooms. Although it had been at least three years since she had needed to crash there, time seemed to melt away.

First she knocked at the door. If Mireille had not received her e-mails, Annie didn't want to scare her.

No answer.

Annie pushed the bell and heard the gentle chime through the door.

She put her key in. If Mireille had left her key in the lock on the other side, she would not be able to get in, but she was sure Marc would put her up for the night. Even his parents would have if they were there but it would be with a fake welcome.

The key turned.

The apartment opened onto a room that Annie considered not to be the best use of space. It had no windows and the kitchen, living room, bedroom and bath all opened off it. She had used the entry as a study and she could tell by the desk and bookcases that Mireille had kept it the same way. Staying here was strange because Mireille had kept so many of Annie's old things, then added her own, making Annie feel as if she were *almost* home.

The block of flats was in what Annie had called the international ghetto because it was located in walking distance of so many of the alphabet UN agencies like WIPO, ILO, WHO and the equally alphabetically fluent nongovernmental organizations. Workers from secretaries to diplomats in these organizations found it convenient staying in the district often not more than two to four years before being transferred to some other country. They bought inexpensive but attractive flat-pack furnishings and accessories from discount furniture and home decorating stores to make comfortable homes for their sojourns in Geneva then discarded them. Annie was able to furnish almost her entire flat, with the exception of her mattress, from these discards. So much was thrown out she only had to wait for the red throw rug that she wanted for the kitchen: it had appeared in the trash, and she had scooped it up. To this day, it was still in the kitchen.

However, Mireille was nowhere in the apartment. The bed was unmade, which Annie found strange. Since her friend was neurotically neat, to the point that Annie joked that Mireille made her bed even before she got out of it, the tussled sheets worried her.

Mireille had e-mailed her that her dog had gone to the great dog-biscuit factory in the sky about three months ago, so she couldn't be out meeting his needs of nature. There were no doggy dishes indicating that she had replaced Titian with another canine, although she had e-mailed Annie she was thinking of getting a female puppy which she would name either Georgia or O'Keefe.

Not wanting to pry, but prying anyway, Annie opened the hall closet.

No surprises.

Mireille's all-black wardrobe was there. When they had first met in their second year at Geneva University, sitting in the tiered lecture hall of a European art-history course taught by none other than Herr Professor Dr. Urs Stoller, Mireille had black hair halfway down her back and dressed in prints so bright that people looking at her might have wanted to put on sunglasses. Over the years, she had transformed her look.

First, the long hair was replaced by a bob worn by her namesake, the French singer Mireille Mathieu. Then all her clothing became black, although she would add scarves reminiscent of her earlier sunglasses-necessitating wardrobe.

A small suitcase was on the top shelf. That meant nothing since there was other storage in the *cave* where each flat had a space in the bowels of the building. The space doubled as the legally required underground bomb shelter. Annie still had a few things in it that she had not moved down to her nest in Argelès-sur-mer, not far from the Spanish border on the Mediterranean. Mireille could have taken a suitcase, a backpack, whatever if she went away unexpectedly.

The glass door to the kitchen was closed. Annie saw that there were dishes in the sink, two plates, two sets of knives and forks, two champagne glasses. Opening the refrigerator, she saw a half-drunk bottle of champagne with a spoon dangling down the neck, a so-so way to keep the bubbles bubbly.

That there were no dirty pans was not a surprise, for Mireille was one of those cooks who cleaned as she went. Because she had obviously eaten at the small table with whomever was there by the placemats and napkins, Annie knew her friend well enough to know she wouldn't want the detritus of the meal preparation showing.

Annie knew from their e-mail correspondence that there was someone in Mireille's life, someone she never wanted to talk about in detail, but mentioned in a line thrown out but not followed up on. Annie had guessed he was married.

A closer look at the dirty serving dish in the sink showed the meal had been a pasta dish.

Back in the entrance, Annie noticed that the computer was asleep but not off. She tapped it, not wanting to read anything personal, but worry overcame her desire to protect her friend's privacy.

What came up was Mireille's thesis, a complete analysis of Brueghel's work. Mireille and Annie had talked about it enough. One day, when snow made going out an unpleasant idea, Annie had helped her friend count and describe the number of different hats worn by the painter's subjects. A quick look at the screen showed Mireille was in the middle of describing all the household items shown in the paintings. When Mireille finished, she would be a world authority on everything the painter put into his work: clothes, buildings, colors, trees, tools, animals and who knows what else.

The bed linens were where they had always been kept. Annie made up the couch, put on her pajamas and sank into the comfort of a vertical position with a sigh. After a twelve-hour trip that should have taken seven at the most and the unsettling discovery of a missing friend, bed felt wonderful.

Oops.

What if Mireille did come home? A body on the couch would scare her. Annie got up and pulled a piece of paper from the paper tray and a pen from the jar of pens next to the computer screen.

I am asleep on the couch.

Annie

Scotch tape was harder to find, but she located it in a kitchen drawer along with a screwdriver, hammer, stamps, nails, needles, miscellaneous spools of thread. She taped it to the door and fell back into the bed.

CHAPTER 3

Geneva, Switzerland

The Number Three Gardiol-Champel trolley stopped at Place Neuve. Although the sun was just coming up, two men were already moving life-size chess pieces around a giant stone board behind the thin, iron, gold-tipped bars that bordered the park. Their business suits amused Annie as she imagined they were trying to get in a last-minute moment of pleasure before being locked into some stuffy office.

She turned her back to them as she crossed the street and mounted the road running along a several-stories-high wall, which had once marked the edge of the Vieille Ville. In 1602 French soldiers had been stopped from scaling the walls by an old woman who threw a pot of vegetable soup on them, an image Annie, the history fanatic, always had loved. Today there was no soup, just wet, slippery cobblestones from a rainstorm that had awakened her in the middle of the night.

The old stone house that had been converted into Carsonwell Auctioneers was at the top of the hill.

When a secretary answered her ring she introduced herself. The woman, dressed in a conservative gray woolen business suit with a gray-and-dusty-rose scarf around her shoulders, was probably in her mid-forties. "The boys have been expecting you. I'm Antoinette Piccard." "The boys," like Annie, were in their early thirties. Maybe Antoinette acted as a mother to "The boys."

Before she could usher Annie inside, a man dressed in a perfectly tailored suit with perfectly cut hair, albeit it falling over his collar, rushed out and kissed her three times on alternating cheeks. He held her by both shoulders in front of him so he could look at her. "Annie, Annie. We've so missed you."

"Thomas, I feel the same."

"When Conrad told me you would be working for us again I was thrilled. And Damien and I want you to come for an *apéro*. He has said we can't let you come back to Genève without a proper welcome from your old friends."

"You guys are still together."

"Just like any old married couple, only without the ceremony. Enough. A tour, so much has changed."

He showed her into the room where the auctions were held. The floor-to-ceiling windows with their small panes of glass were covered with maroon velvet drapes held back with complementary rose tassels. The chairs were in the style of Louis XIV, except each was equipped with a side table like in a school study hall and each bore a touch pad.

"See how modern we are. The buyers can peruse our catalog or they can watch the items as they are being sold. If they want to bid the old way by waving a paddle, winking, or scratching themselves they can. Or"—he drew out the *or* into a multisyllabic word—"or they can just touch this pad and their bid is registered. Conrad can see it on his screen at the lectern." He dragged her to the front of the room between the two windows.

Another man came in. He was in shirt sleeves, but his shirt was so starched that no wrinkle would dare sully the material. "Annie." He held out his arms. She rushed into them.

"Conrad."

He led her into his office. Instead of going behind his desk, he led her to the couch. The furniture was also antique in sharp contrast to the computers, which were color coordinated to the furniture. If any one of the kings of France walked in, they would be comfortable with the environment, providing they could adjust to a keyboard in place of a plume to sign documents.

"You're graying at the temples. That's uncomfortable. We're all the same age."

He laughed. "It's fake. I color it. I think it gives me *gravitas.*"

Annie laughed. Conrad Carsonwell was nothing if not a showman. From the time they were at university together, he had had a flair that no one else did. And nerve.

After graduation, having inherited business sense from his father along with a healthy bank account in Swiss Francs and love/knowledge of art and antiques from his mother, he went ahead and opened this auction house: an auction house that in nine short years was rivaling the Geneva branches of Sotheby's and Christie's.

Part of his success was that he was the first to put his catalog online with not only price and provenance but with in-depth descriptions as well. Whenever possible he told stories. A necklace might have been worn by a Serbian princess at a ball the night before the shooting that began World War I. If he knew what Picasso ate for breakfast when painting a work about to go under the gavel, it was added to the information. The catalog was also available in fourteen different languages, even though most of his customers were fluent in at least English and French. Prices came up automatically in the currency of the language of the country that the person was connecting from, but could easily be converted with a mouse click.

Nothing had been left to chance. He had run focus groups on whether to name the house Carsonwell Auctioneers or Conrad Auction House in five countries and although he went with their decision, every now and then he would sigh and say he still preferred the Conrad Auction House. His renovation of the house had nearly driven three contractors to nervous breakdowns.

Not that Carsonwell Auctioneers had been an overnight success. Conrad had gone through most of his inheritance before he was in the black.

"How is Veronika?" Annie referred to Conrad's wife, who also had been at the University of Geneva with them. She had studied international law, but worked for the firm both in getting materials into Switzerland as well as schmoozing with the clients in one of the seven languages that rolled off her tongue. A diplomat's daughter, she was comfortable with the powerful. In the early days when Thomas, Mireille, Conrad, Annie and Veronika were all working together, it had been heady and exciting.

"She's fine except she insists on being pregnant too many times."

"Have you said that to her?"

"If I had, you would not be sitting here talking to me. You would be visiting my grave. And your fiancé, I can't remember his name?"

"Roger." Annie gave it the French pronunciation Ru-shay. "Fine." She had forgotten to text him to tell him she arrived safely, but since they had talked while she sat in a café in Lyon waiting for her train, she was sure he would not be worried. Slowly she had broken him of being overprotective and of getting upset when she took tech-writing/translation assignments all over Europe, necessitating her absence from his daily life.

"Marriage date?"

"As far in the future as I can manage."

"Cold feet?"

"Nope, just things are good, why shake them up?"

"I still wish you'd never left us."

Annie did not need to go into the reasons with Conrad. He knew that although she had loved the work she did for him—researching the history of various antiques and writing stories about them in English and translating them into Dutch, German and French—she did not like working fourteen-hour days and fighting for her four-week vacation although it was decreed by law. Once Annie had found her nest in Argelès, she realized that she could live on far less money and worked only about six months a year. The rest of the time she delved into whatever historical subject caught her fancy.

"Well, I do like the idea of an occasional assignment from you. It's much more fun than writing about how to use software." She didn't add more profitable. Now that Carsonwell Auctioneers was in the black she was billing him almost a hundred Swiss Franc (CHF) per hour, a lot above her usual fifty-to-eighty-CHF fee.

Thomas came in with a Syrian mosaic wooden tray with inlaid mother of pearl on which there were three tea cups, a teapot, creamer and sugar bowl. A lemon was sliced so thinly it was possible to see through it. Three almond croissants were on a doily and plate. The tongs for the sugar cubes were real silver.

"Clarice Cliff, Crocus Stamford, art-deco design for all," Annie said picking up her cup.

"You remember your training here," Conrad poured a cup of tea and handed it to Annie. "Still take it straight?"

"Only with a cup around it." And as she grasped the triangle-wedged handle she added, "I have this fantasy, that I am at a *vide grenier* or a *marché aux puces,* and I find a complete set of Clarice Cliff dishes and the seller has no idea of what he has and I can pick it up for centimes."

"That is a fantasy," Thomas said.

"Not necessarily. A French person might not know about her."

30

Thomas took the cup that Conrad poured for him. "Mireille hasn't come in yet."

"I'm staying at her place. She wasn't home when I got there last night." She told them how she had found the flat.

Conrad frowned. "Wednesday, late in the day, she hung up the telephone and started to cry. She ran out saying she was taking the rest of the week off."

"I thought she would be back today, though," Thomas said. "It's that man again." He leaned forward and lowered his voice, although there was no one to overhear. "She has this lover she won't tell us anything about. I suspect he's married but he keeps her in a constant state of agitation."

The Mireille that Annie had known was the one who kept men in a state of agitation.

"Should we call the police or something?"

"If we don't hear from her by Wednesday," Conrad said. "Take your tea and let me show you the room where you need to start your work."

CHAPTER 4

Geneva, Switzerland

Annie tapped in the code at her old apartment building's entrance. Spending nine hours in concentrated research and writing had left her exhausted. She had tackled the easiest items first, the opposite of how she normally worked. However, since Veronika had to translate Annie's work into Russian, Spanish and Italian and Rima into Arabic and Tomoni into Japanese, that would give them a head start while she began the really heavy research needed.

Then she had begged off from having an *apéro* with Thomas and Damien. Thomas had admitted he was tired too and was looking forward to going home, taking a shower and crawling into bed with a book. "Even Damien running through the bedroom stark naked wouldn't arouse me," he'd said.

"Then aren't you glad I said not tonight dear, I've a headache," Annie teased.

He'd hugged her and said, "Which is why we are such good friends."

Good friends were those who understood, Annie thought, as she passed the bank of mailboxes.

Her cell phone vibrated. It was an SMS from Gaëlle, her fiancé's almost fourteen-year-old daughter, with whom Annie had a relationship that could not be described as mother-sister-friend-counselor but was a little bit of them all.

"Papa is pissed at u," it read. Since last Christmas when

Gaëlle and her father had made her first trip to the US to join Annie and her parents for the holidays, she loved using American slang—a change from before when she didn't want to use English at all. Now she was dreaming of going to an American university.

Roger wanted to discourage her, but Annie had a different approach. She encouraged the girl to look at universities. Annie guessed that when Gaëlle figured out that a single course at an American university would cost about as much as an entire year at a French one and that she would lose her government allowance if she left the country, reality would probably take over. And if that didn't discourage the girl, Annie was fully prepared to work out how much Gaëlle would have to earn between now and finishing her *bac* to be able to afford it.

"If you tell her no, she will just get all teenagey," Annie had told Roger. "But if you let her work it out, it will be her decision, and maybe, just maybe, she'll be able to pull it off."

"Do you really believe she could?" he'd asked.

"No, but on the off-chance she could, I wouldn't want to stand in her way. Meanwhile, she thinks we are supportive, which in a way we are."

Roger did one of his humphs. Annie reminded him yet again that he had never been a teenage girl so she could understand how Gaëlle's beady little mind worked better than he could and she could help him prepare for, or even circumvent, whatever Gaëlle was thinking.

She dialed his number. "I know I was wrong when I didn't call you last night or this morning," she started out, knowing full well that when she admitted being wrong, he couldn't complain, or not complain as much as he would have, had she blustered her way through. She went on to explain about Mireille's disappearance.

Roger did not particularly like Mireille, finding her too

intense, although he did admire that she worked full time while trying to write her thesis. Lazy did not sit well with the Argelès police chief.

His professionalism kicked in. "Has she done anything like that before?"

"No." The elevator came, but Annie let it go. She was not sure how strong the signal would be inside. "Do you think it is too soon to call the police?"

"Have you talked to all her friends?"

Mireille did not have many friends. There were the people from university: Conrad, Veronika, Thomas, all of whom had moved from university life to auction life. There was Andrea someone or other from Scotland. She thought Mireille had mentioned her as a Hash Harrier, a group that Mireille ran with sometimes when she just couldn't stand sitting at a computer any longer. But Mireille might have talked about her going back to Scotland. Making friends with internationals in Geneva was often a short-term prospect as people were transferred in and out.

"What about her parents?" he asked.

Annie had met them a few times. Mireille's father was a businessman who operated a water-bottling company. Her mother was Madame Bottling Company who had glommed onto Annie because Madame BC loved all things American. That Madame BC had spent much more time in the States in the past ten years than Annie had didn't seem to bother Mireille's mother at all.

Mireille had complained about her parents. They wanted her married with children, not exploring some stupid painter who had died centuries before. Art was for museum outings with their various social clubs, not for a profession.

"I don't want to worry them if she's just taken off to get a break."

Someone called the elevator and it disappeared.

"What do Thomas and Conrad say?"

"They didn't seem all that worried, more annoyed with so much work to do for the next auction. It's a biggie that could bring anywhere from five to seven million dollars."

Roger whistled.

"The stuff is beautiful: furniture, figurines, Fabergé eggs that once belonged to the Tsar, dishes, paintings."

"Am I going to lose you to Prince Charming?"

"I've found mine already." The elevator came down and went up again. "Besides the boys say that this client is in his seventies and has blown much of the family fortune in dissolute ways. It is also rumored he's gay, but other than that you have every reason to be jealous."

"I better let you go. I love you, you know."

"I love you too."

By the time Annie had pocketed the phone, the elevator was back down. She used her key to let herself into the apartment to find the beds made, the dishes done and Mireille dressed in black sweats sitting in a chair, her feet on the bed with her laptop between her knees and thighs. "Annie!" She jumped up, almost knocking the chair over, but pausing to place the computer safely on the bed before hugging Annie.

Mireille looked awful: pale, eyes swollen, blotchy skin.

"I'll make tea." Mireille went into the kitchen and took down the Chinese metal teapot and a red bag of ginger tea fastened with a gold tie. She filled the pot with hot tap water then flipped on the kettle that was resting on the counter.

At university, tea was the backdrop to their conversations be they about men, music, homework, papers, sports, politics and/or religion. Nothing but nothing was discussed without tea. When the water boiled, Mireille poured the water over the leaves and placed it on a tray with cups and a package of chocolate cookies.

"Where the hell were you?"

"I didn't see your e-mail. I didn't know you were coming in. I just ran out to my parents." She spooned the tea into the metal strainer resting in the opening of the pot. "I told them I had the flu."

"Do you?"

Mireille shook her head.

"Let's go into the living room."

Annie's bed, which she had left in disarray, was now neat, although Mireille had not turned it back into the couch. The girls sat opposite each other, cross-legged with the tray between them.

"Talk."

Mireille let out a long sigh. "I've been having an affair and I broke it off."

Annie let the silence hang.

"And he was married."

"Which is why you broke it off?"

"Hell, no! I did it because he was stealing my work. I wrote a paper and he submitted it under his name."

"A professor?"

Mireille nodded. "We were together three years. He kept saying he was going to leave his wife. She was a bitch."

"They all say that."

"I know her. She is."

Annie so wanted to ask who, but waited in hopes that Mireille would tell her.

Mireille, instead of saying anything, lifted the cup to her lips. Rather than sipping it she blew on it and the steam, caught by the lamplight, feathered her face.

"Do you want to tell me what happened?"

"We had worked on this paper together, about Brueghel's depiction of village life. He made a couple of suggestions, but it was ninety-nine-point-nine-nine percent my work. Then he took it and sent it to a publisher under his name, without giving me any credit at all and had the nerve . . ." She started to cry, spilling the tea.

Annie took the cup and held Mireille's hand.

"I'd made us a dinner, and he showed me the published paper, like he expected that I should be thrilled. He'd changed a bit of the opening, and two lines in the conclusion. He knew that I am trying to become the current authority on Brueghel. He knew. He *knew.*"

Annie was at a loss as to what to say. It was not the first time some executive, some professor claimed credit for an underling's work.

When Mireille regained control she said, "I threw him out. Then I ran to my parents to hide out."

Annie remembered Conrad saying that Mireille had received a phone call at work and ran out saying she wouldn't be back for a few days. "Did you talk to him at work?"

"Before he came over for dinner. He had the nerve to tell me not to be babyish over some work he wanted me to redo for the umpty-umpth time, that he was coming for dinner and that I would forget all about it."

"And stupid me, I made dinner, champagne even, thinking that maybe he might . . . he might . . . I don't know, accept what I'd done. I'd backed it up enough."

"Have you heard from him?"

"He texted me for a couple of days, sent e-mails, but nothing since Sunday, thank God. Of course that's not the worse part."

Annie cocked her head.

"I'm pregnant."

Annie didn't know what to say.

"And there's more."

Annie wasn't sure what could be added.

"I'm keeping it."

"What have your parents said?"

"I haven't told them. You know them."

Annie did. They were ultra-straight people of the old Calvinistic school. There was little room for any moral lapses. "Perhaps since you're their only child and you will be producing a grandchild . . ."

"You always were an optimist. But there's still more bad news. The father is my thesis advisor."

The all-too-obvious realization struck Annie like a physical blow. "Holy shit! Stoller."

"Our beloved neighbor, Marc's father."

"Holy, holy shit!"

"Promise me, promise me, you won't tell anyone who the father is."

"I won't."

"Promise me you won't tell anyone about the baby until I'm ready."

"I promise."

CHAPTER 5

Geneva, Switzerland
October 27, 1553

"Where have you been?" Aunt Mathilde held the baby Jeanne in her arms as she walked out of the kitchen. "Your Uncle Jacques will not like his dinner being late."

Five-year-old Louis ran around and around the kitchen table, out the hall and up the stairs. "Stop it!" Aunt Mathilde called after him, but the little boy continued to the top of the house where he could not hear his mother.

Elizabeth apologized. She wanted nothing more than to escape to the room which she shared with Sarah, her nineteen-year-old cousin. Eleven-year-old Mathieu and seven-year-old Pierre were at catechism class, held after their normal school day. Regular school was not for girls, but learning about God was the responsibility of everyone in the city, and Cousin Sarah now taught religion to young girls. If anything she was more pious than her mother, but without the hardness. She should have been married, but an illness that left her right leg withered eliminated suitors, and even her father's economic status had not been enough to encourage a proposal from anyone.

Elizabeth knew that her uncle hoped to entice the young lawyer, Guillaume Dumont, who worked in his practice, to pursue Sarah. Although the young man had often been invited to dine with the family many a night at her aunt's repeated suggestions, her uncle reported back that Monsieur Dumont had this or that commitment and could not accept the invitations. This made her aunt harrumph and mumble that Monsieur Dumont should be so lucky to have a good home-cooked meal rather than eat in the cafés dotted around the city for travelers or try and prepare something himself in the rooms he rented not far from Uncle Jacques's office.

Using all her willpower, Elizabeth tried not to show her frustration. When she would have time to draw today's events she had no idea. Jean-Michel had slipped her more paper that she tucked under her dress next to her bare skin. She had to stand behind a tree to do it on a deserted path as the clock struck five. People still had another two or three hours to work so no one was to-ing and fro-ing.

Maybe on Sunday there would be time. Maybe, just maybe, she could plead a headache to avoid the long hours for Sunday prayers or not take the walk with the family after church. Maybe she could pretend to twist her ankle. But she wanted to get the scene down today before she forgot some of the details.

Where could she twist her ankle? On the cobblestones outside Saint Pierre's on the way into the church? On the way out? Then she could hobble the short distance to her uncle's house, one that she could never quite bring herself to think of as her home.

"Pay attention, girl. You're more flighty than your mother and that's saying a lot," Aunt Mathilde said.

Elizabeth handed Aunt Mathilde the basket of beef bones, still with meat attached, that the butcher had placed in her basket along with the onions and cabbages she had bought along the rue Molard.

"I suppose almost everyone went to the execution," Aunt Mathilde said. "Bad business, that."

"You don't approve that he was burned?"

"Of course I approve: he was a heretic. But that it is no reason to close a shop."

Elizabeth took off her cape and hung it on a peg. Those pegs usually used by Sarah, the boys and Uncle Jacques were empty. The gray wool smelled damp. Her aunt spent most of her days in the house since she had become pregnant yet again, so she would never learn that although Elizabeth hadn't lied, she hadn't told the truth, either. "Let me help get the soup started." Elizabeth had found changing the subject often deflected the criticism that was heaped on her or at least changed the type of criticism.

"Get the table ready, I'll do the soup, but you add the wine to the water." Her aunt headed for the kitchen. "And afterward close all the shutters. Keep the damp out."

Elizabeth put out enough spoons for everyone to dip into the soup pot. The stone house was long and narrow. The ground floor held an entrance and the dining room. The kitchen was in the basement. Her uncle's study and the master bedroom were on the next floor. The top floor held two bedrooms: the three boys slept in one; Elizabeth shared the other with Sarah and baby Jeanne. She wanted to ask when her older cousin would be back from the catechism classes that she herself was now too old to attend, thank goodness, but experience taught her to stay as quiet as possible, speaking only when spoken to. However, she would have time to hide the paper. Making the bed daily that she and Sarah shared had ingratiated her with her cousin, but Elizabeth did it to keep the older girl from looking under her mattress.

She started at the top floor and worked her way down. The windows had glass panes, showing the status of the family or at least the success of her uncle, just like the family ate off plates not trenchers of bread as poorer people did.

As she opened the window to reach for the wooden-slatted shutters, she strained to see the fountain at the Place du Bourg-de-Four, but it was invisible in the fog that had crept in since she had arrived home. She could smell the lake and the fires from the many metal workshops that produced cauldrons, breastplates for the soldiers and the metal bars for doors and windows. The wind was going in the wrong direction for her to smell the fire of the execution and even if it were blowing toward them, it would have mingled with the fires from all the other household chimneys.

A few shapes could be seen moving around the street like ghosts. Shivering, she pulled the shutters together and threw the bar across them, shut the windows and drew the heavy wool curtain. Nothing would make the room warm, but at least the worst cold was relegated to the outside.

"What is taking you so long?" Aunt Mathilde's voice wafted up the stairs.

"I am just straightening something out." She hoped her aunt would not ask for more details. As a child she never lied, but she had never felt she needed to protect herself back then either.

Elizabeth wished her uncle Jacques would finish the evening prayers. Her knees were cold against the stone floor. He was giving thanks for everything that happened during the day, and his day had a lot of tiny details. Then he launched into his requests to be more understanding of God's will before praying against all the imagined sinning that went on around him.

Elizabeth knew at one time her uncle had thought of becoming a pastor, but his family wanted him and his brother, her father, to follow the law, so follow the law they did. Uncle Jacques used the story to convince his own children that they should always be obedient.

"Amen."

Elizabeth resisted the urge to let out a sigh of relief. She got up and joined the family in wishing each other good night.

Uncle Jacques helped his pregnant wife stand. Elizabeth suspected that she had become pregnant within days of her recovery from her last miscarriage.

Outside nine bells boomed from the church, signaling the start of curfew—not that anyone in the household would consider being outside at that hour.

The boys helped their father stoke the fire for the night. Sarah hobbled up the stairs ahead of her. Good. If she were in bed first, there would be some warmth under the covers when she climbed in. Baby Jeanne, no longer teething and fussy, had been asleep upstairs for the last two hours. Grateful the day was over, Elizabeth headed up to her room.

With her back to her cousin, Elizabeth slipped on her nightdress over her clothes before even taking off her apron. Then off came the jumper-like overdress and the blouse.

Sarah's breathing told Elizabeth that her cousin was asleep. She didn't snore, but when in deep sleep made little putt-putts. That everyone slept early no matter what the season was to be expected. The family rose at four for morning prayers, followed by chores, breakfast and the boys leaving to be at school by six. Uncle Jacques always left immediately after prayers.

While the putt-putts continued, Elizabeth slipped out of bed. There was a loose plank under the bed where she had hidden her string-wrapped lead and the colored sticks that Jean-Michel had given her when those that she brought from the farm had been confiscated by her aunt. She pulled a piece of paper from under her side of the mattress.

Tiptoeing past the bedroom of her aunt and uncle, she went to the kitchen. The coals from the fire produced little warmth and less light. In her secret box she also had a candle that she lit from the red ember. Taking her cape and Sarah's down from their pegs, she wrapped one around her shoulders and the other around her legs.

Praying no one would wander downstairs, she began to sketch out what she had seen at the burning. She would not be able to add the color in this light—Sunday, after she twisted her ankle.

CHAPTER 6

Geneva, Switzerland

When Annie awoke the next morning to a harsh noise, it took her a few seconds to realize where she was. The curtains at the windows were not the ones in her Argelès nest nor were they the ones in Roger's bedroom. They reminded her of the ones in the flat she had lived in while she was at university.

Then she realized: she was in the old flat with her old curtains, and the noise was the alarm that Mireille had set because both women felt after talking much too late that they would never wake up on their own. Why couldn't Mireille wake up to music instead of the horrible buzzing? It stopped and she heard her friend dash into the bathroom followed by the sounds of throwing up.

This was not a wonderful start to a day.

The toilet flushed, water ran and the bathroom door opened. Mireille stood in the doorway. She wore sweats for her pajamas. Her normally smooth black hair was tousled. Without makeup, she was not only pale; her skin was almost translucent. "Want some coffee?"

"Can you stand to make it?" Annie asked.

"If I eat a piece of toast first it usually stays down. Besides, I've got to get back to work. The boys give me leeway, but they've limits."

"They were annoyed you weren't in yesterday, but only mildly. Do they know about the baby?" Annie had debated us-

45

ing the word pregnant, but since Mireille had said she planned to carry it to term then keep it, the word baby seemed better. Her friend, despite her upset at her lover, had told Annie she always wanted children and in her early thirties her biological time clock, if not ticking, was getting wound up to tick. Once she got her doctorate and published her findings she would be in demand as an expert on Brueghel, guaranteeing her an income. She would never be rich, but she would have enough for her and the baby, or at least that is what she'd told Annie last night.

Annie threw off the duvet. The heat had already come up. She wished she had been able to give her friend better advice, or any advice, but Mireille's situation was so far from her own, all she could do was ask her friend if she had thought of this or that. Annie knew she was one of the few people in the world that had no money worries. Between her chosen lifestyle, Roger and her parents, she had plenty of cushions, something that Mireille did not have. Her friend's parents were for standing on your own two feet, laying in the bed you made and other clichés that said don't you dare come to us for help. She had eaten just enough meals with them during her university days when Mireille didn't want to face them alone to know that their strict moral code would have made Jean Calvin look like a raging liberal.

Annie lay in bed, her mind roaming from one idea to another: I want coffee, better her than me, and I hope she knows what she's doing, not in that order. Mireille had always been focused on whatever she was doing at the moment—be it studying for an exam or going for a hike in the Geneva countryside. Her postponement of getting her doctorate had been planned as well, because she wanted to work at Carsonwell Auctioneers to get real life experience. It only confirmed her educational goals.

The environment she'd rediscovered yesterday at Carsonwell's made Annie almost regret the choices that she made in her own life, but she knew from her many assignments at different corporations all over Europe that most working environments weren't like Carsonwell's. "I'll make the coffee and toast. You take a shower."

The women sat at the kitchen table that overlooked a field, the Route de Ferney and on the other side of the street a small white *château* only visible after the leaves fell. In the center of the table was a coffeepot, a toast rack, a pot of honey and a pad of sweet butter. The coffee had been poured into bowls, French style.

"I have far less morning sickness," Mireille said. "I figure in another week or so it will just be a memory. And I stay awake more."

"Like last night?"

"Getting to bed at two in the morning wasn't the smartest thing, but we had so much to catch up and we never got to you."

"My life has been dull in comparison." Annie dribbled honey on the toast. The honeypot was a Clarice Cliff shaped like a beehive, decorated with tiny fruits on the cover. Love of Cliff's designs was one of the things that she and Mireille shared. "Is this real?"

"Oh, yes. Conrad let me pull it out of an estate auction— with the permission of the clients, of course." She held it high to show a small crack that was just large enough to reduce the value but not large enough to make the pot dysfunctional.

"Well, at least you are eclectic. A twentieth-century art-deco potter and a sixteenth-century painter."

"Consistency is for little goblin minds, or something like that." Mireille took a swallow of her coffee. "My God!"

"What?" Annie wondered what other shocker her friend could come up with, but Mireille had jumped up from the table, taken the small step stool and was fumbling about on the top shelf of the hall closet.

"Be careful, you're rummaging for two," Annie said.

"Got it." Mireille extracted a dusty old leather folder. She washed and dried the countertop before laying the folio down. It was tied with leather strings. With what seemed to Annie almost reverence, Mireille gently tugged on them and opened the folder. Annie stood next to Mireille, her mouth open.

There were six drawings in soft colors. The edge of the paper on each was yellowed and cracked, but the center had somehow been preserved. "May I touch them?"

Mireille opened the hold-it-all drawer and brought out two pairs of surgical gloves, handing a pair to Annie.

There was a naked man, probably not much more than twenty in all his anatomical glory. Another was a still life of a book and candle.

"This one looks like it was drawn out a window in the old town."

"I've found the building. I can show you on our way home tonight. Wait till you get the last one." She handed it to Annie.

It was a charcoal drawing looking down on a crowd. In the center a man was being burned at the stake. All were signed with writing that could have been *Elizabeth H,* but some of the letters were so badly faded they were almost impossible to read. The pages were without dates.

"Where did you get these?"

"The old used bookstore on Sismondi. Do you remember it?"

Annie couldn't have forgotten it with its dark interior that smelled of other times. Sometimes there were prints. Monsieur Galy used to own it. The old man treated each book as if it were a work of art, a miracle put together even if it was only a ten-year-old paperback. But he also carried valuable books.

"When he died, his nephew took it over. Really snotty kid who doesn't know anything from anything."

"He inherited the store?"

"I suspect so. I suspect he took it over thinking it wouldn't be much work. I went in there about three months ago after I read the old man died. I knew there were some old books on Brueghel that I'd been eyeing and I thought I better scoop them up before he threw them away. The kid was throwing stuff out. I grabbed a first edition Henry James, and a second edition of Zola's *Confessions de Claude*. The kid said if I wanted them so badly it would cost twenty CHF." An expression crossed her face that could only be described as a smirk. "Conrad is saving them for a book auction and he thinks they'll bring in at least ten times that. I would never have screwed the old man, but the nephew?"

"Open game?"

"Open game."

"Did you show the drawings to Conrad?"

"I wanted to show them first to Urs, who wasn't all that excited. He said he would try and sell them for me, but he wasn't optimistic. I think that was when I first saw what I should have seen long before."

Annie wanted to say, but resisted saying, what took you so long to discover what a bastard Urs Stoller was? She hadn't liked him when he was her professor of art history, although he was a great teacher. She didn't like the way he ignored Marc. And nothing Mireille had told her made her feel any better about Urs. "And the drawings? Where'd you get them?"

"I stole them."

"Stole them?"

"Well, partially. I saw them in the trash. The snotty nephew was carrying the trash out to the alley behind the store. As soon as the store closed I snuck into the alley and grabbed them."

"And Urs thought they were worthless?"

Mireille nodded. "He claimed to have had a Parisian expert evaluate them."

"And you believed him?"

"That was the second click. I mentioned them to Conrad. He has the name of someone who can really evaluate them. I trust people Conrad trusts."

"And you're keeping them in your closet?"

"I still have to show them to him. Conrad said I should leave them in his safe. At some point I will take them back and get them appraised. Conrad said if they had any value he'd put them in an auction for me."

"We should take them to work with us today."

Mireille looked out the window. A light drizzle gave the fields and *château* the feel of an impressionist painting, only with even more muted colors. "When the weather is better."

CHAPTER 7

Geneva, Switzerland

Thomas only flamed when he was around someone he thought might be gay. Annie was sure Thomas could have had a starring role in *La Cage aux Folles,* as the Prince-not-so-charming Ruppert whined his way through the mountain of details that he needed to share with Carsonwell's.

Conrad, Thomas and Annie had all they could do to keep the prince on topic as he wandered off with his stories that had nothing to do with the objects they were planning to sell.

Someone should have told him he wasn't all that an important prince, Anne thought. His heritage was from a small German area swallowed up by a larger state which in turn had become a tiny part of Baden-Württemberg. Still, he was part of the royal families that sometimes ended up on the cover of *Hello.* How he had ended up in Geneva in a small *château* probably had a lot to do with marriages to other nobility. It was not a history that she had any desire to trace.

Portly, with most-likely dyed black hair and jowly, he looked his age, which was rumored to be around seventy. When he left to go the bathroom, Thomas whispered to her, "He's gay, all right."

"Are you sure?"

"Takes one to know one. Although I've never seen him at any clubs—not that I frequent them since I've been with Damien," Thomas said in what Annie thought was a normal speaking pat-

51

tern. Sometimes she wondered about Thomas. If there were chameleon genes for humans, she was sure he had a number of them. She'd heard him switch accents and interests as easily as he changed his clothes.

"But he's a widower with two children," Conrad said.

"Had to keep the line going." Thomas stood as Prince Ruppert ambled back in followed by Antoinette carrying a tray with a silver tea service and Limoges china, playing her role of subservient secretary to the hilt. A prince would not expect any of the upper-level staff to serve him or themselves, which is what happened when they were working together without visitors. Whoever felt like tea or coffee made it and offered to share. More than once Conrad had made coffee for his staff, including his secretary.

Annie smoothed her skirt. Unlike many of her assignments, she was expected to dress expensively when clients were around, not that easy to do with her street *marché* wardrobe. Still the chocolate wool skirt and sweater set off by an orange, brown and beige scarf fastened with a pin plucked from a display case by Thomas to complete her outfit worked. However, the pin would bring a quarter of her annual income at auction. She knew that she had carried off the image, meeting the cultural coding requirements for the prince. Had she not had anthropology and communication courses, she might have resented the necessity to playact, but instead she felt grateful that this type of game occupied such a small part of her life.

"I still don't see why this is necessary." As Prince Ruppert muttered in German, he cocked his head at Thomas, who, Annie thought, batted his eyelashes.

"We can show you our market research on how adding stories increases the bidding," Thomas said also in German.

"We want to make sure you get as much money as you possibly can," Conrad said.

"As do you," Prince Ruppert practically sniffed.

Annie wanted to say *asshole* in German and French, but Thomas moved his hand as if to pat the prince's knee and stopped mid-air. "Then we all have the same goal, don't we?" He handed Prince Ruppert a plate of almond croissants and let his hand linger a moment more than normal. "Let's look at the photos."

The collection had already been photographed by Mireille. Originally they'd used a professional photographer. Conrad wasn't being chintzy using Mireille. He honestly felt her work was better than the photographers he'd used in the past. Her love of doing the photos showed. Some were straight photos, but she also would put coffee in coffee cups, flowers in a vase, two dolls positioned on a couch with a children's tea-party set on the table in front of them.

The estimate for this auction was low-balled at five million CHF, which would bring the house ten percent from the seller and ten from the buyers.

Prince Ruppert shuffled through the pages of photos with a sigh. Then he stopped. "This one: I believe Princess Sophie of Hanover sat on this chair when Graf Ludwig proposed. That was the family legend. She was supposed to be more beautiful than even Princess Sissi. The year was probably 1832."

Annie did some rapid Googling and found there was a portrait of Princess Sophie in the Gemäldegalerie in Berlin. She made a note to try and get the right to add a reproduction of the portrait to the catalog. "That is exactly what we are looking for. Did they have a happy marriage?"

Prince Ruppert shook his head as he continued to delve into his memories.

A ruby-and-diamond necklace, handed down for generations, had been lost and finally was found behind a *schrank*. How it got there was never known.

A tea service had been used to serve *König* Wilhelm just before the start of World War I.

A sword was reported to have been used during the Hundred Years' War.

All together, Thomas and Annie wormed one hundred twenty-one stories out of the prince.

When he was gone, Mireille came into the room. "How did it go?"

Thomas wiggled his hand back and forth. "It could have been worse." His flame had died; his voice's inflection was back to normal.

When Mireille left the room, Thomas asked, "How is Mireille really? She doesn't seem normal. As her friend can you find out?"

"As her friend I need to keep her confidence."

"You're no fun at all."

CHAPTER 8

Geneva, Switzerland
December 25, 1556

Elizabeth woke when Sarah opened the shutters then slammed the windows shut, but not before a frigid blast of air crossed the room to where Elizabeth was huddled under the covers.

"It's snowing hard," Sarah said as she reached for her dress.

"Prayers, hurry." Uncle Jacques opened the door without knocking. Elizabeth scrambled out of bed. The two girls dressed as fast as they could, more to not get colder than just to make prayers.

Elizabeth tried not to think that it was Christmas as she almost ran down the stairs. Running in the house was not allowed, even if the five-year-old often did anyway and was only told to stop in a voice that said ignoring the directive was a choice.

Although it was forbidden to celebrate Christmas, her mother and father had followed much of the English tradition, eating a special meal, singing and exchanging small presents that they had made. On their last Christmas together, two years ago, her father had brought the most wonderful colored pencils she had ever seen from England. Those were the pencils her aunt had confiscated, demanding with a tut-tut that Elizabeth go to her room and retrieve any others she might have hidden away.

Last Christmas, after her father had not been heard of for weeks, her mother had gone to her uncle and he had put out enquiries, but nothing had happened.

Her mother had been saying they should go back to England, back to her family where even under the very religious Catholic Queen Mary, smiling wasn't illegal. However, before her mother could make the arrangements to sell the land and find transportation to the channel, Elizabeth's brother had died and her mother had become ill with nonstop vomiting until she no longer had the strength to breathe.

After the burial, Uncle Jacques had sat down with Elizabeth.

"We will rent out the farm. That money will be yours, of course, except for my administrative costs." What he didn't say was that she would have no access to it.

"My mother thought she had a buyer."

"No, land should always stay in the family. It will work for your dowry."

"But my grandfather is expecting me."

"We have written him and told them that your place is with us. Besides, your Aunt Mathilde can use your help."

Without any money under her control, Elizabeth had no choice but to move into the house of her aunt and uncle. She tried finding a courier to tell her grandfather of her predicament. Her mother had stayed on good terms with her family despite their disapproval of her marriage and her moving so far away. That disapproval did not extend to her father, whom they had liked except for his taking their daughter and sister to another country.

So far she had not been able to write, but giving up was not in her character.

Her aunt did not join them for prayers. The end of her pregnancy was not going well. Elizabeth did what she could to help out, but nothing met the rigorous household standards.

Despite her woolen dress and shawl, she felt cold not just from the temperature but in her soul.

Prayers over, the family was seated around the table nibbling on yesterday's bread, already hard until dipped into a bowl of milk, to break their fast. Uncle Jacques prepared to leave for his office, the papers he had been working on last night before bed bundled into a leather case to protect them from the snow falling outside and stuck under his arm. His last words were to go up and see if her aunt needed anything.

The boys were chattering in Latin, talking about Elizabeth and thinking she did not understand, but she did, for her mother had given her lessons, insisting that she needed to be as clever as any man.

"Let's get her in trouble," Mathieu said.

"How?" Pierre asked.

Five-year-old Louis whined, "I don't understand what you're saying."

"You'll be learning Latin soon enough," Pierre said. "Papa won't have any of us not knowing Latin, Greek and French."

"No choice. Just be happy you don't have to go to school yet," Mathieu said.

Louis's pout showed he did not appreciate staying home while his two big brothers got to go somewhere every day while he was excluded.

Elizabeth stopped preparing the tray for her aunt. "Don't even think of playing a trick on me."

"How did you know?" Pierre asked.

She wasn't about to tell them how her mother had both her and her brother conjugating Latin verbs along with other chores. "I know everything. Now get off to school or you'll be late." The school was only a few minutes' walk from the house, but the punishment was swift for any boy who arrived even a few seconds beyond the ringing of the seventh-hour bell.

With a flurry of activity the boys put on their cloaks, grabbed their books and were out the door.

Elizabeth continued the preparation of the tray which also contained bread soaked in milk for baby Jeanne, a sleepy child who seldom woke before eight. With Aunt Mathilde not being well, Elizabeth had more than enough time to do what needed to be done.

Upstairs, her aunt had propped herself up in bed against the wooden headboard. Her stomach formed a large mound under the covers that she had pulled up to her armpits. She had a shawl wrapped around her shoulders, and her sleeping cap covered her hair that was braided to prevent snarling.

The walls were unadorned plaster, whitewashed only at the end of summer, giving the room a bit of brightness. "Thank you for the bread," she said. "Has everyone left?"

"Yes."

"The boys remembered everything?"

"As far as I can tell. How are you feeling?"

"I wish the pregnancy was over. What a waste of time laying abed like this is."

Elizabeth nodded. Aunt Mathilde said that every day. However, since she started bleeding, the doctor had insisted she stay in bed to keep the baby in the womb for as long as possible.

"Did my husband say when he would be home?"

"I believe he has to stop at the church. The under pastor is worried that the workmen are not getting the paint off the walls fast enough." Elizabeth didn't say how much she preferred the colored walls that were rapidly being turned to cold, plain stone. Gray seemed to be the essence of her life these days.

"And what do you think they expect him to do? Start rubbing those popish decorations off himself?"

58

Long ago Elizabeth had learned not to contradict or give an opinion. When her parents were alive—and just maybe her father still was although she doubted it—they would spend an occasional day with her aunt, uncle and cousins, usually a command Sunday dinner. On route, her mother would complain, and her father would jolly her out of it and beg her mother not to start any disputes.

Elizabeth's mother was not one to give in easily, but once she realized that nothing she said would make the slightest change in Jacques's or Mathilde's point of view, she would sit silently until it was time to leave, then splutter all the way back.

Elizabeth's father would laugh, kiss her mother's nose, and, once home, contentment would be restored.

Elizabeth took the bowl from the tray. "Here's the baby's breakfast, when she wakes up. Last night you said you wanted me to do the shopping first thing, but I can wait and feed the baby."

"I think the shopping is more important."

"I really can wait."

"All the good onions and cabbages will be gone. At this time of year . . ."

Elizabeth tuned her aunt out, busying herself with opening the curtains, then the windows and finally the shutters.

"Close that window before I freeze." Aunt Mathilde pulled the covers to her neck.

"When I was at the shop yesterday there were some chestnuts." Her mother had always roasted chestnuts on Christmas day and used them in the goose that she roasted on the spit over the fire. Maybe, if her aunt would agree, this would be a bit of a secret Christmas.

"Much too expensive. Get going now, and don't dawdle."

As Elizabeth walked down the stairs, she wondered why her aunt and uncle were so tight with money. Everything came down to exactly what something cost. Buy a rotten onion if it were cheaper. She knew her uncle's business was going well. Her father was careful with money, but he always managed to bring back something from his trips for her and her mother, a ribbon, a book, once even a perfume bottle from which, when the stopper was removed, the smell of a flower garden tickled Elizabeth's nose. Her mother had put a dab behind each of Elizabeth's ears.

She picked up her basket, wrapped herself in her cloak and let herself out into the sleet. The small fountain at the center of the Place du Bourg-de-Four was overflowing from the storm the night before, spilling water onto the dirt, leaving ice-crusted mud for water carriers to step in. But on a day like this, putting a pot outside the stoop to gather water saved going to the well at all.

Moisture seeped through her shoes turning her feet icy cold. She headed down the hill toward the Place du Molard. The lake, which she loved looking at with its changing colors, and the Jura Mountains beyond, were totally invisible. Sleet cut at her face. She pulled her cloak tighter around her head and she tried to walk as close as possible to the stone buildings.

"Elizabeth!"

She stopped and turned to see Jean-Michel running toward her. He almost slipped but righted himself before he went down on the cobblestones.

"I have to talk to you. Where can we go?"

Certainly not the café where word would get back to her uncle even before the first sentence was out of Jean-Michel's mouth. The fact that she and Jean-Michel were neighbors would not still the tongues.

She looked around. The shoe shop door was closed, but they could see the shoemaker inside. He had lit candles near his iron last, where he was slicing at a leather sole to fit the shape of the last. She and Jean-Michel exchanged looks and ducked in.

The bell over the door tinkled.

"Bonjour les deux," Antoine said. He was one of the refugees who had run from France tired of the persecution of his religion, which was not all that strong, but strong enough to be accepted by the Genevois. He was three years older than Jean-Michel, who had befriended him and helped him find the space to open the shoe shop. "I didn't expect any customers today. Good time to get caught up."

His accent was not the thick, singsongy patois that the local Genevois spoke, but bore traces of French, his mother tongue. Because of her parents, Elizabeth spoke French, patois and English and they often joked about how many ways they had to communicate. There was never an excuse not to find a word in one of the languages to convey the exact meaning they wanted to express.

Antoine waved his hand over the shoes stuck in small cubby holes behind him. He had a wheel, a grindstone, and several hammers. Nails of different sizes were also stuck in small wooden boxes on his work table. The place smelled of leather.

"I need to talk to Elizabeth and . . ."

". . . where her family won't know about it. Go upstairs as usual." He pulled back a curtain that led to a narrow staircase.

At the top of the stairs was a single room with a table, a chair, a bed, a small fireplace. Jutting out from the fireplace was an iron bar. A small cauldron hung on the bar over a smoldering log. Jean-Michel peeked in. "Soup."

What little light there was in the room was supplied by a crack in the wooden shutters. Antoine, having left everything but his tools in his flight from France, had put into his business whatever money came his way. Although he was considered a real craftsman with reasonable prices, it took time to be accepted.

Refugees who worked hard were readily taken into the community, but those that didn't were quickly ostracized by the townspeople. Antoine was considered hardworking, but loyalty to Yves, the old shoemaker, was great, even if the old man's work was getting shoddier as his eyesight failed. Some families were beginning to do business with both, letting Antoine make the new shoes while Yves was relegated to repairs.

The single candle on the table could have been lit, but Elizabeth and Jean-Michel felt it would be taking advantage of their friend.

"Light the candle." Antoine's voice floated up the stairs.

Instead Jean-Michel went to Elizabeth and gathered her in his arms pressing her head against his chest, which was as wet as her face. "Your uncle said no, I couldn't marry you."

"I know. I heard him and my aunt talking about it." She didn't want to marry Jean-Michel, but in the last few weeks she had begun to see it as an escape from her aunt and uncle's control.

"Do you know why?"

"They say you are after my money to set up your own print shop."

He pushed her away holding her by her shoulders and bent slightly so their faces were opposite. In the dim light she could make out his features.

"You don't believe that?"

"What I believe is they want to keep my farm and its rents in the family."

He nodded. "I love you."

She knew that and showed him with a kiss. His hand went down to her breast but she drew it away.

"I know, I shouldn't," he said. "We can continue to meet here, when we can each get away."

It was here that he often passed her the paper and drawing

supplies. In the warm weather she had drawn him, sitting by the window. His portrait filled the right side of the paper and the left had the half-opened shutter with the tree in full bloom as the background. She had done the drawing first in pencil then a second with colored chalk that he gave her.

"What choice do we have?" Her voice was insistent.

"None, for now," he said.

She knew he was correct. Until his apprenticeship was up, until he could open his own print shop, he could not support her. They could not go against her uncle. If only there were a way that both of them could go to England.

He turned the key in the lock and kissed her again, but when his hand went to her breast this time, she did not stop him.

CHAPTER 9

Geneva, Switzerland

As soon as Annie and Mireille entered their apartment, they went around to each radiator to turn up the heat.

"I'm hitting the shower to warm up," Mireille said.

Although the walk from the Number Three trolley had been less than three minutes, the *Bise* was blowing hard that night. Had the heat on the trolley been working, it might not have been so bad. But the heat was off, leaving the girls thoroughly chilled.

"If this is October, I'll hate to see how December will be," Mireille called from the bathroom.

Because the water had started running, Annie did not bother to answer as she lowered the shutters as tightly as she could, but they still rattled. She drew the drapes to add another layer of insulation from the bitter night.

Then there was a scratching at the door, which she barely heard over the noise in the flat, the wind and the running shower. She opened it to see Marc.

"Mama is home and she wants to invite you to dinner. Nothing fancy, but she hasn't seen you for so long." The shower stopped running.

"I don't know, I'm pretty tired."

"Please. She's making *sopa de Apio y guisantes*. It will be like old times." He blushed. "I feel a bit funny because she didn't include Mireille."

Annie did love Maria-Elena's pea-and-celery soup. But old times? While she had lived there, the sixth floor had been unusual by Geneva standards where many people didn't know their neighbors. During her time in residence, everyone but the Finnish diplomat would get together for meals, go to the movies in different combinations and swap off laundry days. It had driven the concierge crazy to find Andrea doing laundry in Gina's time slot or Mario using Hannah's. Finally he took down the schedule posted on the laundry room's door with the names in various blocks and replaced it with one where seven empty blocks said, "Sixth-floor tenants only."

Maria-Elena and Urs had been the least involved. Mireille stepped out of the bathroom in a terry-cloth robe and towel wrapped around her wet hair. "Good thing I heard voices and didn't come out naked."

From Marc's blush, Annie suspected he might have preferred that.

"I've been asked to dinner, but I told him I was tired." She wondered if Maria-Elena knew Mireille was her husband's lover.

"Go ahead. I really have a headache. I suspect it is the damned *Bise*," Mireille said. "Marc, it's okay. Just because Annie is staying here, we don't have to be invited as a couple."

"Come on, Annie, please," Marc said.

Annie followed him down the hall. His parents' flat was the largest on the floor: three bedrooms, two baths, a toilet, dining room, kitchen, living room and two balconies. The front door faced the kitchen where Maria-Elena was spinning lettuce dry. She came out and kissed Annie three times on the cheeks but kept her wet hands away from her former neighbor.

Once seated at the table, which included a salad and a roast chicken bought from the supermarket co-op Migros, as well as the promised soup, they searched for topics, never that easy. Annie knew nothing about Maria-Elena's work as a researcher for Renatus Pharmaceuticals and Maria-Elena acted as if tech writers were all incompetent and out to waste her time with unnecessarily bad descriptions and deliberately left-out vital steps.

Annie would be the first to admit there was some bad tech writing out there, usually by companies who would not pay for people who understood that it was a skill that required training and intelligence. However, it was more the way Maria-Elena attacked the profession that bothered Annie.

Annie, on the other hand, was not a big fan of Maria-Elena's company, which had hidden some bad side effects of a drug that was supposed to help heart patients. It did help the heart but had led to blood clots. To be fair to Maria-Elena—something Annie didn't really *want* to do—her neighbor had joined the firm well *after* the drug went off the market.

Her main antipathy to Maria-Elena was the way she treated Marc. His needs had always come last in the family priorities. Even the au pairs were not always that interested in him, which is one reason he had sought Annie out: she listened to his idea to win friends by handing out lollipops at school; why he really didn't like skiing but had no choice but to go on the annual school ski trips; how he didn't like holiday camps where he had to spend his summers; how much he loved swimming in the lake; what costume he wanted to wear for *L'Escalade*. Together they had carved pumpkins for Halloween when the holiday first made its appearance in Geneva, only to have his mother worry about it rotting too fast.

Urs was not much better, so wrapped up in his research and students. He did take Marc to his swimming meets, never mind that he had forced Marc to participate in them even though Marc hated competition. And he had tried to teach him tennis. The two of them at least shared an interest in art, but Marc was more interested in creating it than learning about its history.

"Where's Urs?" Annie asked as Maria-Elena spooned soup into bowls.

"We don't know," Marc said.

"Hush," Maria-Elena said.

"Well, we don't," Marc protested.

Maria-Elena's next remark was about dirty laundry and the public.

Marc slumped down in his chair, doing as good a sulky teenager as Gaëlle had ever projected.

"Sit up," his mother said.

Maria-Elena glanced into the living room. "Marc, how many times do I have to tell you not to put your shoes on the coffee table. It's bad luck."

"Sorry," he muttered and got up and put them in the hall by the door.

"I'm going to be here for a few weeks. Do you want to come over and see the new computer games I've got on my laptop?" Annie asked.

"Are they all stupid word games?"

"Marc!" his mother said.

"It's okay. It's a routine with us. I've one where you build a factory and take over the world of commerce."

Marc raised one eyebrow. "You should see the ones I have. They have well-known actors for the voices and a bonus where they talk about their characters. You'd love it."

"After dinner," Maria-Elena said.

"Your parents called," Mireille said, as soon as Annie got back.

Annie sat on the corner of the bed where Mireille was reading the latest Musso novel. "What did they say?"

"They'll be here next Wednesday. Seems your dad's partner picked up a big contract and they need your dad to do some work."

For a change, Annie thought, although she wasn't being critical. Her father, once given a very golden handshake by Digital Equipment Corporation before it disappeared, had built a successful consulting business then made sure others could do what he could do, rewarded them well, and set about enjoying his life. The last year or so that meant spending time in Caleb's Landing in a house they'd inherited from Dave Young's aunt. Her mother had joined an artists' co-op, and Annie had come to the conclusion that her parents would spend less and less time in Geneva, leaving her none too happy.

"Your dad said it works out well, because the couple subletting their house can move out at the end of the month as their new home will be ready early. But your folks need a place to stay for a few days and thought you could reserve something for them."

"Okay."

"Not necessary. I chose the John Knox Centre and arranged for them to have a room where they can cook if they want. And, of course, we'll have them over here."

"This is good news. I prefer sharing a continent with my parents."

68

CHAPTER 10

Geneva, Switzerland

"Mireille, wake up. It's a beautiful day." Annie went into her friend's bedroom with a cup of tea and crackers.

The black head turned to show a sleepy face. "It's October. It's Geneva. This does not go with a beautiful day."

Annie went over to the window and rolled up the shutters. "I do not speak with a forked tongue." When Mireille looked confused, she added. "It is what American Indians say when they run into liars."

Mireille ate the crackers then swallowed some of the tea. "Hmmm, I don't feel like throwing up. I like having maid service."

The two women walked with their coats open to the Number Three Gardiol-Champel trolley which was waiting in place. They each grabbed a copy of *20 Minutes,* the free newspaper available at almost all the bus stops throughout the city and suburbs.

"Damn, I meant to take the paintings and drawings in on the first good day."

"You could go back," Annie said.

Mireille glanced at her watch. "We lingered too long over breakfast."

Since this was the beginning of the line, there was a plenty of room in the cars, although as they waited, men and women in business clothes and briefcases arrived. In this area more people worked in the international agencies, which were in walking distance. The Number Three trolley went downtown carrying those that worked in other parts of the city. The women walked to the very back and sat down on the orange plaid plush seats.

Both looked at their papers. "The sniffing dogs found drugs at Cointrin," Mireille said.

"They are talking about increasing the number of lessons a dog owner needs before getting a license for his pooch," Annie said.

"Another accident outside Lausanne," Mireille said. The way they report the accidents, they might as well use a form and simply fill in the name of the driver and route."

"Finn is going to be daddy again." Annie mentioned one of the Bernese bears always on display for tourists. The animals made the headlines on a regular basis.

"Wow. Page six," Mireille said.

Annie skipped ahead to see that they had pulled a body out of the lake near the *plage*. No identification, but he was described as being extremely well dressed, about fifty, gray-haired and in good form. "He still had his shoes on," she said, thinking that it was an interesting detail.

"Horrible way to die," Mireille said. "Kinda makes doing the Find the Seven Errors and Sudoku puzzles on the last page seem unimportant doesn't it?"

They got off at Bel-Air this time, crossing over to the fountain and the street leading up to the Vieille Ville where they could walk up to Carsonwell's, stopping at the *pâtisserie* to pick up croissants for the staff.

By the time they arrived at the auction house they were late. As soon as they crossed the threshold, they heard Thomas and Conrad arguing. When they looked into the office, Conrad was leaning across his desk. Thomas, on the other side, was leaning back in his chair, his hands holding his head.

"I don't care that you are gay. I don't want you dating clients," Conrad yelled.

"Who in their right mind would want to date Prince Ruppert?" Thomas asked. "I have high standards. I don't care if he is an aristocrat, or even if he will make us a bundle on the auction. He's repulsive. Never mind that I'm in love with Damien."

"Then you shouldn't have flirted with him. He could pull everything out and take it to Christie's or Sotheby's."

Thomas sat up straight. "Won't happen. He signed a contract. Did you forget?"

"No. And I hope he won't either."

The phone rang and Antoinette came in to say that Prince Ruppert was on the phone for Thomas. "Again. This is the fifth time. He wants Thomas, not Conrad, not Annie, not Mireille, not me."

Conrad reached for the phone and oozed his greeting. "I'm terribly sorry but Thomas is preparing to go out of town to talk with a client . . . I am not sure, because he needs to check in with an appraiser . . . Italy . . . of course, I can give him the message that you called . . . I don't think he'll be back before the auction . . . he is overdue for a holiday, and I suggested that he take it while he was in Italy . . . I am sorry, we don't give out contact information for our staff even to an extremely valuable client like yourself." Conrad looked heavenward as if hoping for some kind of intervention.

After he hung up, Mireille asked, "And what will you do if Prince Ruppert shows up on our doorstep and Thomas answers the bell?"

"I'll say he came back unexpectedly." Conrad turned to Thomas. "You have to control being so cute and adorable around horny princes."

With that, Annie went to her office, switched on the computer

and started to research the artist of a miniature painting that
showed two little girls in long dresses sitting by a stream. On
the opposite bank a horse watched them.

Nothing existed in the reference books, and there was nothing on the Internet: nothing, nothing, nothing. Annie turned to
the computer and wrote.

"A summer day, a warm breeze, the smell of freshly cut hay
sweeps across the river. A horse watches as two little girls share
secrets. Although nothing is known about the artist, Pierrette
Montaine, she is thought to be French." She then started the
history of how the painting was acquired. The little girls would
not bring in a lot of money, perhaps just a few hundred. The
gallery would never handle a single unknown artist's work like
that, but as part of the bigger collection, they would use it as a
loss leader, so to speak. So to speak was one of Conrad's favorite
expressions. Annie found herself picking up on it.

When the doorbell rang, Annie, being the closest, answered
it. Chloë, one of their friends from university who had gone on
to teach in the art-history department, stood there. Annie
glanced at the grandfather clock. It was 12:36. The morning
had escaped her.

"Are you going to let me in?" Chloë asked. When Annie stood
aside, she swooped in. Chloë, although chunky, darted every-
where, often knocking things over as she went. Annie's eyes
took in anything breakable in the room.

"Didn't Mireille tell you?"

"Tell me what?"

"We're all going to lunch. I need some Mortimer's chocolate
cake."

Mireille entered the room and the routine cheek kisses were
accomplished with minimum fuss as Thomas and Conrad came
into the reception area. Another round of cheek kisses followed
by the usual pleasantries passed back and forth.

The women put on their coats but before they could leave, Chloë said, "I can't wait another minute to tell you. The police came to *Uni* today. The body they found in the lake was Dr. Stoller's."

Annie heard a small thud and when she turned around, Mireille was crumpled on the floor.

CHAPTER 11

Geneva, Switzerland

"I've never seen anyone faint like that," Thomas said as he carried Mireille out of the room. "In fact, I never saw anyone faint." Annie, Antoinette, Chlöe and Conrad followed him.

Thomas placed Mireille on the white brocade-covered couch in Conrad's office. Her skin, paler than its normal white, seemed to erase any boundaries between the material and her face. Thomas went into the small washroom just outside the office and wet a paper towel which he placed so gently on Mireille's forehead that it almost fluttered down. Annie brought a glass of water, but when she offered it, Mireille brushed her away with a wave of her hand.

"Leave us alone for a few minutes," Annie said. Antoinette, Conrad, Chlöe and Thomas exchanged glances before leaving.

"Urs is dead." Mireille's voice, which—when she wanted it to—could summon those buried in the cemetery, was barely audible. "Dead. My baby's father is dead. He'll never see his second child."

Annie didn't remind Mireille that she had said she planned to raise the child alone.

"I know we broke up, but I thought he would be around." Tears ran down her cheeks. "I want to go home."

"Just lay there and I'll see if one of the boys can drive us home."

Downstairs, Annie saw that Conrad, Thomas and Antoinette

were sitting on Victorian chairs from an English collection that would go under the hammer after Prince Ruppert's auction. The three pieces had been reupholstered in a flowered patterned so busy that a person's eyes could get tired just looking at it.

Thomas jumped up. "How is she?"

"Feeling terrible."

"I never expected her to react like that. She and Urs were always at each other's throats. There were times when I thought she hated him," Antoinette said. "She gave too much importance to her advisor. Not that I want to speak ill of the dead but . . ."

"Because he drowned doesn't make him any nicer. I had a lot of run-ins with him, too," Annie said. "He may have been a brilliant teacher and researcher, but he had the people skills of a . . . a . . ."

"Cockroach?" Thomas suggested. "Angry bear? Mosquito?"

Annie shrugged. "All of the above, depending on the day."

"There were times I heard him screaming at her over the phone," Antoinette said. "More than once. Of course, she claimed he screamed at everyone, but I never thought she would faint."

If Annie could have taken back her next words, she would have. "That's because she's pregnant." She clapped her hand over her mouth. "Oh, my God. I shouldn't have said that."

"I knew it, I knew it," Thomas said. "She was throwing up mornings and claimed it was the flu. No one has the flu that long. I told Damien: he thought so too."

Thomas drove Annie and Mireille home and left them at the front door saying, "If you need anything just text me."

Mireille headed straight for bed, only slipping off her shoes and crawling under the duvet. As Annie made tea, she could hear Mireille sobbing. Her first impulse was to go to her, but then she decided it was better to let her cry herself out. When the sobs diminished to hiccups, Annie went in with the tray.

Mireille propelled herself up in bed. Her white skin looked as if she had big patches of poison ivy or chicken pox clusters. "I suppose you think I'm silly."

"Why would I think that?"

"Because I broke up with him?"

Annie sat the tray down on the far side of the bed and crawled under the covers next to Mireille. "You loved him. You've known him for years, not just as a lover, but as a teacher, neighbor and your thesis advisor. You saw many different sides of him."

"He was a bastard for the way he stole my work."

For a minute Annie thought Mireille might start crying again, but she could see that the emotion that was rising to the surface was anger, probably healthy, she thought. "And because you left him angry, it's harder."

Mireille nodded several times, her eyes filling, but she wiped the tears away with the back of her hand in the same way a five-year-old trying to be brave would.

"Finish your tea and try and get some sleep."

When Mireille was asleep, Annie left her a note that she was going to the Migros to pick up some food. Then she softly shut the door behind her. The grocery store was across from the Number Three trolley stop. Annie bought two roast chickens and, from the deli counter, picked out two packages of carrot salad and two containers of *rösti*, then packed them into two separate bags which she had to buy, cursing herself for forgetting her own bags. The cashier, a woman who looked bored, wrote the date on the bag. "You know when they wear out we'll replace them?"

Annie nodded. She had forgotten bags enough times that she could almost start her own bag store from those she had had to buy rather than go home clutching her purchases in her arms.

Those that she had would never wear out because they were so seldom used.

Back on the sixth floor she walked to the end of the hall and knocked on the Stoller door. Marc answered without his normal radiant grin and stood in the open crack blocking the view of the inside.

Annie held up one bag. "I brought a complete meal so your mom doesn't have to cook. I don't want to come in or anything."

"*Merci*. Mom's not up to seeing anyone," he whispered to Annie.

"I understand." Annie started to go then stopped and looked at Marc. "If you need to talk, call me on my cell anytime. I don't care if it is three in the morning."

CHAPTER 12

Geneva, Switzerland
June 5, 1556

Elizabeth wanted to skip and dance as she forced herself to walk sedately down toward the lake, which sparkled in the sun. It looked like hundreds of thousands of candles were burning just below the surface. The Juras behind the lake had no more snow but stretched green above the water.

She was free for two hours. Jeanne was asleep. Her aunt, newly pregnant yet again and worn out from taking care of the baby that was always sick, was taking a nap. Her boy cousins were at school: poor them, locked up in a stuffy room. She felt sorry for the teacher who was trying to contain Louis who had just started going to school with his brothers. Sarah was at Saint Pierre's, undoubtedly doing some good work or maybe just polishing her halo.

In a moment of generosity her aunt had encouraged her to take a walk along the lake for her health, saying Elizabeth looked a bit peaked. Maybe it was because she had rubbed white chalk dust on her face.

She ducked into the shoemaker's after checking to make sure no one was looking, including from the windows of the houses across the street. Antoine had filled out since she first met him. When he'd arrived in Geneva he had been scrawny, probably from his struggle to walk all the way from Toulouse, hiding in barns and begging food where he could or trading food and a bed for a shoe repair.

"I could have made better time without my tools, but then how would I work?" he would ask anyone willing to listen to his stories of which they were many. Hearing about the awful Catholics that persecuted Protestants was one of the few things that seemed to make the Genevois happy.

Antoine's back was to the door and he was hovering over a last with a piece of thick black leather that he was shaping to the wood. To the back of the shop was shelf after shelf of lasts, one for each of his customers who wanted their new shoes to fit properly. They were labeled, including one with the name Jean Calvin. From the day Calvin had become a client in February, the boxes for lasts had filled quickly as had Antoine's coffers. "I didn't know you were coming today."

"I didn't either. I'm supposed to be walking by the lake."

"I'll get Jean-Michel. Go upstairs before anyone sees you."

She heard the bell on the door tinkle as she slipped behind the curtain and mounted the stairs. Antoine not only let her meet Jean-Michel there, he let her leave all her drawing supplies. Sometimes she could only work for fifteen minutes or less, but she considered each minute a gift. Her favorite model was Jean-Michel, but their time was more often spent holding each other.

The bell tinkled again, followed by footsteps on the stairs. Jean-Michel came bounding into the room. He wore his ink-stained apron, which he pulled off before gathering her in his arms.

"I've a new client coming in an hour," he said. In February he had opened his own print shop, but he only had one small press. He could not produce the religious books that the man he had been apprenticed to did, but he was able to handle many smaller pamphlets that his old boss sent his way for a small commission. He held her at arm's length. "Are you ill?"

She laughed as she rubbed the chalk from her face. "Only to make my aunt think I needed to take a walk. She believes fresh morning air is the cure to everything."

"Do you want to work on the drawing?" He pointed to the paper that she'd left on a shelf along with her art supplies.

What she wanted to do was to lie down on the bed with him, but with the time as short as it was, best to put it to her other passion. At least they were together. She posed him on the stool by the window.

What she wanted to do was to draw his body naked again: the body she loved, the body she had let enter hers despite all the rules against making love without being married. But then drawing naked people of any sex was also a taboo. In her mind she saw him without clothes, each muscle embedded in her memory.

"How is the baby?" He shifted his position on the stool. He found it impossible to sit still unless he could talk. She had long ago given up on his being quiet. Plus his voice, rich and deep, almost stroked her with its sound.

"Not well. He does not seem to grow and eats very little."

"And his foot?"

"Despite the brace, twisted. The second they take it off, it turns the wrong way. Don't move."

Her hand moved in little dashes, adding a tiny line to capture a hair out of place, a curve to his ear. She smudged the chalk under his chin to make a shadow. "Our only hope is to go to England, you know."

"And how are we going to do that with no money?" She noticed he did not chide her for jumping from subject to subject. "Everything I have is in my print shop."

She kept the chalk moving, but worked more on the frame of the window that stopped above his head. The light made his hair look like he wore a halo. "Like Antoine did to come here.

Walk, sleep in fields."

"And when we get to the Channel? Only Christ can walk across water."

"We can offer to work for our passage. Once we reach England my mother's family will take us in."

He broke his pose to go to her. "I love you." Forgetting that time was short, he undressed her and laid her on Antoine's bed. They had made love once, knowing that if they were caught they would be imprisoned—at best. Like always, at the last moment he pulled out.

"Two Calvinists walking through Catholic France . . . ," he said. "We could be killed."

Her head was now nestled in his arm and he stroked her hair.

"We could be killed for what we just did here, too," she said.

"When my shop makes more money, we'll marry."

She knew that was too far away. She hopped out of bed.

"Where are you going?"

She took a new piece of paper and began to draw him nude on the bed.

"The under pastor approached my uncle about marrying me, and he too was turned down. I'm more convinced than ever that my uncle does not want to let go of the rents from my father's farm." The smell of printers' ink, his sweat and semen mixed together was a better odor than the flowers outside the door on her family's farm, she thought.

"Which means it is hopeless that we will ever be together."

"I don't believe in hopeless." She looked into his eyes. With her fingers, she tried to wipe the frown off his face, but she couldn't.

CHAPTER 13

Geneva, Switzerland

Annie's parents staggered off the plane at Genève Aéroport. Her mother Susan, her blonde hair more disheveled than usual, said, "We missed our Frankfort connection because the plane was late taking off from Boston, and we ran into winds. I hate those up-and-down flights."

"I do too." Annie pushed their overburdened baggage caddy toward the parking lot. The amount of luggage told her that her parents would be in Geneva for a while. Both had mastered the art of traveling with one bag or less for anything up to a month.

"Art supplies for your mother," Dave said tapping one suitcase. "Even with the overweight cost, it is cheaper than buying the stuff here."

As they piled the bags in the trunk of the taxi to drive to the John Knox Centre, Dave said, "We can drop you at the flat." He had a nine-o'clock shadow, making him look a bit like some of the actors on television who thought it was fashionable to look scruffy.

"I can walk back from John Knox. I need some thinking time anyway." Annie wanted to tell them about Urs Stoller's murder.

They had met the professor in the elevator of her building years ago when she was a student. They had gotten off on the ground floor, and Urs had gone down to the basement for his car, she'd assumed. "That's the professor who is brilliant and a bastard."

82

"B and B," Dave had said.

Another time they had run into the family at the Café du Soleil and shared a table. On the walk back to Annie's, Dave had commented, "Not just brilliant and a bastard. Add arrogant."

"Makes him a BAB," Susan had said.

No, she would wait until they had rested a bit. However, she could not tell them about Mireille. Her parents were often the confidants of her friends who could not talk to their own parents. As much as she wanted her mother's advice on how best to help her friend, she felt it was Mireille's secret to share. All Annie's friends teased her that they were sure that even waterboarding would not make her reveal a secret she'd promised to keep, which made her feel even worse about her telling Thomas and Conrad, even if Mireille had forgiven her.

They pulled into the parking lot in front of a long stretch of grass. The low wooden building almost looked as if it could be a western ranch house. Nearby was a farm which raised buffalo, a fact that startled more than one airline passenger who saw the beasts as their planes came in, leaving them wondering if their plane had taken a wrong turn and landed in the American west.

As soon as her parents were settled, Annie started the seventeen-minute walk back to her apartment, past the small stone mansions surrounded by hedges or stone walls. The sky had turned a dark blue, but how long that would last she had no more idea than she had as to how to tell Mireille that the police thought Urs had been murdered.

She needn't have worried. When she let herself into the flat, Mireille was sitting in the living room with two men. Before she could introduce them to Annie, the men stood.

"I'm Detective Inspector Luca Fortini. This is my partner Christian Morat." Morat was the younger of the two men by decades. They were almost stereotypical of a TV detective series.

The older Fortini's black curls were streaked with gray. He looked if he could have starred in any Italian film as a Mafia don and he wore a world-weary expression.

Morat was blond and had an angel-on-a-Christmas-card look about him, a bit pudgy and smiley.

Fortini didn't look as if smiling was part of his repertoire.

Two identity cards came out. Annie looked at them, aware that she had no idea what a Genevois police identity card looked like.

"They're here about Professor Stoller," Mireille said. "They're talking to me because he was overseeing my thesis."

"And your name?" the policeman with the Italian name asked. His accent was slightly Italian, but also that of a person who had lived in Geneva for many years.

Morat took out a notebook and seemed to be taking down every word.

"Annie Young."

"And how do you know Mademoiselle Bosset, Mademoiselle Young?"

"Right now, I'm staying with her."

"Then you both knew Herr Professor Dr. Urs Stoller."

"He's our neighbor. Annie had him as a prof at *Uni*. And he's my thesis advisor. Why?" Mireille said.

Fortini saw the *20 Minutes* paper on the coffee table in front of the couch. He picked it up. The front page showed a photo of the *plage* and men huddled around a body bag. "This interested you enough to keep it?"

"Of course: I wanted to read about it, both because we knew him and because this affects my thesis. But I kept it more for the Sudoku," Mireille said.

"This isn't the Sudoku page," Fortini said.

"Look around, Monsieur Fortini," Annie said. "You will see old copies of *Paris Match*, *Voici*, *Art Aujourd'hui*, open to different places. The detectives did glance around the room which was littered with papers, books and magazines."

"The paper said the body had no identification," Annie said. "How did you identify him?"

"His suit was tailor made and the prof's name was sewn into the label. From there we . . . ," Morat said until Fortini held up his hand.

If Annie had any doubts about who was the boss, they were gone. "I feel so sorry for his wife and son, especially his son. When I lived here all the time, Marc used to come down a lot."

"You once lived here?" Fortini asked.

"I sublet from Annie," Mireille said. "But when she comes to Geneva, she often stays with me."

"Where do you live now?" Fortini asked.

Annie explained how she owned a place in the South of France and how she traveled to work for several weeks at a time to different clients located all over Europe.

Fortini turned to Mireille. "How close were you to the professor?"

"I had him for several courses. He was my thesis advisor, as you know. I'm in the finishing stages for my doctorate," Mireille said. But when she looked at Annie, Annie raised her eyebrows, although neither detective was looking at her.

"What is it on?" Morat asked.

"Brueghel. I am, among other things, quantifying the use of color, costume, men, women, household items, farm items and then taking them to try and explain how even when he painted a religious topic, it was an insight into the daily life of the period where and when Brueghel lived and worked."

Morat, who stopped scribbling, picked up a book of Brueghel paintings that was well marked up with notes and checks. He opened his mouth, but Fortini barged in. "How would you describe your working relationship with the professor?"

Morat put the book down and went back to his note taking.

"Like all students. Sometimes I would think I finished a certain theme and he would send me digging for more research. That is how it usually is with a thesis."

"At the university they said you and he had had a number of fights over a paper he published."

Mireille looked at Annie who barged in. "It is not unusual for profs to use students' work in their papers. I hate the system."

"Isn't that dangerous, challenging the person who could stop you from getting your degree?"

"He promised that the next time he used my research for a paper he was publishing, he would give me an acknowledgment," Mireille said. "We'd finished with the matter."

Annie knew better than to add sarcastically that he damn well *should have* given an acknowledgment because Mireille wrote the whole damn thing. Surely the police didn't suspect Mireille? And what if they discovered she had had an affair with Urs and was pregnant by him? Even if Mireille had a motive, how could she have dragged Urs into a boat and dumped him overboard? She was too small and he was too big. She would have had to do it before Annie got there. But, then again, Annie didn't know how long Urs had been in the water. And even if she did, Mireille was fanatic about all forms of life. Once she'd carried a captured mouse outside the apartment rather than kill it.

"I saw Marc a little while ago, and he told me his father didn't drown but was murdered? What was the weapon?"

Morat started to speak but withered under Fortini's stare.

Mireille paled even more. "I hope he didn't suffer."

"We don't know except that he was dead when he went into the water, which is why we think he was murdered," Morat said and kept his eyes away from Fortini's.

"Is there anything else you want to ask us?" Annie asked.

"Maybe later," Fortini said.

As soon as the door closed, Annie said, "If they find out about the affair and baby, they will be back."

CHAPTER 14

Geneva, Switzerland
October 6, 1556

Elizabeth was worried. Her monthlies had not come and she felt sick most mornings, something she did her best to hide. Seeing her aunt lurch from pregnancy to pregnancy left her little doubt that she too was expecting.

Keeping secrets in Geneva was next to impossible, but she had carried off her secret meetings with Jean-Michel, although for a short time there had been rumors about her and Antoine because she popped into the shop as often as she could. However, sometimes she was there just to draw. Wagging tongues were silenced when Antoine married Marie, and the couple gave credit to Elizabeth for bringing them together, thus explaining her many visits.

Marie's presence had made their meetings easier because Elizabeth claimed she was visiting her friend whenever she went into the shop. Jean-Michel had started coming in the back way. Marie would go downstairs to work in the shop leaving the two alone.

Aunt Mathilde and Uncle Jacques saw the young couple as a good influence on their niece, citing how hard Antoine worked after starting from nothing. "God must approve of him, letting him succeed the way he has." Monetary success was always a sign of God's blessing, in their opinion. That blessing did not extend to Elizabeth, however, who never met with their approval.

"The butter you bought yesterday is rancid," Aunt Mathilde said. She held the slab out to her niece to sniff. "Didn't you check it?"

"I thought I did." Elizabeth remembered talking to Marie as the man who ran the *crémerie* wrapped up the piece in cloth. He easily could have changed the good slab for a rancid one. The smell caused a wave of nausea.

"Take it back. Make a scene. The more customers, the better. Let everyone know he cheated you."

For once Aunt Mathilde was between pregnancies, having miscarried twice since June. "Take Jeanne with you, I feel a headache coming on." Aunt Mathilde sank into a chair. "There are times I think this family is cursed."

After the last miscarriage, her aunt had become more disagreeable. Each time when Elizabeth thought her aunt had reached the peak of unpleasantness, she would do something else. Elizabeth was forbidden now to sleep anywhere but in front of the fire, which was a blessing in summer because the entry was cooler than the stifling top floors, but not in winter. Her aunt insisted that the blankets were needed for her own children. Little Jeanne now slept in bed with Sarah upstairs in the place that Elizabeth once occupied.

In her kinder thoughts Elizabeth tried to believe it was because her aunt suffered from headaches, the noise the boys made when home, the fussing of the younger ones, which drove her to her bedroom with a cool cloth on her forehead. When the headaches struck she said light stabbed her brain.

Jeanne, the youngest girl at almost four, loved to go out, and when she heard her mother tell Elizabeth to take her, she jumped up and ran to get her cloak and Elizabeth's, coming back dragging them behind her. Elizabeth put Jeanne's on first,

making sure that her bonnet was tightly tied under her chin and
the cloak buttoned up to her neck. The child's arms poked
through the holes cut for the purpose.

"I want to go see the boats. I want to see the boats."

Elizabeth was not surprised. Her little cousin loved watching
the boats from Bern unload the wheat that stocked the mills
which supplied the *boulangeries.* Depending on the time of year
they brought onions, cabbages and carrots. The number of boats
had increased because with the influx of French Protestant
refugees, Geneva could not feed itself, and even if Elizabeth did
not find the unloading interesting, she loved watching Jeanne's
eyes grow wide with excitement.

"I want to see the boats." The child stamped her foot and
pushed out her lower lip as she crossed her arms.

Elizabeth knew if she took her, her aunt would be angry that
they had taken so much time. If she didn't take her, Jeanne
would complain and her aunt would be angry that she had not
fulfilled the child's wishes. Elizabeth suspected that Jeanne was
her aunt's favorite, but then, she too adored the little girl.

"I want to see the boats. Can we, please? Please?" Elizabeth
loved the way the child changed techniques. If foot stamping
failed, then being winsome was the next thing she tried.

Well, if Aunt Mathilde was going to be angry, better that at
least Jeanne be happy.

"We can go."

As they walked out of the house, Jeanne dashed into the
street just as a horse galloped by. Usually horses walked within
the walls, but this one seemed in a hurry. Or maybe the young
man on it wanted to show off. Elizabeth grabbed the child out
of harm's way. "Hold my hand," she ordered.

She headed toward the lake where the *crémerie* was. They
would go see the boats first, then the *crémerie,* because she
didn't want to risk something going wrong with the butter again.

She had to pass Jean-Michel's shop, but on the front door was a be-back-after-lunch sign. Too bad. She might have snuck a few words with him, although with Jeanne along, she would have to be careful of how she phrased everything.

She wanted to hire a messenger to send a letter to her grand-father telling of her predicament and asking him to send for her. Then Uncle Jacques would have no choice but to send her to her grandfather. When she told Jean-Michel, he replied that it was the craziest idea he'd ever heard. He was working too hard to waste money on a fool's errand. And even if by some remote chance the messenger did get word to Elizabeth's grand-father, and even if the grandfather sent for her that was no guarantee that her uncle would let her go.

Her next idea was to hire a messenger to bring a letter sup-posedly from her grandfather in England, but one that she would have written herself, saying that he wanted his daughter and his grandchildren with him. Her grandfather would explain that he had been attacked, hit on the head and lost his memory for a time but was just regaining his health and needed their care. He had realized how much he had missed his daughter and before he died he wanted to meet his grandchildren.

Jean-Michel's reaction to that was even if the impossible hap-pened and her uncle believed the letter was real and did not recognize the fake messenger and agreed to let her go to England, and they did end up in England, where would he work?

How different were English printing methods?

He couldn't speak the tongue of the Anglos, so how could he communicate with customers?

What if her grandfather didn't have room for them? Then how would they live?

What would happen if Elizabeth became pregnant in a strange country? And now that England was Catholic again under

Queen Mary, and Protestants were losing their lives in droves according to rumors that reached Geneva, how safe would two Calvinists be?

His last argument was, "I'm just beginning to make my way here and if even half of what I plan happens, we will have the blessings of God upon us."

Elizabeth, annoyed at his lack of imagination, worried about his phrasing. He talked more and more about God this or God that as many of the Protestants did. If they stubbed their toes, it was as if their God had pushed them, and Elizabeth, like her mother, could not believe that a God that created the universe was about to hurt a person as punishment or some minor sign of disfavor.

But the idea of the fake letter had triggered another. Maybe she could go on her own. Although she had never been to England, she could picture the moors where her mother had spent her summers running free. In the winter, of course, she returned to the village near London, where her grandfather lived next to a beautiful church with stained-glass windows and there was music and happiness, or at least that was what her mother had said. She had talked about her uncle's jewelry business, which was how she had met Elizabeth's father. Her maternal uncle had entertained her father, Yves, when he was there talking about the jeweler buying the Swiss watches and had invited his brother's family.

In her most fearful moments, Elizabeth wondered if her grandfather were dead. Had Mary purged him as being too Protestant? Or had he returned at least outwardly to the Catholic faith? That was not a fear she would share with Jean-Michel, who could conjure up more than enough excuses and problems on his own.

Then again she remembered what her mother had told her about life under Henry VIII and how her father had had no real problem going from accepting the king in place of the pope as the church leader. Her mother had also told her that her father had come to the conclusion as a young man that God and man-made religions had little to do with each other. Her grandfather was the one who had made sure that Elizabeth's mother could read and speak French and Latin, that she knew how to play music as well as the necessary household arts which all women must perform.

For a moment Elizabeth let memories of her mother's stories flood through her. How Elizabeth's father met his future wife at a dinner featuring roast lamb and how it was a love-at-first-sight story. Most couples married for other reasons: putting pieces of land together, their parents were in the same guild—practical reasons that had little to do with love.

But if Elizabeth's parents had been that rare commodity—a love match—so had her mother's parents. Her grandmother had been bringing her own father's dinner to him at the small jewelry shop he owned. He'd had a guest from Oxford, a student and son of an old friend. After that the student found many a reason to come to the town and to court Elizabeth's grand-mother. Not that the courtship had gone smoothly. A student was not a good prospect, but when he secured himself a post as Saint George's historian, the couple was allowed to marry.

Her mother had told her over and over the stories of couples falling madly in love as she sat on the edge of her bed before Elizabeth went to sleep. But her favorite love story would always be her mother and father's. When her mother got to the part how both parents had the same reaction when their eyes first met, Elizabeth always wanted to cry because of the beauty of it. Had her parents lived would they all be in England now?

Her mother had convinced her father that being among the dour Calvinists was not the way to live. Life was full of beauty. Laughter should not be a sin.

She shivered fearing that Jean-Michel was taking on the dour characteristics of other Genevois. She put her hand on her stomach. Now that she was pregnant, traipsing across France alone was out of the question even dressed as a man, but she had another idea to flirt with. She must convince Jean-Michel that, for the sake of the baby, they had to escape. She couldn't do it today with Jeanne with her, but hopefully tomorrow.

Unlike Jean-Michel, her father had thought the idea of moving his family back to England was a good one. He'd begun to inquire about selling or leasing his farm and all he needed to do was to tell his brother. Her father had promised her mother that he would tell him, then go on his last mission. Afterwards, he would come back for the family with all the plans in place.

He never did come back. In fact, he had never come back from telling his brother, but sent the first of two notes saying he had to leave for England directly from work along with a list of things her mother needed to pack and give to the messenger who waited. The second note had arrived when he had crossed the channel.

Elizabeth had never seen her father again. As these memories filtered through her mind, she wondered if Uncle Jacques were somehow responsible for her father's death.

Still, she couldn't imagine her uncle, who was so religious, breaking the commandment, "Thou shall not kill."

"Someday, I am going on a boat and go to the end of the lake." Jeanne broke into Elizabeth's thoughts.

"Are you now?" Elizabeth asked.

"And I'm hot."

"I didn't think it was so warm when we left." She untied the child's cloak and carried it over the same arm that held the basket with the rancid butter.

A small café where business people met with their clients to drink a glass of wine, beer or cider and to make business deals was on the left side of the street facing the lake. Usually it was peopled with only men, but on rare occasions wives and children would be included. In the summer they sat outside on benches and at tables, their feet stretched out, or they hunched over talking so that their noses almost touched.

Because it was warmer than normal, the café had placed three tables outside in the sun although they were sheltered from any wind by a stone wall. Sitting at one was Jean-Michel, a man and a young girl. The man, who was wealthy and a pillar of the church, owned one of the new watchmaking ateliers: it was said that even the King of France had one of his watches. He was also sickeningly pious, ferreting out sin and calling the sinner to task, whenever he found it. He and Calvin were said to be so close that if one reached for a handkerchief, the other would sneeze.

His four sons were also in the watchmaking business. The girl, Françoise, sitting there with her hand under Jean-Michel's, was his only daughter. No one needed to tell Elizabeth that the girl adored Elizabeth's fiancé, albeit unofficial thanks to her uncle who had refused permission once again last month. It was the hand-touching that knotted Elizabeth's stomach. It was too much like he had done with her when they first knew they were in love. He looked up and saw her: his eyes widened.

At that instant, she knew that she had lost him. And Jean-Michel knew she knew. He jumped up so fast that the bench fell over. Françoise needed to grab at the table to not end up on the ground. Elizabeth assumed he stopped to pick it up, but she wasn't looking as she hustled down the hill dragging Jeanne, who began to cry.

"Wait," Jean-Michel called.

Putting one foot in front of the other as fast as she could with Jeanne tripping because she could not keep up with the pace, Elizabeth made her way down the hill toward the lake.

95

The child tripped, fell, then was dragged to her feet. Elizabeth was engulfed, a swirl of pain without a physical source.

Jean-Michel caught up with the duo as they reached the lake's edge. He twirled around and she watched his mouth move as he said what she knew he would. It wasn't necessary to hear the words.

"Go away, just go away." She bent down to wipe Jeanne's tears and to hide her own.

He lifted her by the shoulders and held his face too close to hers. "I have to marry. I can't wait for you any longer. Your idea of going to England is crazy."

He started to walk away but after a few steps turned. "I still love you, you know."

She watched him make his way up the hill. For a moment, she wondered what he would say to his future wife and father-in-law to explain running out on them like that. She hoped they would understand only too well.

Elizabeth loved the lake because it had as many moods as there were days: glass flat, slightly bumping or it could get angry and throw its waves onto the rocks. Some days it was gray, but other times it looked like the sky had fallen asleep in the water. Or after a storm, it was brown from the mud that had been churned up.

Under other circumstances, Elizabeth would have taken the time to enjoy the reflection of the mountains in the water and how the lake was calm, so calm that it looked as if it were a carpet to be trod upon.

How could the water be so calm, when her life was in turmoil? She had found herself at the water's edge, not along the beach area, but where several large rocks protected the village when winter storms caused the lake to throw temper tantrums.

What was she going to do now? Her pregnancy would be discovered.

Where was Jeanne? In her pain she had totally forgotten the child. She called loudly but there was no answer. Then she glanced to the rocks where the little girl was inching her way along the boulders.

Jeanne waved. "I can almost see the boats 'Lizabet."

"Stay there! Don't move!" Elizabeth screamed just as the child tumbled head first with her feet disappearing over the rock's edge.

The rocks were slippery as Elizabeth propelled herself over them. At the edge she saw the little girl facedown. Most women could not swim. Their clothes would hamper their movements, and any clothes that would give them freedom of movement would be too immodest.

Elizabeth's mother thought that was only more Calvinistic nonsense and had fashioned an outfit for both her children and had taught them how to paddle in the pond behind their fields. Sundays the whole family would picnic by the pond then swim when they got too hot. Isn't-this-better-than-being-on-your-knees-all-day, her mother would bait her husband, and he would laugh and reply, "As long as no one sees us."

Elizabeth plunged into the water and turned the child face up. However, the rocks were too high for her to climb onto them. She screamed for help as she treaded the water holding Jeanne's head above the surface. The water was bloody from where the little girl's head had struck a rock, probably knocking her unconscious. Elizabeth was sure she had not been in the water long enough to get water into her lungs.

No one heard her screaming. The only thing to do was to swim until she reached a place where there were no high rocks and she could climb out. Her clothes were drenched, hampering her movements, but she struggled until she came to shallow water and walked ashore carrying the child.

Laying Jeanne on the grass already brown from the night

frosts, she could see that she was breathing. Although the day was warmer than most October days, it still was chilly and her wet clothes clung like icicles from the roof.

Jeanne moaned. To Elizabeth the sound was music. Brushing the child's wet tendrils from her face, she whispered her name. The child's eyes fluttered and she let out a sigh.

The soft clip clop of a horse's hooves against the path made Elizabeth look up. "Help me! Help me! Over here!"

The gray-haired rider looked around. As soon as he saw them, he dismounted and ran over.

"What happened?" he asked.

She told him.

"Let's get you home." He mounted his horse and held his arms out for Jeanne and then pulled Elizabeth up on the saddle.

"She's wicked. She's evil." Aunt Mathilde's voice rose up the stairs. "I want her out of the house."

Elizabeth, who was huddled at the top of the stairs, could not hear her uncle's reply. Jeanne had been put to bed, the doctor called. He said she would be all right, only that the rocks had knocked her unconscious. Of course there was the danger of pneumonia. Aunt Mathilde had refused to let him look at Elizabeth, whom she said deserved whatever cold she caught. That Elizabeth had saved Jeanne's life did not override the anger that the toddler should never have been able to fall into water in the first place.

For once, Elizabeth was in agreement with her aunt.

CHAPTER 15

Geneva, Switzerland

After removing any cups with liquids from the desktop, Mireille undid the shredded black ribbon that was holding the two pieces of fortified brown and black leather together. The material almost looked moldy. She stood in front of Conrad's desk. Thomas was to her left, Annie to her right.

"It took you long enough to bring this back in," Conrad said. Like the others he wore surgical gloves.

"I had no intention of carrying this around in the rain. And it wasn't like I didn't have anything else on my mind. Sometimes I wished I'd never gone back to *Uni* for my doctorate."

"No, you don't wish you weren't studying. Then you wouldn't have anything to bitch about." Thomas stood to peer over Mireille's shoulder.

The first was a lightly colored painting of a crowd sketched from a higher place. In the middle of the crowd a man's face could be seen through flames.

Conrad let out a long whistle. "From the clothes I'd say sixteenth century. What do you think, Annie?"

Annie, who had come to the same conclusion when Mireille first showed her the portfolio, knew Conrad liked to lead in discoveries. He did not take well to being bested and she saw no reason not to humor him. "You're probably right. Look at the women's head coverings. Of course that doesn't mean it couldn't have been done more recently and merely copied sixteenth-century clothing."

"But there are different styles that seem to go beyond class. When did the strict dress requirements come in, anyone know?" Conrad asked.

"Sometime after Calvin's death in 1564," Annie said.

"Not bad. I'm impressed," Thomas said.

"Don't be. I did a paper on the clothing edicts and these don't fit, which is why I am guessing these are before Calvin died," Annie said.

"Urs said his appraiser said that these drawings were probably no more than fifty or seventy-five years old and someone was mimicking an earlier period."

"I don't think so," Thomas said. "Or at least the paper is older."

"I've verified the paper," Mireille said, "but Urs said someone could have found old paper."

Conrad nodded. "True, but it doesn't feel like it."

"And there have been some incredible forgeries over the years, but if you're going to do a forgery, wouldn't it be better to do say Rembrandt or Van Gogh . . . not an unknown artist?" Thomas took out a jeweler's glass and looked closer.

"Where did you say you got them, again?" Conrad asked.

"The old bookstore. You know the one. We went there once when you were looking for some texts on Saint Pierre's. The owner told me they'd been found in the trash when the building across from the Lutheran Church was being renovated."

"The one in the Vieille Ville?" Conrad asked.

"His father grabbed them, thinking someone would like them, but died almost immediately after getting them. The new owner considered them junk."

"Look at the faces of the people to the right of the guy being burned. Those expressions are wonderful." Thomas looked up from where he was studying them. "And it is done in a few lines and shadows."

Mireille gently moved the drawing aside revealing a second one of a young man, sitting with one knee raised and his sexual organs in full display.

"My turn to whistle," Annie said. "Not typical sixteenth century. Calvin would have had a heart attack at the thought that this was going on."

Thomas held one up. "This one is done up in the Place du Bourg-de-Four. You can see some of the same houses."

One by one Mireille went through them all, pointing out what could easily be identified as the Vieille Ville, buildings still standing or the view of the lake and Juras. Two were of a shoemaker tapping with his hammer against a sole. Three other scenes were Mary Cassatt–type scenes of women with their children doing household tasks, but they were on the same piece of paper. Three children all slept in the same bed in the sketch on the back.

"Offhand, I would say all of them are by the same artist," Thomas said, "despite the variety of topics."

"Interesting how he uses both sides of the paper."

"Maybe he couldn't afford more paper?" Thomas half asked, half offered.

"She. Some are initialed. Some signed. See here." Mireille pointed to a very tiny *E something* on the corner of one of the drawings that were done in pastels rather than just charcoal. Some had *E.H.* Others had *E—b-th H.* or *E: Hu—te*. The letters were blurred at best. Most had no signature at all.

"The name is Elizabeth H.," Mireille said. She pulled out the ones with the faint signatures.

Conrad opened the middle drawer of his desk and located his magnifying glass. "*P.* I think that is a *P.*" He handed the glass to Annie.

"Not a *P,* but an *H.*" Annie examined another drawing with the tiny initials. *"H."*

"If they are mid-sixteenth century, the artist would have had problems sharing his, er, *her* work. Calvin was not a lover of art or graven images," Thomas said. "I'm surprised that the artist would dare sign any of these."

"Assuming the artist was of that century and came from here," Conrad said. "Historically, we might have a chance of tracing down the artist if there were some kind of process against her. Or maybe through the burning of this man. Annie, when did they stop burning people?"

"I think the last witch burned in Switzerland was Anna Goldi out in the eastern part of Switzerland sometimes in the sixteen hundreds. During Calvin's time, there were quite a few burnings, some famous, some not."

Mireille was lifting each paper and looking at both sides over and over.

"What's wrong?" Conrad asked.

"Annie, when you looked at these at home, did you see several still lifes? Not just fruit, but kitchen items? One of a well in the middle of the square with a woman drawing water?" Mireille asked.

Annie shook her head. Mireille had been taking a shower when Annie went through the portfolio piece by piece.

"Did you check it when you picked them up from the person who analyzed the paper?" Thomas asked.

"Urs picked them up. I was so disappointed in the evaluation, I just put the whole portfolio aside when he returned it to me—until Annie came. I was tempted to store them in my *cave* or throw them out, even."

"Well, thank God you didn't," Conrad said. "From now on we don't touch them at all, even wearing gloves, and I want to get a real appraisal not just on the age of the paper. I think we can find out more about them because of all the clues in the drawings themselves. And who painted them."

"With the little we have to go on, it might be pushing it," Annie said. "However, it will be fun to try."

CHAPTER 16

Geneva, Switzerland

Celebratory red. Now, that would shock everyone, Maria-Elena Stoller thought as she took the dress out of her closet. She held it against herself as she looked in the mirror.

Her sister Sophia walked in. "You can't be planning to wear *that!*"

Damn, Maria-Elena had thought her sister was still asleep in Urs's office, the third bedroom in the flat that held the futon where she hoped her sister and brother-in-law had had an uncomfortable jet-lagged night. They were representing her family, doing the done thing by coming from Uruguay for the funeral.

Between the time the body was found and released by the police, her family had had plenty of time to decide who would go. Certainly not her parents, who although on speaking terms, still hadn't forgiven her for staying in Switzerland to marry *that professor-person* instead of the man they had picked for her. Even if the marriage hadn't turned out like she had dreamed, it had given her a much more interesting life, not to mention her career. With a little luck within a year she would be head researcher with Renatus Pharmaceutical International instead of assistant head. The current head was seldom in the lab, having had a cerebral hemorrhage, but the company was holding the post gathering the insurance they were being paid for keeping him on board. However, everyone knew that Maria-Elena was already doing the job.

"It should be a long time before you can wear red," Sophia sniffed. Maria-Elena's older sister was acting just like the stereotypical older sister and a disapproving one at that.

"I know that, but red does look better on me than black."

"Still," Sophie said going through the closet and pulling out a black suit. It had been custom made for Maria-Elena by the courtier in Eaux Vives, not a big name, but she had had him design a few things for her before he retired. In the lab, whatever she wore was hidden under her lab coat, but she made sure when she attended any management meeting that she was dressed to kill, probably a poor choice of words considering what had happened to her not-so-dear-poor-dead Urs.

She would have no trouble pretending to be the grieving widow any more than she had had trouble pretending to be the devoted wife. Her acting skills had been honed as a daughter: she had pretended she was an obedient daughter before doing what she wished when there were no witnesses.

Not that she rebelled with drugs or boys, but rather with her plans to study and live abroad and not follow the route prescribed for her.

"I was planning on wearing that suit, and you will find a gray blouse toward the back of the closet," she said to Sophia.

Marc knocked on his mother's door and came in without waiting to be invited. "The caterer is here."

"Have them set up in the kitchen." She expected a mob, between her colleagues and her husband's, all of whom would probably return to the house. She was under no illusions that her husband's arrogance had endeared him to many of the university faculty, but they would come because it was proper. She wondered how many of his mistresses would show up. None, she hoped. She hated pretending that she didn't know.

Her cell phone played the first few notes of Beethoven's "Ode to Joy"—more appropriate than the black suit she was about to wear.

"*Allo.*"

"How are you holding up?" Garth said.

"Zebras are descending," she said as she turned her back to Sophia.

"That means you can't talk."

"I will get through the next few hours. Do you need directions to the church?" As if anyone could miss Saint Pierre's rising as it did above the city at the top of the hill where the Vieille Ville resembled the time of Calvin if one forgot electric wires and motorcycles parked nearby.

"Can whoever you are with hear me?"

"No."

"Good, I love you."

"I understand. I feel the same way."

"You love you too?"

"You know what I mean."

CHAPTER 17

Geneva, Switzerland

Christian Morat was alone in his and Fortini's office at the new Genevan police station opened only two months before. The building was ultramodern, but the furniture, transferred from the old station, was antique. However, each of the twenty battered desks had a modern plasma screen.

The night shift had come and was out on the street. The day shift had disappeared home to dinners and televisions. Only the person assigned to phone duty sat at the entrance and he was engrossed in a book.

Morat was Googling Urs Stoller and had over one thousand hits that came up in English, French, Italian, Spanish and German. The professor certainly had carved out a reputation for himself in the academic world, Morat thought. Unlike many of the older detectives, Morat loved the computer, the Internet and his cell phone. At home he had the latest everything. At one point he had thought of going into computer programming, but instead gave in to his father's pressure to get a law degree and then ended up joining the police force more on a whim than anything else. That it annoyed his father was only a fringe benefit.

His boss reminded him a bit of his father, cranky, not particularly interested in anything that had happened after the twentieth century had become the twenty-first. If Inspector Fortini ignored modern techniques, he did have a good instinct that he sometimes buried under stubbornness.

Morat felt sorry for his boss. The man lived in fear of the Big Boss, a smart woman who had left Interpol to be closer to her aging parents.

Morat wasn't afraid of the Big Boss at all. The few times they had talked in the canteen he knew that they had the same philosophy toward police work. But she wouldn't tolerate sidestepping the hierarchy of the department.

It wasn't that Fortini was a bad *flic*. In fact, he was damned good. Morat knew he could learn a lot from him. He also knew that if Fortini did not always have to prove that he was superior, Morat could teach him a few things too. Together they could be a great team. Morat had not given up on the idea that with time he would be able to demonstrate to Fortini what he, Morat, the future Chief of Police of Geneva, could offer.

Morat kept his ambitions to himself. He was not so fixated on his future career that he did not enjoy his current work. He loved unraveling a case, which was not that much different than unraveling a computer glitch. In a way he felt a bit like he was living in one of those television detective series with mismatched partners: the old experienced grump and the new enthusiastic cool-looking rookie.

Except this wasn't television. They had a real murder, his first, to solve. Most of the murders in Switzerland were either domestic violence or committed by criminals from the former-Eastern-bloc countries. He didn't want to be racist, but the stats bore him out. For a moment he thought, when people talk about domestic violence they aren't accused of being husband-ist or anti-husband or sexist. More husbands killed their wives than the other way around. Still the murder rate in the country was only about two hundred or so, maybe a little higher in a bad year. He did not expect to be overworked so he must make every minute of the investigation count.

Car thefts and robberies, those were something else. There were many, often committed by rings of criminals from across the borders. God, there he went again sounding like a racist or in this case a nationalist. In theory he liked the idea of open borders, he liked the idea of offering asylum to those that needed it, but he had to be realistic that some of the immigrants were criminals. Some Swiss were criminals too, but nobody ever suggested throwing the criminal Swiss out of Switzerland. Anyway, immigration wasn't his problem tonight. Tonight he wanted to know more about Herr Professor Dr. Urs Stoller.

The autopsy report had not helped. The professor had died of massive hemorrhaging, caused by an overdose of an unknown drug in his system, a blood thinner. An examination of several on the market given to treat various kinds of heart disease did not lead to a match. The report said that the blood had lost its ability to clot as if the professor suffered from hemophilia, which according to his medical records, he did not. There were no pinpricks to indicate an injection. The stomach contents had revealed he had residues of pasta in his stomach and intestine. He was a big man, and heavy enough to show he enjoyed eating, although he wasn't fat.

There was no water in his lungs. Because of the cold water there was no way that the medical examiner could estimate the time or even the day of his death. Being bounced around in the water affected lividity, and rigor mortis was long gone, but he had no way of knowing how long. One of the professor's hands had parts of its fingers missing, probably from tiny fish considering the professor a good meal. The other hand was gloved and the only other exposed skin was his face because the professor went into the water fully clothed, not just in a suit but in a scarf and overcoat.

That he was found near the Bains de Pâquis probably meant that he was dumped to the right of the Jet d'Eau if the person had their back to the Salève mountain. The *Bise* had been blowing and the water would have flowed in that direction, or so he thought. Morat went back to the Internet and Googled currents in Lac Léman where he found that they varied and that although they were more on the surface, they could move the water up to two meters below the surface as well. Water temperatures ran about five degrees centigrade at this time of year. Okay, so the professor could have been put in the water any number of places.

He started reading about Stoller, his publications, his presentations at different academic forums, his use as an expert to certify the authenticity of the works of painters from the thirteenth to sixteenth centuries.

Much of it was repetitious and boring. He was tired, but he wanted to have startling information for Fortini in the morning, though this looked less and less likely. If he pointed out anything he found out, Fortini would perhaps stop treating him like the village idiot.

He decided to type up his notes from the different people they had questioned. His mother had insisted he learn shorthand the summer he was twelve so he could take good notes in school when his laptop was unavailable. At the time he had sulked and complained, but now he thanked her every time he interviewed a witness.

Morat labeled each page with the name of the person to whom they'd spoken, their address, telephone, e-mail information and a brief description along with their relationship to the professor. Despite Fortini's scowls, Morat had asked each person for a visiting card, which, once everything was printed out, he stapled to the appropriate sheet.

Sometimes he wondered if, rather than in the crime division, he might not have been better working with the technical group that specialized in Internet and computer crimes and frauds. There were no Fortini characters in that group.

The clock on his computer read 21:42. Oops. He was supposed to meet his girlfriend at the piano bar in the Hotel d'Angleterre at 20:30. He turned on his cell. A message read, "You've stood me up for the last time."

He hit call, but he only got her message box. He texted his apology but questioned his sincerity. The relationship had been rocky—fueled by her objections to his working hours and his objection to her lack of understanding.

As he entered his notes, he decided to create a spreadsheet because all the people they talked with had seemed to use identical phrases about Stoller: best in his field, talented, does not mingle with other faculty members (said in a variety of ways), demanding, moody, arrogant. None used the phrase "not nice to speak ill of the dead" but there was an implication that if they were looking for a friend of Herr Professor Dr. Urs Stoller they must keep looking.

The spreadsheet proved he was correct. On the right, there was a list of the names, on the top the phrases and almost all the boxes were checked for each person.

No one said they hated the professor, but the undercurrent of distaste was there. He had thought that Fortini should have asked if any of them had any disagreements with the professor. He considered barging in and asking the question himself, but did not want to face another tongue-lashing. And although he fully expected Fortini to sneer at this spreadsheet as a waste of time, he also expected that Fortini would look at it when Morat wasn't watching.

That done he went back to reading about the professor, noting each new fact, creating a timeline of his life.

By the time he finished, the computer clock said 23:23: time to shut the computer down and go home. However, he checked his personal and professional e-mails. There was one from his newly ex-girlfriend, saying that she would have a mutual friend drop off the few things he had left at her apartment.

In his professional box there were notices for meetings and one from the Big Boss. She had written that starting next Monday there would be a new French policeman joining Fortini and Morat as part of the European Police Exchange program.

Now that would be interesting, Morat thought as he pressed the off button.

CHAPTER 18

Geneva, Switzerland
December 1556

Had God come down and said to Elizabeth, "Tell me what happened during November," she could not have listed anything except a blur of impressions.

A memory of coughing and coughing the night after she had pulled Jeanne from the icy Lac Léman was followed by her finding herself in the dingy alcove behind her uncle's study on a mattress. No candle lit anything, but sometimes, *maybe*, there was a sliver of light at the bottom of the curtain that separated her from where *maybe* she heard her uncle's quill scratching against a paper, his chair screaking against the floor as he moved it back. Maybe a book slammed.

She couldn't be sure of any of those details: they could just as easily have been part of the dreams where Jean-Michel walked down the street with his new bride wearing the sketches she did of him at Antoine's. Or she would be blocked from going upstairs to draw over the shoe repair shop by her uncle, or the lake rose up the hill to flood the house and approach the alcove where she was sleeping.

Never had breathing hurt so much, so when she repeatedly awoke from sleep, she imagined someone had tied a rope around her chest. Did her cousin Sarah really spoon gruel into her mouth, saying over and over, "You must eat"?

Did her aunt tell her uncle it was a waste for him to pay for a doctor? Did the handsome young doctor from Lyon, François Grandjean, come and tell her uncle that he had real training at a university, not like some of the doctors who were apprenticed to practicing doctors who had probably taught themselves?

Did he put his head on her chest then prescribe powders that he watched her take? Was he there when she soaked the bed with blood and did he throw everyone out while he cleaned her? Did her aunt mourn the loss of the bedding and did Dr. Grandjean tell her it was part of the illness that she had coughed up that much blood?

How often did she feel her uncle standing over her? Was it her imagination that he had held a folded-up blanket just above her face then threw it aside and stormed out of the study slamming the door?

How many of her uncle's conversations with people in his study were real? He could not have met with a man who claimed to be willing to get rid of an adversary like he had done with his brother? "Don't speak of that," she thought her uncle had said.

"Another letter from England," she thought she'd heard her aunt whisper. Had she imagined that her uncle told her to burn it like the others? Then she slept again with more dreams of the grandfather, whom she had never met, finally answering the letters she had managed to send secretly to him. He had come and carried her away across the channel and she saw the Yorkshire moors that her mother had told her about and the church in the village near London.

Sometimes she thought the house had to be on fire she was so hot and other times there were not enough fires and blankets in the world to warm her.

And then the coughing slowed. Her cousin *did* feed her. The doctor *did* come and smiled at her progress. Some days she stayed awake almost an hour at a time.

Sarah came more often and talked to her about what was

happening in the house. How one of her brothers got in trouble at school for not doing his Latin homework three days in a row, how the lake was freezing over, how the first snow fell. There were no windows in the alcove, but Sarah opened the curtain hanging behind her uncle's desk so some of the limited daylight could come in.

Dr. Grandjean entered the room. "You look better." He put his hand on her head. "I think your fever is gone. We must work on getting you out of bed."

"Do you think she's ready?" Sarah asked.

Elizabeth had not seen her cousin standing at the door.

"Maybe we should say a prayer first."

Two heads droned on with thanks for Elizabeth's deliverance and a fervent hope recovery would continue, amen.

"Help me get her up," Dr. Grandjean said.

Elizabeth touched her nightgown. It was floor length, long-sleeved with a tie that kept it tight around her neck. It was not the one she had worn to bed the night she was taken ill.

The doctor and her cousin hoisted her up. Sarah held her left arm. The doctor was on the right. He had one arm around her waist, whilst gripping her by the waist with his other.

"The room is spinning," Elizabeth said.

The threesome paused.

"We won't let go," the doctor said. "I want you to make it to the window."

The few steps seemed longer than the trip to the farm of Elizabeth's parents in the countryside outside Geneva's walls. Her legs felt like rolled wet sheets trying to support an oak table. From nowhere, her uncle's chair was behind her. She sank into it.

Outside she could see the fountain, a long icicle dripping from the nozzle. The cobblestones where people had walked were covered with dirty snow, but the sides of the street were white. Three horses walked by, one led by its bridle, the other two ridden by soldiers.

Elizabeth shut her eyes. The activity was almost too much.

"She's falling asleep," Sarah said.

Elizabeth had no idea what time she awoke back on her mattress in the alcove or how long she had been sleeping. The house was quiet.

Little by little, her strength returned. The doctor was told he need not come back, but he had replied that since he had already been paid, it was part of his service, but his appearances were less frequent.

By late December, Elizabeth was allowed to return to the bed upstairs. No more bedding down by the hearth, the doctor had said to her aunt when Elizabeth could overhear. She began doing small chores, setting and clearing the table. The dishes, which were a signal of the wealth of the family, were not too heavy to lift. She was no longer excused from prayers.

The last day in December she was ready to go out for the first time. "Make sure you are warm enough," Sarah told her.

Aunt Mathilde harrumphed that if Elizabeth were too stupid to know that, she deserved to fall sick again.

The door closed behind Elizabeth. The sky above was a brilliant blue with none of the gray that covered the city so often during winter days. Sometimes in December, January and February, it seemed to Elizabeth that a gray thick blanket got stuck on the Juras and Alps, allowing no sunshine through.

Her chore was simple: go to the *boulangerie* near Saint Pierre's. The crisp air cleaned her lungs of the smoky inside of the house, although a fresh pile of horse droppings was less pleasant to inhale. As she approached the *boulangerie,* the yeasty smell of baking bread drifted out.

Dr. Grandjean was coming from the direction of the church, his head down. He moved at a fast pace, his boots clicking against the cobblestones. Only when he almost ran into Elizabeth did he notice her. "You're out. This is wonderful."

"I must thank you for all you did," Elizabeth said.

He looked up and down the street. A housewife with her basket full of leeks passed them by. "I will never tell anyone your secret."

"My secret?"

"The baby you lost. I was able to clean you up and get it out of the house."

CHAPTER 19

Geneva, Switzerland

Annie threw off her black hat, more of a woolen beret, and pulled off her black mittens. "Okay, I did the proper thing. Good thing my normal coat is black, perfect for a funeral."

Mireille was sitting at her desk, her laptop open to a page of text and reproductions of Brueghel's paintings, *Peasant Wedding Banquet* and the *Wedding at Cana*, propped up in front of her. "Glad you're back. Look at these paintings and tell me what is strange."

"Strange?" Annie looked closely at the two reproductions.

"Nonreligious more or less, peasants there. Same subject, a wedding."

"People are eating. In most art of this period there might be food, but no one eats it. It was as if it were an unwritten taboo."

Annie looked at the man with a spoon held to his mouth. "This guy is eating, all right." She looked more closely. "I see bowls and spoons and even plates, not trenchers."

"I wish I knew what they were eating. In *Wedding Banquet* the servers are carrying individual dishes of something white."

"Might be some kind of grain. Don't you want to know about the funeral?"

Mireille stood up and went to the kitchen to put the kettle on.

"Do you want me to tell you about it?" Annie called into the kitchen.

"What?"

Maybe Mireille didn't want to deal with the death of her baby's father. She imagined her mother saying that wasn't healthy. Things not faced today would bite you in the bum later. Annie had to smile: that her mother was no prude when it came to words like ass, but she preferred the alliteration of the words bum and bite. Literary merit or not, she still would not let Annie bury things that should be dealt with. And as Annie was Mireille's good friend she felt she should do the same. "The funeral, silly." Keeping it as light as possible might allow her to get further.

"If you want." The clatter of mugs and the opening and shutting of the refrigerator's door almost hid the "If you must."

"Funerals depress me so maybe talking will help me shake it." Annie got up and stood at the kitchen door watching Mireille place each item on the tray arranging and rearranging until she found a balance. Avoidance, she thought. Big Time.

"I think the entire *fac* was there, but no one looked very sad. I kept thinking of the joke that people went to make sure the bastard was dead." She clamped her hand over her mouth. "I'm sorry. He was your lover and the father . . ."

"Which doesn't make him any nicer," Mireille said. "I saw a side of him others didn't or maybe I brought out some tiny part of sweetness in him."

Annie didn't say she doubted that there was any sweetness there. At least Mireille was talking. "Marc did pretty well. He was able to give his eulogy. But there is something going on between him and his mother. Their eyes never met, he never touched her. She was flanked by her sister and brother-in-law. And of course the Swiss German relatives were there."

Mireille pushed past Annie as she carried the tray into the living room. Annie followed.

"Neither Stoller would qualify as parent of the year. I was

never as close to Marc as you were, but he was always quick to help if he saw me carrying something heavy. He would be polite and ask about my work and a couple of times we discussed computer games. But you were the one who gave him a refuge," Mireille said.

Annie started to pour a cup of tea, but it wasn't strong enough. She returned the liquid to the pot. "He was—is—a good kid. I'm sorry for him."

"Me too. At least I know my baby is not losing a good father. By the way, next Thursday I've an appointment with Dr. Baudoin—Jean, not Benôit."

"To be your thesis advisor?"

"Yes."

"He should be good." Damn, the subject has been changed, Annie thought.

"Meanwhile I want to get as much done as I can to show him, so he won't push me too far in another direction. I've asked the boys if they can do without me for a few days. Which brings up . . ."

Annie knew what Mireille was getting at. If she stayed, even though she had the right, her friend would be more apt to take a tea break, mention something and they would be off talking and Mireille would lose valuable time. Holding her hand to her head, she said, "I'm getting a vibration, let me think . . . you are wondering tactfully . . . how long I'm staying?"

Mireille laughed. "I know we've our deal that you can stay here anytime you're in Geneva and as you're a sublessor I won't renege."

"This is not a problem. My parents will move back into their house tomorrow, and I will enjoy spending some time with them." She put down her mug. "I need to go to the Stollers' for the polite after-funeral feed. Marc made it a point to make sure

I was coming."

"Go support Marc."

There was a constant murmur in the Stoller apartment when Annie entered. People were crammed together and two waiters tried to force their way through the crowd carrying trays, reminding Annie of the Brueghel painting. If it weren't a funeral, it could have been a cocktail party.

Annie searched the crowd for Marc but didn't see him. She walked down the hall to his room. The door was closed. She knocked.

"Who is it?"

"Annie."

"Come in."

He was on his bed and made no move to get up, but shifted his legs so she could sit down. He had changed into jeans and a sweatshirt. His feet were bare. "I couldn't take it anymore."

"Want to talk about it?"

He shrugged.

Annie said nothing.

"Want me to go?"

He shook his head.

"Want me to talk?"

"As long as you don't say anything, like 'you poor boy' or 'now you're the head of the house.' "

"No danger. And I won't tell you how you feel or are meant to feel, either. I've not lost my parents, and my relationship with my parents has always been good, so I don't know."

He nodded but didn't meet her eyes. Like all of Annie's friends, Dave and Susan Young had included Marc in their warmth. He had often gone with them all on ski weekends.

"Someone once told me that it is easier to lose someone that you get along with than someone with whom you've had problems."

Marc looked directly at Annie. "I suppose it has something to do with guilt."

"Got it in one." She reverted to the phrase they used when they were playing computer games.

"Sometimes I thought I hated him. Sometimes I did *hate* him."

"Congrats. That makes you a normal kid."

"Did you ever hate your parents?"

"My parents aren't normal parents, but yes and believe it or not it was because they were so nice, I couldn't complain to my friends about them. Also because we moved around so much it made our family much closer than most families. Although, come to think of it, every time my father came home and named a new city in a new country with a new language, and I had to give up my friends yet again, the word hate would cover how I felt, at least until I got readjusted."

He said nothing and even though Annie let the silence hang hoping he would fill it, he didn't.

"I guess I gotta go touch base with your mother." It hit Annie then that she always called Maria-Elena "your mother" never "your mom." She stood up and as she put her hand on the door she heard him sit up. She turned around to see him sitting with his knees pressed against his chest, his arms around his legs and his head resting on his knees.

"Watch the great actress pretend how sad she is my father is dead," he said. "If they gave Oscars for performances of make-believe grieving widows at funerals, she would qualify."

Long ago Annie had learned not to deny people their feelings. She could have said he was being harsh, but she agreed with him. "Nominations won't be out until early next year."

For the first time since she entered the room, he smiled.

"Marc, I'm going over to stay with my parents tomorrow. You've my cell. You can call me anytime."

For the first time he grinned. "I know *that*."

CHAPTER 20

Geneva, Switzerland

Annie pushed the *arrêt demandé* button on the triple long E/Hermance bus as it approached the Corsier Port stop. Although the bus was supposed to stop automatically, sometimes if the driver thought no one wanted to get on or off he would breeze through to the next stop. Although Annie would not have minded walking back, this time she had her suitcase on wheels and her computer case slung over her shoulder. Her parents would have picked her up at Mireille's had she asked, but she wanted to surprise them.

She had no worry that they would be anything but delighted to have her back in her old room for a few weeks, although her old room had changed from her school days when posters of the group Pow Wow and the 2B3 boy band decorated her walls. Her mother said she'd "adultified" the room for guests by hanging her own paintings, but her old furniture, curtains and duvet covers had remained intact.

Annie started down the hill toward her parents' house and let out a long sigh of contentment. Granted Argelès was her "real" home now, but the view of the lake, peeking through the trees with the Jura Mountains rising behind, always aroused her appreciation of the beauty, except now it was just getting dark and all the colors were muted. Tomorrow when she woke, the first thing she would do would be to look at the lake off her parents' balcony.

"Your wandering offspring has returned," she called out as soon as she entered the front door.

"We're in the living room," her father said.

Annie walked the few steps into the living room. Her parents were sitting on the couch next to the fireplace where a fire had turned into coals. Three glasses of wine, a pitcher and the remains of a shrimp platter were on the coffee table.

"My God, what are you doing here?" Annie asked as Roger stood up and held his arms out. She flew into them, but repeated the question.

"Well, you know how you're always rushing off to an assignment somewhere different and how I've never liked it."

"If you can't lick them, join them," Dave Young said as he poured his daughter a glass of wine.

"I don't understand."

"There's a police exchange program in Europe. I've been assigned to the Genevan police force for the next few weeks. I figure if you can do it, I can do it."

Annie sipped her wine, which was hot and spiced and felt good after the chill of the October air. "And you didn't tell me?"

"I didn't know if it would come through. It happened at the last minute, and I did want to surprise you."

He certainly had.

"He asked us to keep the secret. We've put a double bed in your old room," Dave said.

"But if I hadn't come home to surprise you guys?" Annie asked.

"We knew about the funeral today, so we figured we'd come get you later tonight," Susan said.

"What about Gaëlle?" Annie couldn't imagine Roger leaving his teenage daughter alone for that long period of time.

"She's staying with the Martinezes, although she'll be coming up here for long weekends twice during the period. Also she has a two-week exchange program with a school in Austria while I'm gone. She sends her love, by the way. And don't yell at her for not telling you. I swore her to secrecy and you know how she loves surprises."

Annie knew. "When do you start?"

"Tomorrow."

When Annie put her suitcase and laptop in her old room the double bed made the room seem as if the walls had moved inwards. She walked to her window and looked through the sheer curtains at the trees outside. A stray cat sat in the driveway. For so many years she had felt like that stray cat, not quite belonging anywhere: now more and more she knew where she belonged, having discovered that it was people who anchored her, not place.

Maybe that change had happened when she bought her own flat: somewhere to where she could return besides wherever her parents lived. And more and more she unearthed the same feeling when she stayed at Roger and Gaëlle's.

She noticed that her mother had folded the two duvets, German style, in half. They were the guest covers for adults who visited.

Roger came up behind her. "Do you mind my being here?"

She turned around and put her arms around his neck. "Not at all." The truth of what she said surprised her, and she wondered why she had fought against being part of their couple for so long. Dumbness was the only answer she could come up with.

CHAPTER 21

Geneva, Switzerland
June 1557

"Get out, get out!" A strand of Aunt Mathilde's hair fell down her neck. She flapped her apron then pushed and shoved Elizabeth out of the kitchen. "You'll turn the milk just by touching it." With each "get out" her voice grew louder and louder.

Elizabeth fled into the summer sun. For a moment she leaned against the door not sure what to do. The situation in the house could not grow much worse. Her aunt blamed her for the last baby's death. The infant had emerged from the womb with half the head missing or so it seemed. Elizabeth could not bring herself to do more than glance at the body. Her aunt had said it was Elizabeth's fault.

Elizabeth was no longer allowed to do any chores nor join them in prayers. At first she thought this was a good thing, because she could go to Antoine's and draw and paint. Despite Jean-Michel's marriage, the printer still provided her with the paper and colors she needed, but usually through Antoine. Jean-Michel's wife was convinced that Elizabeth was trying to seduce her husband.

All Elizabeth wanted to do was to go to England. After she recovered from her illness, she tried writing her grandfather again, explaining that his letters had not been passed on and giving him Antoine's address. Half of her had hoped what she'd heard during her illness about his writing her at her uncle's and the destruction of those letters was only her fevered brain's imagination. Half of her was convinced it was not the case at all, that her uncle did not want her to be in contact with her maternal relatives.

The noon sun beat down on her as she picked her way over the cobblestones. She had run out barefoot only pausing to grab her shoes that were with the rest of the family's footwear by the door. The cobblestones burned her feet until she got a few feet from the house where she could slip them on.

This was the third day of the *canicule,* when even the dankest house with the thickest walls was not immune from the high temperatures. Few people were on the street, preferring to do whatever they had to do early in the morning or late in the afternoon.

Below, the lake glimmered. Its surface was so smooth that it looked as if she could walk on it. Maybe if she went down and dipped her feet in it, the icy waters would cool her. No, better to use the time on her latest drawing, her escape into sanity, she called it.

She arrived at the shoemaker's just as he was bringing in the display of leathers from outside. His business had increased—his reputation for quality the reason. "Come inside quickly before you melt, Elizabeth." Antoine almost pulled her inside.

The shop was only a few degrees cooler. The smell of leather permeated everything. She heard Antoine click the lock behind her. When she turned she saw him put the large key on the counter next to the hammer that he used to tap nails into the soles. He handed her a metal cylinder with wax sealing the top. "We can melt it or scrape it, whichever you prefer."

"Scrape, but what is it?"

"A courier brought it this morning. Got me out of bed just before dawn. Do you have any idea how early dawn is? The birds start singing at four bells."

Despite the bad morning, Elizabeth laughed. "You obviously don't live in my house. We wake the birds up in summer and insult them for being so lazy in winter. Anyway, what is this?"

Antoine, instead of answering, took one of his knives and started working on the seal. Under the wax layer was a wood stopper which he pried open. A paper was rolled inside. He handed it to Elizabeth.

She skimmed it, relishing the signature, then sat down on his work stool to read it word by word. It was written in English and French. Although her mother had taught her English, she still was far more comfortable in French, but savored that she was sharing thoughts with the man she had waited to hear from for so long in his own language and his own hand.

March 3, in the year of our Lord 1557
My Dearest Elizabeth,

Even though we have never met, I will call thee Dearest Elizabeth. It was with great sadness that I learned of the passing of my grandson and my darling Anne and of the disappearance of thine father. In many ways I was not surprised when thine father did not appear as scheduled, and letters to my daughter went unanswered. I feared the worst.

I have written that first paragraph in each of the five letters I have sent thee, in fear that none reached thee and alas, I was right.

Do not despair. I am coming for thee myself. Although at 60 I am still in relatively good health, my bones are stiff. As much as I hate to wait, I must until my son is back from a mission to France and we will both come, for he says I must not travel the distance alone.

Obviously thine uncle has tried to appropriate your inheritance. None of this is as important as thine safety, but although Calvin's Geneva may be known for being very religious, they are not known for being just. Look what they did to Servetus.

England has had its own problems with religion, but we seem to be on a saner course at the moment as long as we accept the Catholic faith.

Do not say to anyone that I am coming. I trust from thine last letter that the person who thou asked me to address this to is safe and worthy.

> *We will bring thee home to England,*
> *Grandfather Tobias Smythe*
> *Saint George's Church*
> *Beckenham*

Elizabeth read and reread it and did not realize she had been crying, until Antoine handed her a not-too-clean handkerchief.

"Are those good or bad tears?" he asked.

"Good."

CHAPTER 22

Geneva, Switzerland

Annie was tearing through the website that described the history of decoupage to help her with the copy for the cabinet that was covered with cutout angels on a black-lacquered background. The piece had been well preserved except for a small nick on the corner. It was French, probably from Marie Antoinette's time. The queen was said to have not only popularized the technique, but to have practiced it herself, as an early proponent of do-it-yourself. Annie thought how wonderful it would be for the sale if they could authenticate that Marie Antoinette had done this piece, but there was no reason to think so. The workmanship with its several layers of sanding and varnishing was far too professional for an amateur and a blurred signature bore no resemblance to the royal name.

She could get some interesting catalog copy. Both Conrad and Thomas were convinced that this catalog would be a sales item in itself with all the information she had gleaned.

The front door bell rang, causing Annie only to look up for a moment. Footsteps, the door opening, a murmur of voices and the closing of the door were followed by more footsteps which sounded like they went into Conrad's office.

On the screen it talked about how decoupage was morphing into a modern format called photomontage where works of art were created from cutouts of paper and turned into scenes. And there was even a computer format. That certainly wasn't the case with this cabinet. As always, Annie found it hard to resist wandering from one subject to another rather than focusing.

"Annie, Annie, guess what?" Conrad stood in the doorway with Mireille's wooden portfolio of sketches.

"What?"

"That was Marshall, the art expert we sent Mireille's drawings to. He authenticated them as coming from Calvin's time. And more."

He put them next to Annie's laptop. "Look at this." The ancient ribbons that held the wooden covers together on all four sides had been untied. Before he opened the cover, he slipped on the surgical gloves that he always used to touch precious items. The drawings and pastels were there.

"Marshall said he found this under the paper lining of the cover." He held up a yellowed sheet of paper. "Had it been face up we would have lost the content because of the glue, but it was face down against the wood."

"What is it?" Annie looked in her top drawer for her own surgical gloves.

"A letter. I think it is from the artist's grandfather. It may mean we've a better chance of discovering the identity of the person who signed the drawings. Marshall says he is sure they were all done by the same person."

"Mireille might just make herself some good money with this."

"And a place in art history as well, even without her Brueghel research."

CHAPTER 23

Geneva, Switzerland

At the rue Carl Vogt office of the Genevan police, Roger Perret was directed to another building, about a block away, where the detectives and top brass had just been moved. The building itself was nondescript, one of those square stucco buildings that could be anything. However, inside it was nothing like any police station he had ever seen.

Once he was directed past the reception area, there were private offices arranged pod-like. He could see that each desk was set out with flat-screen computers. That and the absence of file cabinets made him think everything was computerized. He stopped, as the receptionist told him to, at number twelve with the names Fortini and Morat on the door.

"If he is such a hotshot detective, how come he was demoted from Paris to a dinky little French coastal village?" The words came through the rather flimsy door.

"When I Googled him, they said he requested a transfer . . ."

Roger knocked. Two desks were back to back in front of a large window. The shutters were half rolled down to keep the morning sun from swamping the office. Despite the cold air outside, the sun had warmed the office to the point that both the younger and older man had their ties loosened and their shirt sleeves rolled up. Roger introduced himself.

"Fortini, and this is Morat," the older man said.

They all shook hands.

Morat offered to get Roger a cup of coffee, which he accepted. When the younger man was back Roger asked, "So what are we working on?"

"A professor was murdered. He had an overdose of blood thinner in his system, but we haven't been able to trace the exact type. Maybe it's new on the market. His body was dumped in the lake," Fortini said.

"And where are we in the investigation?"

"The medicine caused massive hemorrhages. No water in the lungs, and the cold of the water makes it difficult to tell how long he had been dead, but long enough for a few of the fish to nibble away."

"Suspects?" Roger asked. He didn't let on how much he knew already about the case from Annie.

Morat did something with the computer and turned the computer screen toward Roger. "It's strange. We interviewed all his colleagues, and it seemed almost like they were robots. I did a spreadsheet on how many of the same phrases they used, like "best in his field," "knew his stuff," "great lecturer.""

"You and your spreadsheets," Fortini mumbled.

"That's the younger generation for you," Roger said. "I'm just beginning to learn the computer, but with kids around, they can do a lot of it for us." Had he been able to win the confidence of both with this? He wasn't sure, but he suspected Fortini was a curmudgeon, and well versed in tried-and-true tactics, while Morat was an itching-to-succeed kid driving Fortini crazy with his enthusiasm. Maybe Fortini was even a bit threatened by Morat.

"Did you record the interviews?"

"I take shorthand. It almost got rusty but when my law profs wouldn't let me use a laptop or tape recorder in their classes, it kept me up to speed so I pretty much have a word-for-word record of each interview."

Well-educated the younger one, Roger thought. Probably another reason Fortini might resent the young man.

"Which only you can read," Fortini said.

"I transcribed it. I sent it to you by e-mail. Have they given you an e-mail here yet, Roger?"

"Not yet. My personal is roger-dot-perret-at-hotmail-dot-f-r."

"I'm not sure we should be sending police business to private e-mails," Fortini said.

"I can give you my Argelès police e-mail. I'll be checking it daily."

Fortini sighed. "I suppose the personal one will be okay."

"Thanks. Once I read it, I won't have to annoy either of you for information you both know." The word *either* was important if he wasn't to get in the middle of an intergenerational professional war. "Is that how you picked up the rote-like responses of his colleagues?"

Morat nodded. "I got the feeling none of them liked him because other phrases, and these were the exact words, 'didn't intermingle much' and 'kept to himself,' also came up: it seemed to me that there was almost a sneer or that the words 'the bastard' should have been used immediately after."

Aha, an intuitive type of *flic*. He bet Fortini was the facts-only type of *flic*. "Fortini, what about the family?"

"Wife and son. The wife is a big-shot researcher for some pharmaceutical company. Foreigner, Latin America, Uruguay."

"She didn't seem all that broken up about her husband. No tears at the funeral," Morat said. "Lots of dabbing at dry eyes at the grave site."

"Are you of the look-to-the-family-first type of *flic?*" Roger asked. "Financial gain?"

Morat glanced at Fortini before speaking and when he didn't get a negative reaction said, "As far as we can tell, the family has no major debts. They own two cars outright. We don't know about insurance on the good professor yet."

"Do they own a house or apartment?" Roger asked.

"No, but that's not that unusual what with the way the tax code is here," Morat said. When Roger frowned, Morat explained, "If you own your own place, you take the rent you would have earned had you rented it and add it to your taxable income even though you don't get the money and are living in the apartment."

His statement jogged Roger's memory of complaints from the Youngs on the subject.

"They did have a chalet across the border, but that was sold about four years ago. They never used it, and for some reason never rented it either," Fortini said. "The proceeds are in a bank account. The professor didn't play the stock market: a big-shot academic without financial smarts."

When Fortini smirked, Roger made the assumption that the man might not like those with more education that he had, but he never relied on his assumptions and retested them until he could turn them into facts.

"Any idea how and where the drug was administered and how he got in the lake?"

"On the drug, probably swallowed because it was in the stomach and intestine. As for the lake, no idea," Fortini said. "He was a big man, so it would take someone with strength."

"So what's next? I'm not here to take over, you're the boss."

Fortini almost smiled. "There are other cases we're working on. We've had quite a few break-ins, and we think it is a Roma gang. Why don't you look through the files? Morat will set you up with your own computer. Get you a password thingie."

Roger nodded. He needed to talk to Morat alone, and he was sure Annie had some ideas about the Stoller marriage. Although he wanted to keep an open mind, so many times in the case of murder it was a family member.

This would be an interesting exchange.

CHAPTER 24

Geneva, Switzerland

"I can't believe it," Mireille said. She sat on the couch in Conrad's office, where she had come immediately after they called her with the news of the letter. She stared at the letter. "We really might be able to find out who did these drawings."

"And the dates mean that the man being burned *might* be Michel Servetus," Annie said.

"Urs must have used a cheap expert who didn't recognize the value," Mireille said.

Annie clenched her fists as if to keep in the words "or he was trying to cheat you." Instead she asked, "Did you ever see the appraisal?"

Mireille was silent for a moment then shook her head. "You know what worried me? There are two drawings I didn't get back from Urs. He said the expert must have kept them, but he died before I could find out who he was. I suppose at some point I could ask his wife, but . . ." Mireille let out a long sigh. "Strangely enough, I do miss him a little bit. He would have had such insight into all this. We used to have such wonderful discussions."

Annie wanted to say even bastards can create a good memory or two, but did not see how it would help. "I've some ideas on how to go about it."

Mireille cocked her head.

"First, we check and see if there is still a Saint George's

138

Church in Beckenham and see if they have a record of Tobias Smythe. That means you probably should go there. Churches do keep this type of stuff and they *might* have a list of all their old vicars. God, I love the word vicar."

"We don't know if he were a vicar, just that he used the church as a place he wrote the letter from," Mireille said. "And Saint George's might not be a church."

"True, but it is a start. If there is a church and if it has a record of Tobias, there might be a family history and we can find out if his daughter married someone from Geneva and then we *might* be able to find her husband in Geneva's records and then we *might* . . ."

"That's a lot of *mights*. Unfortunately, I don't have time to do it right now," Mireille said.

Annie realized that. Between Mireille's thesis, her work and the baby, her friend had the proverbial full plate. And she doubted that she had the money for a trip to England. "In another week, I'll be through with the catalog, and I would love to do it. With Roger here, I'm not sure how happy he'll be about it though."

"I wouldn't blame him, since he arranged the assignment so you guys would be in the same place at the same time," Mireille said.

CHAPTER 25

Geneva, Switzerland
August 1557

It was all Elizabeth could do not to sing and dance and jump. Her time here would be limited. She was not sure how her grandfather would be received, and she told Antoine when he did arrive not to let her grandfather go to her uncle's.

"Of course not," Antoine replied, his tone implying how could she think him that stupid. His having to flee from Catholic France had taught him cunning as it had most of the many refugees that had come to Geneva over the past few years. "Any idea when he will come?"

"No."

The late-afternoon heat shimmered off the lake, but, typical of rapidly changing Geneva weather, within minutes storm clouds rolled in, lightning sliced the sky and the rain bounced high on the cobblestones and burst the bubbles in the puddles. Elizabeth huddled in a doorway, which offered little protection because of the slant of the rain.

Almost as suddenly, the rain stopped. Two rainbows shone over the lake. The storm had caused a temperature drop and Elizabeth shivered as she headed to her aunt and uncle's house. No wonder Calvin thought God capricious. He was probably influenced by the change-in-an-instant weather.

Inside, the first thing Aunt Mathilde did was yell, "You are getting the floor wet, stupid girl. You don't even have enough sense to come in out of the rain."

At least she was no longer raging about Elizabeth being responsible for everything that went wrong in the house.

The tirade was interrupted by a knock on the door.

"Well, don't just stand there, answer it."

When Elizabeth opened the door, she saw Guillaume Dumont, the lawyer who worked for her uncle. The sun had come out and created a glow behind him. However, his clothes were drenched.

"Your uncle asked me to stop by and tell . . . you're as wet as I am!" Then he blushed. "I shouldn't have said that . . . I'm here to tell your aunt . . . but you are so very beau—" He grew redder. "I'm here to tell your aunt that your uncle will be late. He has to meet with Pastor Calvin. He's not sure what time he'll be back."

He turned and almost stumbled down the stone steps.

CHAPTER 26

Corsier Port, Switzerland

When Annie awoke in her old bedroom, Roger had already left. The house was quiet. Her father had mumbled something about checking in with his office. In the last few years he had delegated enough jobs to the consultants working for him, that his appearances were unnecessary except for this current project. His trusted partner was a workaholic and the lack of division of labor suited both men. Still Dave Young would do what was necessary "to bring home his share of the spoils." As for Annie, she shared her father's attitude: to work to live, not live to work.

A few footsteps overhead suggested that her mother might be painting in her atelier on the top floor. Susan, who had given up a career in commercial art to follow her wandering husband, used the time no longer devoted to earning a regular salary to develop herself as an artist and was after years and years beginning to meet with moderate success.

Annie padded downstairs to the kitchen to make herself breakfast. A tray had been laid out with a dish, a brioche and a pot with loose tea. It was one of those cute pots that sat on top of the cup.

She looked at the whiteboard glued next to the refrigerator, Communication Center, her father called it. The family had used it to track their comings and goings, convey messages and sometimes jokes. No matter where they had lived, there had been a whiteboard.

This morning, Susan had done a rough sketch of the breakfast tray and left a note: "Enjoy your first free day. I'm working till noon, but if you want to go to lunch, I could be talked into treating you to sushi at the Japanese restaurant near Rive."

Annie smiled. She had finished the catalog sooner than she thought she would. Several items she had been researching had fallen into place; the words seemed to write and translate themselves. She told the boys she would be happy to come in, if they needed any fine tuning, but other than that she was done.

Annie made her breakfast and took the tray to her desk. The computer came up, the Wi-Fi kicked in and after making sure that her tea was out of spill-on-the-keyboard distance, she searched for Saint George's Church. She learned that it had been in existence since the twelfth century, a good start.

At first she thought about sending an e-mail, but instead she placed a phone call and asked to speak to the vicar.

"Sebastian Crowe," said a deep voice that would sound wonderful from a pulpit.

Annie told him what she wanted.

"How delightful," the voice said. "We might be able to help. A few years back we put all the old church records on microfilm going back to before God was born. Then about five years ago we transferred the microfilm to CD-ROMs and I guess when a new archiving technology is found, we'll use that too."

"Could I look at them?" She wanted to ask him to burn a copy, but thought that might be a bit over the top.

"I can't let them out of the church, although we do have a set off-site in case of fire. Much safer than when everything was on paper or parchment."

"And if I come over?"

"You can look to your heart's content."

"I will be there as soon as I can arrange a flight from Geneva."

"Geneva," he said. "I spent three months there with a project on the World Council of Churches when I was going for my doctorate."

"I lived around the corner."

"In the international ghetto?"

"If you mean François-Lehman?"

"I do."

A few more exchanges revealed they had both been in the same building, but since so many of the people who worked at the alphabet UN agencies and NGOs lived there, it was not as a big a coincidence as it would seem.

"Can I bring you anything from Geneva?"

He mentioned a brand of chocolate that was not exported.

"Done."

As soon as she hung up she booked a flight on Easy Jet for the next day.

CHAPTER 27

Geneva, Switzerland

Maria-Elena reached into her pocketbook located in her top desk drawer to take out her iPhone. The clock on her computer read 20:22, and she was just about to close it down and head home. Her reports were almost correlated on the new blood-thinning drug, and she was not happy about the results. She still would have preferred to be in the lab more, but her management position guaranteed her financial security now that she was a widow.

Before saying hello, she brushed her medium-length black hair behind her ear, a tick she did hundreds of time each day.

"Hello, love of my life, do you want to go out to dinner?"

"Garth, I'm supposed to be a grieving widow, not gallivanting around town with my lover." She thought she heard a noise in the lab outside her office door. "Hold on."

As she opened her door, the lab door clicked. She ran across the lab and opened the door to the hall just as the elevator doors closed and she watched the red light above read 4, 3, 2, 1, R.

"Are you there?" Garth asked.

"I heard a noise in the lab. I hope someone didn't hear me."

"Probably just the cleaning people."

"Hope so. But it is too early to start being seen together." They'd been so careful. They did lunch together in the company cafeteria maybe twice a month, no more, no less than they might

145

with other colleagues. If they arranged to meet at the door at the end of the day, and anyone was listening he would ask, "Do you want a ride up the hill?"

The Renatus Pharmaceuticals labs were just down the Route de Ferney, five bus stops or a twenty-minute walk from her apartment. Sometimes, if there were lots of people around, she would say, "No thanks, I need to stop at Co-op to buy things for dinner."

Other times they would escape to his apartment in Ferney-Voltaire, just across the French border, but even there they had to be careful because too many internationals lived in Ferney where rents were slightly cheaper.

Geneva might be a city, but as far as the international community was concerned, it was a tiny, tiny town where doing something wrong was almost a guarantee of running into a friend or a friend of a friend. He only called her on her cell phone, never over the office phone. They never used the office e-mail or the office computer for their personal e-mail, anything that might be traced. As much as she would have liked to keep his messages, she deleted everything he wrote or left on her iPhone the moment she'd read or listened to it.

"Please, darling, I've missed you."

"I've missed you too."

"We could go to Nyon for dinner."

"Too close?"

"Saint Cergue?"

She thought about it for a few moments.

"Or we could go to my flat," he said. "You know how long it is since we've made love?"

"Two weeks, six days, twenty-two hours and ten minutes."

"Really? It was a rhetorical question."

"I made it up." He would accept her humor when her family responsibilities kept her from being with him in what might be her free time. "It seems longer."

"I'll sign out now, you wait ten minutes and I will pick you up in front of the co-op. It will be closed." No one from the company lived in the apartment building above the supermarket. She knew because she had checked by asking a friend in human resources for home addresses of all her colleagues allegedly for Christmas cards. Then she had to send them all a card. At least it was only a one-time thing.

She imagined his arms around her, him on top of her, filling her. And, afterwards, his getting wine and cheese and bringing them to her in bed. Marc was staying with a school friend tonight. She did not need to be home. If he drove her back around five, she would have time to change for work.

"Better by the Jardin Botanique entrance. I am leaving now. See you in fifteen."

Maria-Elena leaned back against the wall of the elevator leading up to her apartment. Her watch read 5:17. Would it be worth it to go to bed and sleep for a couple of hours, or should she just shower and go into the lab to get some work done before the staff came in? The mirrors on each side of the elevator showed a satisfied woman, she thought. Her body certainly was.

It wasn't just sex with Garth: it was everything. The way they were interested in the same things, the way he listened to her, the way he made her laugh at a strange twist of words which went beyond the differences in their mother tongues. Until she met him, she had never really thought of the English as having a sense of humor, or if they did, it was a strange one. She had watched the old BBC comedies, trying to find them funny as everyone else seemed to do, but with the exception of the series *Yes, Minister,* which had the stupidities that could be applied to any government anywhere, she found them a complete waste of her time. Marc loved them.

147

Urs certainly never made her laugh, but she hadn't married him to laugh. She had wanted to live abroad, and he, as a visiting lecturer at her university, was her ticket to Europe. It hadn't hurt that he had been handsome, brought in good money, and encouraged her in her own career. As a child she had never been dreamy eyed about being a bride, walking down an aisle in flowing white dress to meet her prince. Maybe it was because she had read enough history to see that this prince married that princess to put their kingdoms together, never for love.

Marriage, she felt, was a business proposition, an alignment of interests much like her parents' marriage had been. They were children of two small business owners. Their parents, her grandparents, had put the grocery stores together, with her father being the future head, and the result had been a good living for all, not the fabulous growth of a chain like you read about in business books or magazines, but successful enough to allow for them all to live comfortably. One of her sisters had married the son of a lawyer: he looked out for their interests. Her brother had taken over the business when her father had retired. Deals. Deals. Deals. That was what life was all about.

She had kept up her part of the deal. She had produced the son her husband had wanted. Her well-run house allowed him a place to work on off hours as well as entertain to meet the social obligations of his faculty position.

For the comfort of it all, she could put up with his cheating and his arrogance. Sleeping with him had been neither a chore nor a pleasure, although sometimes it had been the latter.

Garth had changed her complacency toward almost everything except her work, which she had never been complacent about. That had been her passion, and his passion for marketing was the catalyst that had brought them together. Hired from the United Kingdom, he had embraced international life in a way she'd never considered.

She had run into him over a year ago at the Ferney *marché* where she had gone to pick up a roast chicken one Saturday morning and whatever else she might want for the week. Urs usually worked at his computer Saturday mornings. Marc slept in.

She would hop on the F bus with her shopping trolley. The *marché* seemed almost a time out for her as she ambled up and down the streets devoid of traffic to make way for stands of fruits, vegetables, olives, cheeses and meats.

Garth had been standing by the honey producer who looked like a drawing of a French farmer in a children's storybook. She had recognized him because his picture had been on the company intranet as a new vice president of marketing. His French, although correct, was impossible to understand because of his accent. The honey man couldn't translate Garth's French into his French.

Maria-Elena, who usually would not have bothered, offered to help. What Garth wanted was honey for a cake, but the dark honey he held, the producer was saying, was better for coughs. It was too heavy for a cake. Maria-Elena was both amused and impressed that a man, a successful professional, wanted to make a honey cake.

His purchase made, he'd offered to buy her coffee at the café around the corner from Voltaire's statue. Although she usually didn't remember details, she had corrected his order for a *café au lait* and told him it was called a *renversée* locally and chosen one for herself over her usual espresso.

"Isn't it wonderful shopping like this? Imagine, a honey consultation. That would never happen at a supermarket back home."

"It wouldn't happen at a supermarket here, either."

"But this is an alternative to supermarkets," he said.

Her phone interrupted them. Urs demanded to know where

the hell she was, and what was she planning for lunch? "Do you know it is after one?"

She hadn't thought it was anywhere close to that time. When she glanced out the window of the café, she could see the last of the merchants packing up their stands. Regular traffic was filtering down the street where the stands had been. She and Garth had been talking for two hours at least.

She had said to Urs that she'd run into a colleague from work but was on her way home. Garth had offered to drive her. His apartment was only three blocks away from where they were. She'd rushed to buy one of the last of the fresh roasted chickens, as *Monsieur Poulet* put his equipment back into his truck. Another vendor, who was one of the last to break apart his stand, weighed the potatoes and green beans on his scale which he had already put into his caravan. He had to jump into it to complete the transaction.

From the very beginning it had always been like that with Garth. Hours together seemed like seconds. They never ran out of something to talk about: his reading had been so eclectic that he even knew about the flora and fauna around Geneva, the history of her country, pop and classical music and who knows what all. When she told him how amazed she was at the breadth of his knowledge, he replied that it had no depth; he merely swept over the surface of everything, never exploring deeply.

To her his variety of interests made him a complete contrast to Urs, who burrowed deeply only into his own field. And after spending so much time doing her own tunneling into her field of expertise, she loved peeking into the tunnels Garth opened for her. His sexual allure was not breadth but depth. Not that Maria-Elena had had many lovers, but she suspected even if the number were in the hundreds he would be the most talented.

As the elevator reached the floor of her François Lehman flat she prayed she would not run into the bitchy neighbor who walked her dog before dawn. Fortunately, the beast must have slept in.

Never, upon her return from being with him, did she regret not listening to her instinct to stop being a silly school girl with a crush. Stop being silly was her mantra all that weekend following the meeting at the *marché*, followed by a second mantra—he's wearing a wedding ring—but when she found an e-mail on her computer the next Monday morning suggesting coffee at a morning break, she went. On the way she did two things which she never did: put on lipstick and go to the company cafeteria mid-morning for coffee instead of pouring a cup from the machine in the lab.

Two days later, their relationship had been consummated, which to her sounded like some kind of soup. It was at that point that they decided not to let anyone know and had instituted THE RULES.

1: Only business e-mails on company computers.

2: No phone calls except on their private cells.

3: Texting to be kept at a minimum and erased.

4: No touching at all on company property.

5: No meeting where people might see them, although they did travel to Neuchâtel, Lausanne, Bern and Zurich to walk the streets hand in hand.

Garth had been up-front about his marital situation. His wife had not wanted to move to Switzerland. He missed his two kids: a girl, eleven, and a boy, nine. His marriage was in limbo after fifteen years. Legal separation had been discussed but not activated because Garth was sending money home, took Easy Jet to Stansted Airport once a month to visit his kids, where he stayed in the marital home and only sometimes used the marital bed until, of course, he had met Maria-Elena.

His claims that he was only faithful to Maria-Elena did not ring true to her, but she was sure he was true to her in Geneva and the rest did not concern her. Or at least she put the thought out of her mind. After all, she still responded to Urs's requests and tried not to compare the two men's abilities to arouse her.

That she now found herself very much in love with Garth surprised her. Her disciplined mind often kept her thinking about the what-ifs of their both being single, what would it be like to live with him. These thoughts she kept from him and sometimes tried to keep them from herself.

She turned the key to her apartment.

"Where the hell have you been?" Marc jumped up from the couch and approached his mother. His eyes were red as if he had been crying. "I thought something happened to you. You didn't answer your cell. There was only the answer phone at the office."

"Calm down. I was in the lab and couldn't hear the phone, and I didn't think to tell you because you weren't supposed to be here."

"You still should have told me." He approached as if he wanted to hit her, but instead stomped down the hall and slammed the door to his room. "And I don't believe you."

CHAPTER 28

Geneva, Switzerland
March 1558

"Nothing," Antoine said to Elizabeth that was what he said every day that she was able to pass by: nothing from the grandfather who had promised to come for her. Whenever she could find a messenger, she had sent him letters pleading that the situation with her aunt and uncle was getting worse and worse. They blamed her for costing too much; they blamed her for everything that went wrong in the house—as if she could spoil meat or cause a needle to go missing. She supposed she could steal a needle, but what was the advantage if she had? And as for the meat, it wasn't her fault that her aunt hadn't salted it enough.

And as for costing them—what about the income from her parents' farm? She had tried to go to a lawyer, but the lawyer had told her uncle and he had beaten her for bringing shame on him and the family. After all, he was not only a noted lawyer in the city, he was one of the twenty-five members of *Le Petit Conseil*. Although she could not see her back, she could feel the rough ridges in the places she could touch. And he had turned her around and lashed her once across the breasts and then touched them afterwards with a cloth to supposedly stop the blood.

The bell on the door tinkled and Jean-Michel walked in. Although he was now married, he found enough excuses to talk to her. "Can we go upstairs?" he asked.

Antoine opened the door. The room where they'd made love on Antoine's bed, where she had sketched him naked, had not changed. Antoine still allowed her to keep the crayons and drawings on top of the cupboard for she had more and more time to do her work because her aunt did not want her in the house. Her drawings were still protected between two wooden covers and tied with a ribbon. Now they contained her grandfather's letter too.

Antoine's wife Marie had become her new model. Elizabeth had sketched her making the bed, repairing Antoine's shirt. She had posed her in the same way she had Jean-Michel, staring out the window.

"I really think I need to buy some carrots for tonight," Marie said when she saw that Jean-Michel was with Elizabeth.

Before Elizabeth could say that she didn't think it was necessary to leave them alone, Jean-Michel said, "You're really wonderful, Marie," and blew the woman a kiss.

As soon as the door to the top of the stairs closed behind Marie, Jean-Michel opened his satchel and pulled out pastels in every color of the rainbow. "I ordered them from Paris for you. You know why?"

She picked them up and touched her finger to the tip of the blue one that was like a soft sky. It tinted the top of the swirls of her skin. Each stick was more beautiful than the one before and she imagined how to apply small lines so the colors would blend.

She knew why he had given her these. Only after his wedding did he discover that his wife was not the woman he wanted even if she had brought her father's money into his business. "I cannot talk to her," he would tell Elizabeth. "And she is always after me to buy this or that when I should be pouring every centime back into the business."

"You should have thought of that before," she'd said, trying to ignore the red eyes that told of too much wine. She resisted pointing out that the colored pastels had cost money that he could have poured back into his print shop or used to buy his wife one of the things she was demanding. However, she wanted those wonderful colors. And part of her, although she disliked herself for thinking that way, was glad that he still cared about her.

Although he wanted to make love to her, she denied him despite her own desires. He was married, off limits. Talking was the limit.

"My wife is having a baby," he said.

She felt her stomach contract for if she would let herself admit it, she still loved him, but saw him as a weakling. Her gratitude that she would soon leave Geneva forever was almost as strong as her sadness that her dreams with him—those that she had resisted for so long, then had come to accept and cherish—were now never to be. She wished her grandfather had already come and she was somewhere near Saint George, perhaps in the fields where her mother played as a child while her father was writing some paper or working with a document, if that was what he did. Although her mother talked about how learned her father was, how he worked for the church, Elizabeth was not sure if he were the vicar, the priest or what. Since he had married during the Catholic rule of Henry VII, he couldn't have been a priest and married. It was something she would have to ask him when she finally saw him. She turned back to Jean-Michel. "It will be your baby, too. Are you happy?"

"I wish it were our baby."

She was not going to tell him about their lost baby. Hard enough for her to think about the child she would never hold in her arms. To be honest with herself she knew that it wasn't just him she was trying to protect. He was not trustworthy enough to keep her secret.

He leaned over to kiss her, but she moved away. "I have the same answer. You are *married*. It isn't right."

"Would you sketch me?"

What would be the harm? She stood on tiptoe to reach the top of the cabinet where her paper was and her old pencils. Jean-Michel came up behind her to help, but as soon as he had them, he put them on Antoine's bed, took Elizabeth in his arms and kissed her.

For a minute she let him then pushed him away. "Sit on the bed."

"Do I leave my clothes on?"

"Yes!" Taking the pad, she used one of her old pencils to draw one line after another and his face appeared on paper. His hair was longer than before he had married and his beard, which had been scraggly, had thickened. She wanted to stroke it, but instead recreated it on paper.

"Do you think your wife would accept something I knitted for the baby?" She knew his wife was jealous of her, because he'd told her so. Although the seven deadly sins were of Catholic origin, more than once Jean Calvin had railed against them in his sermons, and said envy was one of the worst. Elizabeth had told Jean-Michel over and over he had to do his part to make sure that his wife did not envy the part of his life that Elizabeth had occupied, but she had no way of knowing if he followed her wishes.

By the time she had captured the lines she wanted on paper and there was only background that she could add, a knock on the door broke her concentration.

"May I come in?" Marie spoke through the wooden door.

Elizabeth opened it with such speed, Marie almost fell in. "It is your home, and we're hiding nothing."

"Too bad," Marie said.

CHAPTER 29

Geneva, Switzerland

When Roger entered the detective office on time in the morning, the receptionist handed him a handwritten note.

Robbery in Pâquis last night. Left Stoller interview files on Morat's desk.

F

Another example of Fortini shoving him aside, giving him busy work and not letting him do anything of consequence.

He shoved the paper in his pocket, used the coffee machine to pour himself an espresso and went back to the table that had been added to the office for him. The file was in a blue cardboard folder, sealed on two ends with attached elastics. Someone had printed out a sheet headed "Stoller Interviews"— neatly listing the names and dates—and glued it to the top. He suspected it was Morat.

For the next hour and a half he read every word. Morat had even noted interviewees' expressions in his transcriptions. Roger would love to have him working on the force in Argelès. The young man had a brilliant future ahead, but Argelès would be too small for him.

By the time he placed the interviews back in the folder, he was aware that they had only interviewed the widow, the son, and colleagues of the victim. What about the students?

Looking at his watch, he made a decision.

"I'm going to the university," he told the receptionist.

The four-hundred-year-old University of Geneva was located in the Parc des Bastions across from the old city wall. The park was surrounded by a ten-foot-high fence made of gold-tipped black-iron poles. On this fall day, two men were playing chess with the giant chess pieces. The tree-lined paths had their share of fallen leaves waiting to be swept away by the city. Knowing how ruthlessly the city was kept clean, Roger suspected that they had been blown off the trees by the wind the night before and at any moment the leaf crew would arrive with their wheelbarrows and rakes. He turned away from the chess players, only to see that he was right. The workmen were arriving to pick up the fallen leaves.

Roger put up his coat collar and wished he had worn a scarf. No signs directed him to the university. In fact, a stranger walking by the buildings on the edge of the park would never have guessed that this was a university campus as well as a park, had not students with books been milling around.

One girl was sitting on a bench. She looked like all students, with long brown hair, jeans and a leather jacket that could have been picked up in any consignment store. She cradled her laptop on her knees as she took advantage of the free Wi-Fi.

Roger sat down on the other edge of the bench not wanting to threaten her, not wanting her to think he was a dirty old man. He reached for the identity badge that the Geneva police had given him. "Would you please talk to me?"

"What do you want to talk to me about?"

"Professor Stoller."

She nodded. "How did you know I was one of his students?"

"I didn't. You were the first student I saw not rushing anywhere."

She glanced at her watch. "And I'm almost late for class. If you come with me we can talk as I walk. If we don't finish, you can sit in. It's his replacement lecturer. Personally, I like the replacement much better than Stoller, although I shouldn't speak ill of the dead, should I?"

"If that's how you really feel . . ."

"I didn't hate the professor, but he was so arrogant. If we didn't know what he knew, his whole manner implied we were ignorant. Now, we were there to learn from him, weren't we? If we knew as much as he did, there would be no reason to take his class, would there?" She didn't wait for an answer as she entered the building which was dark compared to the outside light and led Roger up stairs that were worn in the middle from centuries of student footsteps. "Everyone was afraid to ask him questions, because he treated them so high-handedly. This new man, Dr. Marcel Savary, he acts like our questions are meaningful: a good way to lead into another aspect of the subject. He even thanks us for them rather than rolling his eyes for what he has to suffer in our presence."

By this time they had entered the lecture hall. A desk on a small platform with a screen behind it was in the front of the room. Facing the platform were elevated rows of desks going up two dozen stairs.

A man behind the platform was fiddling with his computer. He smiled at the girl. "Congratulations, Mademoiselle Piccard. You arrived before I started."

She smiled back. "May this gentlemen sit in today?"

"You're interested in the geometry used in medieval paintings?"

"I was hoping you could give me some time after class." Savary had not been on the list of interviewees.

Savary's lecture almost made Roger wish he were back at university and had taken art history. The man could have been an actor in a comedy. He made the paintings come alive, talking about what the lives of the models must have been like, using lines such as "I have to go pee; how long do I have to be part of this stupid triangle?" and using his laser against the screen where the paintings were projected from the laptop to make his point.

The class broke out in laughter several times, and whenever a student raised a hand, Savary quickly answered or turned the question back to the class. Roger was amazed that it was over so quickly.

He and Mademoiselle Piccard sat quietly until the thumping of books and feet disappeared.

After Savary shut down his computer and shuffled his notes back into his briefcase, he asked, "And I've been dying of curiosity. Did Madeleine here have an older boyfriend who is worried about how she has raved about her professor? That is a lot nicer than saying you are an overprotective father."

"He's from the police," Madeleine said.

Savary's smile ran from his face. "I am sorry. I suppose it is about old Stoller."

Roger nodded.

"If you have time, let's go have coffee. Not downstairs. There's a great little tea room across the street."

They were the only ones seated with their espressos in the small tearoom.

"Marcel, don't you think it's time someone told the truth about Dr. Stoller?" she asked, blowing on her espresso.

"They have been," he said. The way he looked at her, Roger guessed they were more than student and professor. The teacher was probably in his late twenties at the most and wore no wedding ring. Madeleine did not strike him as the type of woman that would have considered this a power play on his part nor did he think she might be using him to get a good grade. He had no facts to base this opinion on. "Are you two an item?"

Savary blushed.

"We're engaged. Our parents know, but we have not discussed it with anyone at the school. When Stoller died, I told Marcel about the opening, and he contacted the university. Because he could start the next day, and because another professor had died of a brain tumor, they were so short staffed, that Marcel was brought in to cover the classes. He has a second job at the Musée Cantonale des Beaux Arts in Lausanne, but that is only part-time."

"Jobs for art historians are limited these days," Marcel said. "But I would rather earn less and do what I love than make a bundle, although I'm not sure I'm qualified for any type of bundle-earning."

Roger found himself liking this man, although like and dislike had nothing to do with why he was there.

"All the interviews we've done sound like a recording, praising Stoller."

"The art department protects its own," Madeleine said. "But the man had a world-renowned reputation. Just Google him. His death notice was printed in almost all the major world newspapers."

"But . . ." Roger left it hanging.

"I haven't been here long enough to . . . ," Marcel Savary said.

"He was a bastard. Everyone was afraid to say anything about their work. He would steal their ideas, especially the students working for their degrees under him. I know that is common in academia, but he carried it too far. There is a story that one graduate student killed herself after Stoller published her thesis draft as his own work," Madeleine said.

"Didn't she have a copy?"

"Her computer was stolen. I don't think he had anything to do with the stealing of her computer, but when she went to him for the copies she'd sent him, he said he never kept student work. She dropped out of the program but two years later her thesis became his sixth book."

"*Chérie,* you don't know that for a fact."

"Enough people have said it." Madeleine was not the pouting type. She was the type that snapped back.

Marcel held up his hands. "But that's how gossip spreads."

"Gossip can be based on facts."

Roger admired the way she wouldn't let go when she thought she was right. It reminded him of Annie, making him almost want to take Marcel aside and counsel him on how to handle a powerful woman.

The waitress came by. They ordered three more espressos which appeared within minutes. Roger was beginning to feel wired as he drank his.

"Why do you think everyone was praising him?" Roger asked.

"As I said, they protect their own, and he was great in his field. *Voilà, c'est tout.*" Madeleine downed her espresso. "I'll be late to class." She picked up her books. "If you want to talk to me again, Marcel can give you my cell."

"She's quite a woman," Marcel said, looking after her.

Roger could only nod.

CHAPTER 30

Corsier Port, Switzerland

The doorbell rang over the theme song from the TV series playing on the DVD as Annie opened the split of champagne and Susan placed the tray with shrimp and *foie gras* on the stand between the two chairs in front of the television. They were having a girls' night in while Roger and Dave were having a male bonding night, as Susan termed it, going to a shoot-em-up movie in the city followed by pizza and beer.

Sometimes Annie wondered if she and Roger broke up which one of their couple would her parents choose. Part of it was probably that Roger was halfway between her and her parents in age and was also a parent. Or it could be that they were all just genuinely nice people who enjoyed each other's company, and she should stop being such an idiot and worrying it the way the proverbial dog did with the proverbial bone. Anyway, the girls had the better deal, because it was pouring outside.

"I'll get it." Susan pressed the pause button on the remote.

Annie heard her mother say, "Marc!" and she rushed to the door.

Marc was drenched.

"I walked from Rive," he said. "I need to talk to you, Annie." Even at a fast, fast pace that route would have taken him a good hour or more.

"Before you do anything, you're taking a hot shower. Upstairs. I'll get some of Dave's clothes for you." Susan stood

163

behind the boy and marched him up the bathroom.

The DVD, shrimp, *foie gras* and champagne forgotten, Susan gathered Marc's clothes and put them in the washer. Then while the women waited in the kitchen, Annie made a pot of hot chocolate.

The water stopped running upstairs and Marc appeared in Dave's bathrobe. "I need to talk to Annie." He looked at his hands not at the women. "I don't mean to be rude, Madame Young."

"I have some sketches to do," Susan said and disappeared up the stairs to her attic atelier.

Annie led him into the kitchen where she pointed to one of the modern clear-plastic chairs. Before they had inherited the place at Caleb's Landing, the Youngs had remodeled, transforming their country kitchen into a streamlined white-and-gray twenty-first-century kitchen. She poured him a cup of the hot chocolate and put it on a red placemat. "Drink it; you were thoroughly chilled."

"The shower helped."

"Drink it."

"You're almost as bossy as your mother."

"I learned from the best."

Marc stirred the hot chocolate, getting rid of the milk scum on the top and dropping it in the saucer. He looked around the kitchen. He looked at his hands.

Annie debated letting the silence continue, but couldn't. *"Talk!"*

"My mother is having an affair."

"But your father just died."

"Probably it was going on before. I mean, I don't think . . . I can't know for sure, however . . ."

"What makes you think she is having an affair?"

"She didn't come home until five in the morning. She said

she had some overnight work in the lab, but she never has had to stay all night and besides she has assistants whom she'd tell to do that stuff. And she said she couldn't hear her office phone from the lab, but I've been there and she would have had to be deaf not to hear it. Maybe she had her cell off, but her office phone is loud."

"She could have fallen asleep."

"She looked well fucked."

Annie did not bother to correct his language, and she did not bother to ask him how he knew what "well fucked" looked like. He had always been an imaginative child, putting things together in ways none of his friends did, which often made him feel like an outsider. She was the one who had described what feeling like an outsider felt like. He had been ten at the time, sitting in her easy chair, one leg thrown over the arm and eating a brownie that her mother had baked.

"He hasn't been dead two full weeks, and she is already screwing around. I hate her. I hate her. I hate her."

"I am sure you do at the moment," Annie said.

"You're not going to tell me it is wrong to hate?"

"What I tell you won't change how you feel. I might tell you that when you hate it does more damage to the hater than it does to the hatee. I might also tell you it is good to rage and be angry for a while." She put her hand over his. "But I won't tell you any of that."

He laughed. "Can I stay here? I can't face her."

Annie went to the foot of the stairs leading to Susan's atelier. "Mom, can Marc stay here for a few days?"

"Of course." Susan's voice filtered down the stairs. Annie knew her mother would ask for more information later.

The front door opened, and she saw Marc dash outside in his bare feet and her father's bathrobe. The automatic lights that illuminated the front garden and driveway came on. As she watched, he ducked into the open garage and pulled out a large backpack, the type kids use when they are hiking and camping.

Back in the house he said, "I didn't want to show up with everything in case you said no. It would feel, feel . . ."

"Like you took for granted that we would say yes?"

He nodded. "If it were just you over on François Lehman, I knew you'd say yes. And I know your parents are great and all . . ."

"There is one condition, though."

"What?"

"You need to let your mom know where you are." He saw him open his mouth. "You may hate her right now, but that doesn't mean she hates you. She needs to know that you are safe."

He shook his head. "I can't talk to her."

"Then I'll call her."

He nodded.

As she went to phone Maria-Elena, she realized that Roger would consider having a lover a good motive for murdering a husband.

CHAPTER 31

Corsier Port, Switzerland

"This will be my first pumpkin festival." Roger held Annie's hand as they walked up the hill to the elementary school parking lot past vineyards that were now devoid of grapes. Even before they arrived, they heard the merry-go-round. He had not wanted to go, preferring to look over the Stoller case notes that he brought home for his day off. Annie had coaxed and wheedled him, using as a final argument that beautiful October days in Geneva were gifts which should never be ignored. She also promised to go over the case with him, for he had always found her insights as good as any professional detective.

Booths sold vegetables, arts and crafts, and foods of different nationalities. Children, some with their faces painted, ran around. Adults sat on long benches beside long tables and ate, drank beer or wine and talked.

Annie was periodically stopped by someone she knew from her school years. The elementary school had never been hers, having arrived in Switzerland during her high-school years. The village had no school beyond the sixth year. She had gone first to the school that Calvin had started five hundred years before, then transferred to the international school, because she thought she wanted to go to university in the United States. Once there, she felt as much of an outsider in the country of her birth as she ever had in a "foreign" country. She rushed back to the University of Geneva, which was much more familiar territory.

167

One of her neighbors bustled up. "Is this your fiancé? I heard you were engaged." The woman glanced at Annie's ringless left hand.

"If she'll have me. I'm Roger Perret." He held out his hand.

Annie was once again grateful to him for saying just the right thing when she could not think of anything.

Elodie, a friend from the Calvin *collége,* approached with her husband and their four-year-old twin girls. "It's great seeing you without worrying about a Latin test," Elodie said after they had caught up on the basics of their lives.

Annie stopped at a booth which had framed drawings of some of the local houses, the baker's, the post, the village hall, the church, the boatyard, the dock. "Maybe I should buy one for Argelès."

"So you'll remember your roots?" Roger asked, raising an eyebrow.

"Don't mock me." Annie knew he had listened for hours about how she never felt she belonged a hundred percent anywhere until Argelès and even then it wasn't belonging she felt, but happiness.

The Pumpkin Festival, as much of a great local activity as it was, did not merit hours and hours unless you were at a table with lots of people you knew. The couple walked back down the hill toward the house and the lake.

"It was nice. I like village *fêtes* especially when I am not doing my police thing," Roger said. "Shall we walk along the lake, before we go home?"

Annie nodded. It was one of those perfect days with an almost-royal-blue sky and puff clouds over the lake which sparkled in the sun. Although the leaves on the trees were nowhere as beautiful as those of her New England childhood, because the bright reds were missing, the yellow was brilliant. Roger stopped, hugged her and continued walking.

At the lake, some sailboats and motorboats were moving up and down as a gentle breeze stirred the water. The dock, where the big boats docked as they circled the lake to take on or let off passengers out for a day's cruise, had flower baskets along the rails that protected embarking and debarking passengers from falling into the water. The red geraniums had not yet fallen victim to a fall frost.

"Sometimes my parents will take the 8:35 boat to Lausanne, have breakfast on the boat, get off in Lausanne for lunch then catch the 3:19 back here," Annie said.

"We should try it ourselves," Roger said. "Annie, what are you staring at?"

"The Stoller boat is still in the water. I bet Maria-Elena forgot to have it pulled out."

"Stoller has a boat? There's nothing in the file."

"You mean no one has searched it?"

Roger shook his head. "If they did, there was no mention. I doubt if they even know he had one. I'll have to correct that tomorrow."

As they headed back to the house, which was only a block up from the lake, Annie said, "I guess pumpkin festivals and lake walks are really beneficial to *flics* who have trouble relaxing during a case."

"Guess so. Do you have your key?" he asked as they approached the door. There was no need. It was unlocked.

"Go to your room and we'll talk about it when you're straight," Dave was saying as Annie closed the front door. As Marc disappeared up the stairs, Annie held her hand up in a what's-going-on gesture.

Dave motioned her to the kitchen and shut the door. "Marc came home stoned."

"Where's Mom?"

"You didn't see her at the festival? She walked up with Irena."

"We must have missed each other, or maybe she stopped off at the *boulangerie*. How stoned was Marc?"

"Stoned enough that he couldn't pretend he wasn't."

"And, of course, because you and Mom are ex-hippies, you can recognize stoned."

"Big time."

Annie and Roger and Dave all sat at the kitchen table. "I know it is normal for a kid his age. I think drugs should be legal. It would save you a lot of work." He looked at Roger.

"True, and think of the taxes we could collect. But back to the kid."

"He's just lost his father and in the most unnatural way possible. His mother is a non-nurturing pain in the ass. He's a teenager. I don't want him to go off the rails," Dave said.

"What will you do?" Annie asked.

"Set down house rules. He is welcome to stay indefinitely but no drugs and no alcohol to a point of being drunk."

Roger shook his head. "I'm not sure it will work."

"It might. He doesn't want to go home. He's crazy about you guys and unless he has another place to crash he might go along with it." Annie hoped she was right.

CHAPTER 32

Geneva, Switzerland
September 1558

The first sign of autumn was the leaves floating on the well water. Elizabeth dipped the pail into the liquid. Usually her cousin Sarah did this, because now Aunt Mathilde, instead of wanting Elizabeth out of her sight, more and more wanted to keep her home. Elizabeth could not figure out why. Asking Uncle Jacques would be useless, because unless it pertained to the boys, he always agreed with whatever Aunt Mathilde said. As far as the boys were concerned, both parents looked upon each one of them as if they were Jesus Christ incarnate.

Women, Uncle Jacques often repeated, were all like Eve: temptresses, ignorant and certainly not to be taken seriously. They needed to be guided and prayed over to keep them from sin.

Today, Aunt Mathilde had no choice but to send Elizabeth with Jeanne on errands. Sarah was teaching her catechism class and then was going to dinner at her fiancé's house. They had despaired of her ever marrying, but Gérard Pommier, the son of one of the counselors, had asked for her hand, and because his father served with Uncle Jacques on *Le Petit Conseil*, Uncle Jacques had said yes.

Elizabeth thought it had more to do with the fact that Pommier was a widower with six children and he needed a wife to help him take care of them. He had been turned down by a number of women who did not want to tackle another woman's brood.

Jeanne skipped around the fountain as Elizabeth dipped the pail into the water.

"May I help you carry that?"

Elizabeth looked around to see Guillaume Dumont from her uncle's office. "I am not a weakling, but it is kind of you to offer." She handed him the pail.

"We are both dryer than the last time we met."

She had to think back and then remembered the day she had been drenched and had answered the door and he had been caught by the same storm.

"We've had all summer to dry out."

"Maybe we've learned to stay out of the rain." He lifted the pail.

"Jeanne, come on."

The little girl stopped running around the fountain but started twirling. "If I look at one spot I don't get dizzy and throw up."

"Well, throwing up is not much fun," Guillaume said.

As they walked back to the house, only Jeanne was chattering. She saw a bird, and talked about a horse and asked Guillaume if he had any little girls.

"I'm not married," he said.

"Do you want to be?"

"Jeanne, you shouldn't ask questions like that!" Elizabeth said. Had she not been leaving Geneva, the answer would have interested her.

"How else can I find out?"

"Maybe she should be a lawyer," Guillaume said. "But then women can't be lawyers. It is not God's will."

"I sometimes think God's will is more man's will," Elizabeth let slip.

He gasped.

"No, really. What Bible verse says women should not be lawyers?"

"I don't remember one."

"That proves my point."

"You *do* think like a lawyer also, but you can't go around saying things like that. What will people think?"

"You're right. I should never have said that. Please, don't report me to my uncle."

He put down the bucket for a minute and rubbed his palm where the handle had left a mark. "We've just proven you can't be a lawyer."

She cocked her head.

"A lawyer wouldn't give up so easily."

They both laughed and if as one turned to see where Jeanne was. She'd fallen behind to pick up a very large maple leaf—one large enough to cover her chest.

"I don't think she heard," he said.

"Heard what?" Jeanne asked.

"That bird singing." He pointed to a bird in a tree.

The little girl shook her head.

"The wind is coming up," Elizabeth said.

The two grown-ups laughed at their attempt to distract Jeanne.

"What's funny?" she asked.

"Nothing," he said. "I was laughing because I was happy."

Elizabeth took a long look at him. Definitely, if she were not leaving Geneva she would have been interested in him, but, then again, her uncle would not want her to marry this man and have her rents pass out of his hands.

CHAPTER 33

Beckenham, England

As Annie stood in front of the Victorian B and B, all she could think of was that Charles Dickens would walk by any minute. The flight from Geneva on Easy Jet had been a breeze. Only at the Luton Airport train station had things become difficult. If she'd been in a rush, she would have been annoyed by the announcements. It seemed every train calling from such and such a place due on track A was going to be late and would now be located on track B, C, D and those supposed to stop at B, C, D would be calling somewhere else. Finally she had boarded a train and arrived at her destination, with no appointment until the next morning when she would meet up with Saint George's vicar, Sebastian Crowe.

An elderly woman, who could have taken the role of Mrs. Havisham only without the cobwebs and wedding dress, answered. "You must be Annie Young. Welcome, dearie. I'm Miss Brooke. I'll put the kettle on. Once you've put your suitcase in your room, a good cup of tea will help you settle in."

The inside of the house was as Victorian as the outside, overloaded with knickknacks, flowered wallpaper and overstuffed furniture. Annie's eyes grew tired just looking around. In her room she tested the bed. At least it was comfortable, and the place was clean. No, more than clean. Spotless. The bathroom was out in the hall. She washed her hands and headed downstairs.

"My sister and I have run this B and B since after the war," Miss Brooke told her.

Although Annie thought World War I, she was sure Miss Brooke meant World War II and not the Falklands or the wars in the Persian Gulf.

The old woman's hand shook as she poured the tea into a delicate porcelain cup with violets on the side.

"Biscuit, dear?" She held out a tin with an assortment of chocolate cookies. "Now tell me what brings you to England."

"I've an appointment with Sebastian Crowe at . . ."

Miss Brooke wrinkled her nose. "My vicar. He cares too much about the past. He should spend more time with what is happening today."

Annie nodded, whilst thinking she had come to the right place.

The vicar at Saint George's was an extremely handsome man, maybe in his early forties. His black hair was beginning to grow gray around the temples, and his smile Annie could only call impish.

Automatically she checked the ring finger on his left hand. Even though she was not in the market, it was a reflex. There was a gold band.

"I've been really excited since we talked. You flew over ever so quickly," he said as he led her into his study. It was small, with a yellow stained-glass arched window behind his desk, which was piled with papers. Each pile looked as if it were a breath away from toppling over into even more chaos.

He went on explaining how, when he had become vicar, he had insisted that all the old records, which had long since been transferred to a central depository for safekeeping, be put onto a microfilm. "My parishioners at first thought it was a waste of money, but then we did some research on the different families, and some still live right here. One family has been here since the 1300s when the church was built. We got the kids interested too."

Then it was Annie's turn to explain that they had found drawings from an Elizabeth H., dating back to what they thought was the time of Calvin.

"Drawings during the time of the old sourpuss?"

Startled, Annie looked up from her notebook, where she had just jotted down the date of the church.

"You have to admit times were severe back then. Smiling was almost a burning offense." When he laughed his eyes twinkled. "Now what are we working on to start?"

Annie showed him a photocopy of the letter from Tobias Smythe. "Too bad the top is torn where there might be a date. The original is so brittle that when it was found between the lining and the cover of a portfolio it was a wonder it didn't crumble to bits."

"Sounds like there is a fascinating story, a potential movie, or at least a BBC production," he said.

"One of the sketches looked as if it might be the burning of Michel Servetus."

"Ah, the one who had the nerve to challenge the concept of the Trinity. As Annie nodded, Crowe added, "Calvin really pulled a dirty trick on him, letting him come, and then arresting and burning him as a heretic."

"Wouldn't it be wonderful, if we could prove that it were him?" Annie said.

"Impossible."

"Not necessarily."

The vicar frowned.

"If we can identify the artist, and if Servetus was the only one burned during the artist's lifetime then it would be authenticated." Annie's hope swelled at the idea. Although she knew that most historians had to have university credentials, still being able to discover a pictorial of a historic event long before there was a twenty-four-hour news cycle and phone cameras would be really satisfying. The scenery in the drawing wouldn't be any help, although local historians seemed to know Servetus had been burned near where the Hôpitaux Universitaires de Genève now stood. Plus the value when it sold would help Mireille as a single mom. For a moment, the idea of going back to school for a PhD and the idea of teaching in a university nibbled at her.

Nope.

She liked her life the way it was. Tech writing was challenge enough and working only six months a year suited her fine. Professors couldn't dabble in this or that and she figured if Olympic gold medals were given for historical dabbling, then she would qualify.

"How are we going to work this?" she asked.

"Although I would love to copy the CD-ROMs for you, it is considered church property." He opened the doors to an old wooden cabinet that had two rows of CDs. "Are you a gospel fan?"

"I like it well enough."

He took down several CDs. "You can listen to music if you want while you are looking through the documents. These are the ones that cover the period you're interested in."

"Where do you want me to set up?"

"I'll make room for you in my assistant's office."

"Won't she want the space?"

"*He* . . . and he had an emergency with his mum in Cornwall and won't be back until Monday. That should give you enough time."

Unlike Vicar Crowe's office, the assistant's office was pristine: papers were lined up with soldier-precision, books in the bookcase were in alphabetical order, the computer bore no fingerprints. A photo of an older woman, probably the assistant's mother, was in a silver-filigreed frame.

Annie put her laptop on the desk, and half expected the assistant to come barging in to dust it.

The CD-ROM whirred and came up. Oh shit, she thought. She should not have been surprised at the almost illegible writing of the documents. One of her courses had been in deciphering different medieval scripts in English, French and German. Since handwriting was not stylized in those days, except for Court Hand used by lawyers, it took a certain kind of mind to decipher what the writer was saying. This was not the Chancery Hand of the English courts. She tried to remember which serifs would have been used in the 1500s by clerics taking down records for the churches, and decided that the writing on the different documents was done by anyone who could write at all no matter how good or bad.

She worked backwards eighty years from the burning of Servetus, remembering that the painter's grandfather was sixty when he wrote the letter, but there might be some other family history. Her other assumption was that he was educated and therefore of the middle or upper classes. But the name Smythe or Smith could be a professional application as well, making him a tradesman. Tobias was not that unusual a name for the period, and she located five.

At the same time she was looking for marriages. She found three.

The light was failing. The halogen lamp on the desk looked out of place against the antique furniture and wooden bookshelf-lined walls. Her watch said it was almost five. She had totally forgotten about lunch. She was starved.

The vicar poked his head in.

"My wife wants to know if you want to join us for our tea?

She has a nice piece of fish she bought."

"Yes, thank you."

"It will be ready in a half an hour."

CHAPTER 34

Beckenham, England

Annie's cell phone rang as she walked from the B and B to the church. She dug around in her pocketbook, hoping that the person would not hang up.

Roger let it ring until Annie picked up. "When are you coming home, *Chérie?*"

"No hello, how are you?"

"Bonjour, Chérie. Ça va?"

"Ça va bien, mon cher. I was just thinking of extending my stay a while longer. I haven't found what I'm looking for yet." Annie said nothing to the long sigh that followed.

The silence took her almost a block before Roger spoke, "You know, *Chérie,* I've gotten used to you taking assignments away from me, but when I come to where you are working, it would be nice if you—how do you say?—hung around and not go someplace else."

Damn, he had a point there. It had taken her long enough to get him used to her disappearing to Zurich, Frankfort, Amsterdam, Vienna to do this or that.

"And this isn't even paid work."

He was right again. She was doing it for Mireille. "You're right."

"Excuse me? Is this Annie Young I'm talking to?"

"Smart ass. You're right. I should be in Geneva while you're there."

"I can't believe you gave in."

"Mark the day in history. Anyway, I will try and change my flight to the last Easy Jet out tonight or the first one in the morning. I can always come back after you go home."

As she reached the church, they exchanged farewell endearments.

"I'll put the kettle on," Vicar Crowe said as Annie walked by his office.

First Annie brought up the Easy Jet site using the vicar's Wi-Fi. That there were no seats available until the day after tomorrow made her smile as she booked her ticket because she could text Roger guilt free that she had tried to do as he wanted.

Annie shoved the CD-ROM that she had not finished the night before into her laptop and started scrolling through the documents. The handwriting seemed even less readable.

As the Easy Jet plane circled Genève Aèroport, Annie could see the lights of the apartment complex where she used to live. Because the plane had been late taking off, all the buses had stopped running, so she intended spending the night there in order to show Mireille what she'd found. She had texted her friend as the plane sat on the runway waiting for clearance, and Mireille had texted back, "Can't wait."

It had taken three days of mind-numbing work going through page after page after page of archaically written documents over a hundred-year period. The faintness of some of the writing might have come from the originals, or it could have lost clarity in the copying process. Five Tobias Smythes and four Tobias Smiths had turned up.

She really wished people had been given original names, especially kings. History had too many King Louises, Edwards, Henris and Henrys and they could have done without the Charleses as well. She could not expect the underclasses to have been better.

However, as she traced down each Tobias, she found one that had married an Edyth Constable. They had had six children, four of whom had died before they had turned five. Two survived: a girl, Anne, and a boy, James. Then, among the children of the other Tobiases that she was working on, she came across a marriage record for Anne Smythe, daughter of Tobias and Edyth who married an Yves Huguette of Geneva. Nothing more was found on the new couple: no children, no deaths.

At that point she was sure she'd found the family of the painter of Mireille's portfolio. Her next chore would be to go through the Genevan archives to find if Yves and Anne Huguette had a daughter Elizabeth. But maybe they hadn't lived in Geneva? Maybe they were in neighboring France. Don't make problems, she told herself. Just continue the research in a logical manner.

The flight was almost empty and Annie breezed through customs. She debated walking to Mireille's through the Palexpo park, but it was dark. She was not especially worried about crime, which was minimal, but the night was cold. She grabbed a taxi.

Mireille was in her pajamas, but her computer was open to the spreadsheet where she was tallying more characteristics of Brueghel's paintings.

Annie dropped her bag. "Glad your couch is free."

Mireille checked her watch. "Even if it weren't, it would be. You would never have made the last bus to Corsier." She gathered bedding and started transforming the couch into a bed.

"Don't you want to know exactly what I found?"

"Are we women?"

When Annie told, Mireille clapped her hands together like a child.

"Tobais Smythe had a daughter who married an Yves Huguette of Geneva."

"And the signature on the painting did look like the first letter of the family name could have been *H*. I don't believe it. I don't *believe* it."

"There's no mention of either after that for the next seventy years, which means they could have gone to Geneva—although there is no way we can trace that."

"But maybe there is a record here."

"I plan to check out the state archives here."

"It might be hard to get in, but I imagine that if we got one of the professors at *Uni* to explain it is for scholarly research . . ."

"Tomorrow I need to do some clean-up work for the guys. And I need to get some time with Roger, although he seems to be working straight out on Urs's murder."

Mireille got up and walked out of the living room and into her bedroom. The door shut with a soft click.

Damn, Annie thought. I opened a wound. She got up and tapped on the door. "Mireille. I'm sorry." She wasn't sure what she was sorry for: hurting her feelings, bringing back the pain?

"It's okay. I just need to be alone." Annie could barely hear Mireille's whisper through the door.

CHAPTER 35

Geneva, Switzerland
May 24, 1559

Françoise squeezed her nipple, even though it hurt, hoping a little milk would come. She then put her son's mouth against it. The baby gave a few tentative sucks. His nose was encrusted and it must have pained him because he whimpered whenever she touched it. His breathing could be heard in the next room whenever she left him. He had never been a strong baby, but this latest cold was the worst yet. It seemed that every few days in the three short months of his life a fever, chill or a stomach-ache threw him into misery and the rest of the household along with it.

"How is he?" Jean-Michel popped his head into the kitchen where Françoise and the baby were sitting. He did not have to ask about lunch. Although the fire was crackling against the spring chill, no pots hung from the spikes.

That he did not ask about eating was a good thing, Françoise thought. She was the one that had walked the floor most of the night trying to quiet their son so her husband could sleep. He had too much work to do and it left him exhausted. The shop was just beginning to pay its own way, and he wanted to make sure that everything he did was better than the competition. She watched him cut himself some bread and cheese and pluck a wizened apple from the last of the fall supply that she kept in a barrel near the fire.

Nothing looked good to her. Nothing. She was too tired to eat. Although she loved the baby, it seemed that it had destroyed whatever affection Jean-Michel had had for her.

She was sure he wished he'd married that bitch Elizabeth. She had seen him talking to her on the street with a look that she, his wife, would never inspire in him.

Sometimes she wished she'd never married. Life had been better at home, where her father had felt she should not be burdened with too many chores. That was why they had servants to do those chores, he would say. Do the work yourself and you take away their jobs.

Her mother had insisted she learn all the necessary things to run a household, but that included telling the servants what to do. Jean-Michel was a long way from being able to provide her with even a cleaning woman once a month.

Although she knew it was a sin to be vain, her hands, once soft and white, were now red and chapped from housework. And if her mother had not stepped in to pay a seamstress to let out her dresses that no longer fit after the baby, she would be walking around in rags. Sewing was not a lesson she had paid much attention to, and because her mother always used seamstresses, she had never been forced into learning. She suspected Elizabeth wasn't any good with a needle either.

Elizabeth was weird, what with her upbringing on a farm and how she often spoke out when any well-mannered woman would have kept quiet. And Jean-Michel had let slip that she spoke English and Latin. Imagine a women knowing Latin.

Of course, Françoise never let on how she felt after that first fight about Elizabeth. Jean-Michel was so angry with her it confirmed her fears that he still loved Elizabeth.

She even had accepted that awful blanket that Elizabeth had given the baby when he was born. Although theater was forbidden in Geneva, Françoise felt she could have been an actress with the gratitude she had manifested. It had been easy to rave about its color, a gentle blue like her son's eyes. The blanket was made of a soft wool that almost floated if she dropped it to the floor. Had it come from anyone else, she would have loved it instead of hating it because it came from that bitch. There was something wrong with that woman, the way she could entrance Jean-Michel. Antoine, the shoemaker, was under her spell too.

She knew she should feel sorry for Elizabeth, whose mother, father and brother all died so she had to live with that awful aunt and uncle. She felt if either of them smiled their faces would break, not that God wanted people to go around smiling all the time, but God must want people to appreciate all the wonders he had put before them.

Still, considering how successful Jacques and Mathilde Huguette were, she was sure they were saved, just as she was sure her Jean-Michel was saved.

"I can hold him for a while," her husband said.

"What?"

"Let me hold him. You go take a nap."

Françoise wasn't sure she wanted to turn the baby over to him, but she did. "If he does sleep put him in his cradle, and you can go back to work."

She almost stumbled going to the room off the kitchen that served as their bedroom. She fell onto the mattress and had no recollection of anything until she woke. The room was dark. The kitchen was silent. She wondered if Jean-Michel had taken the baby back to the print shop. He wouldn't do that. Even though it was May, it was much too cold for a sick infant to be outside. She was fully dressed, not having had the energy to take off her clothes before falling asleep, as she walked across the room and into the kitchen.

The baby was in his cradle under the blanket made by the

bitch, but there was no movement, no sound. Picking him up she was surprised at how cold he felt and how blue he looked.

CHAPTER 36

Geneva, Switzerland

Roger put his coffee cup in the dishwasher. "I'm leaving, and not sure what time I'll be back," he called to his future parents-in-law.

Dave Young came up from the basement where he maintained his office. "I'll lock you out."

The tarmac of the driveway was acorn-covered, even though Dave had swept up everything the day before. More leaves fell as Roger walked through the ten-foot brown wooden gate and turned left toward the lake. If he had some time off at any point, he would help Dave rake up the leaves and acorns that seemed to wait until the yard and driveway were clear of their predecessors to fall in droves.

A path between two shoulder-high gray stone walls led directly to the water and to where Urs Stoller's boat was moored.

Roger arrived at the same time as the inspectors Morat and Fortini were getting out of their unmarked police car. The forensic crew of one man and one woman stood along the dock that still had flower-filled boxes along the side.

"How do we get out there, Patron?" the woman asked.

"We need a boat," Fortini growled.

Roger was too good at seeing through people pretending not to be annoyed when they were and Fortini certainly had not been happy that he was not the one to find out the professor had a boat. It was a question any veteran *flic* should have asked when it became obvious the professor had not drowned but had been dumped in the lake.

"I'll see if someone over there can take us out," Morat said and headed to the nearby boatyard. Within a few minutes a small powerboat pulled up at the dock.

The Stoller boat was twenty-four feet long. Unlike most of the boats anchored in view, it did not have sails. Roger wondered if that were a sign of an owner who preferred being in control rather than to be at the mercy of the vagaries of nature.

Sometimes it was possible to go overboard on theory. It could be that Stoller had a chance to buy that particular boat at a time, price and place that was advantageous for him. Roger did not like to think of his unintentional pun on overboard, nor why he preferred to think of Stoller not with his full title Herr Professor Dr. Stoller. Maybe it was his anti-Germanic DNA left over from World War II and his parents' resentment of the destruction of their home in Paris.

No, more likely he just found the victim unappealing, although there was nothing in the etiquette of being a detective that said they would only search for murderers of nice victims. He glanced up to realize they were almost at their destination.

The man who was taking them out to the boat was in his early thirties. "I can't stay but I'll give you my cell for when you're ready to come ashore."

The five police slipped on surgical gloves before they stepped onto the deck. "We don't have a key? Did anyone bring the master keys?" Luc, the forty-year-old male of the two-person forensic crew, asked.

"No one asked the wife?" Fortini asked. His tone was growing less pleasant.

"I did, of course," Magali, the young woman officer, said. "The wife was unhelpful. She said she hated the boat, didn't know where the keys were. Of course she was unhappy that we showed up at her office, but she did go home and find them."

Roger had thought that the second they realized there was a boat that they should have sealed it as a potential crime scene rather than wait a day, but he was the new cop on the block.

"We should have sealed this right after the body was found," Morat murmured, earning a glare from his chief who said so everyone could hear, even on the next boat, "Nice layout."

Pristine was the only word to describe the cabin's condition. It could sleep four, Roger guessed, but at the moment it was set up with a table and seats that could be converted into beds. The galley consisted of a hotplate and a tiny sink opposite the head. A small closet contained a couple of pans and four dishes, bowls, cups. A drawer held a place setting for four. There was one sharp knife, a spatula and a wooden spoon: basics without one thing extra. Curtains covered the small windows on each side. Morat opened them, making the cabin brighter.

That everything was so neat was not a surprise after seeing Stoller's offices in his home and at the university. The man might have been described as obsessive compulsive by the way he arranged his affairs. Even his pencils had been lined up.

One thing wasn't pristine. The trash bin needed to be emptied of two paper napkins. Morat bagged the napkins and labeled them. "If the killer used one of the napkins, we can get them with the DNA."

One by one, they opened each cupboard and hidey hole. Under the seats which could be converted to beds was an opening and inside were three boxes of papers with labels: Brueghel, unknown artists, student work.

"He works here." Magali pointed to a modem before picking up a box of papers that were some kind of manuscript. There were notes in the margin, but the printing was almost as neat as a laser printer's Times New Roman 12.

Roger flipped through the papers one by one as the forensic duo started dusting for fingerprints. There were several blank letterheads from DeFontaine Art Appraisers in Paris along with blank envelopes. "Did Stoller do appraisal work?"

"How the hell should I know?" Fortini said.

"He has blank letterheads." Roger took out his phone and tapped in the number of the appraiser. "There is no DeFontaine Art Appraisers listed in Paris, or if there is, they don't have a telephone with the same number on their letterhead."

"Maybe they went out of business," Fortini said.

Magali who was flipping through another folder said, "But here are completed appraisals made out to Stoller for different paintings and drawings. Signed by a George DuBois."

Roger sat down at the table and Googled the firm. There was nothing. There was a George DuBois furniture store in Paris, and two listings in the phone book. He called both to get answering machines that indicated they were private homes. "I don't think the firm ever existed."

"Maybe the good professor was going to set up a company," Fortini said.

"But who was doing those appraisals then?" Morat asked. No one answered him.

Roger opened the small cabinet above the sink where shaving gear was stashed.

"Look at this," Magali said. She had removed the cushions from the bench in front of the porthole and held up a small white pill with her tweezers. Usually medicine came in silver packets where each pill was pushed out.

"Is it an aspirin?" Fortini asked.

"No mark on it. Maybe this is like what thinned his blood."

Fortini dropped it in a plastic bag and handed it to Magali who was dusting for fingerprints. "Mark it, and see that it gets to the lab as soon as you are finished. Compare it to the unknown drugs in Stoller's system."

"This is strange," Magali said.

"What?" Morat asked.

"There's not a single fingerprint anywhere. The boat has been wiped totally clean."

As the police turned the corner onto the Route d'Hermance heading back to Renatus Pharmaceuticals, Roger saw Marc sitting at the bus stop. "Stop the car."

Morat did and Roger jumped out and pushed Marc into the cruiser. "What do you think you're doing?" When Marc didn't say anything, Roger continued, "You should be in school."

"Didn't feel like it."

"You're going to feel like it, real quick. Monsieur Fortini here will drive you to school. It's Collège Calvin, Morat."

Marc, his arms folded, sat in the backseat of the cruiser with Roger and said nothing for the entire drive, including when they were stalled in traffic along the *quai*. The boy stared out the window as the cruiser pulled up to the school. The sun shone on the renovated building, giving it a golden glow.

"Are you going in of your own free will, or do I drag you?" Roger asked.

Marc slammed out of the car and headed into the building.

When he had disappeared inside, Roger said, "Drive around the corner and let me out."

"Think he's going to do a runner?" Fortini asked.

"I'm sure of it."

Roger stood on the corner and watched to see Marc open the entrance door and look both ways. He didn't see Roger until he walked by the older man.

"I said you were going to school. Now this time I'm going in with you, or you can go back in and decide to stay."

"You can't make me."

"Yes, I can. I can even sit in class with you, but I bet that would embarrass the hell out of you."

Marc turned and went back into the building. Fifteen minutes later when he still hadn't reappeared, Roger walked back to where Morat and Fortini were sitting in a café drinking coffee. "We can get on with business now, gentlemen," he said.

"You want to explain what you were doing with the Stoller kid?" Fortini asked.

"He's staying with my future in-laws. He and my fiancée have been close friends for years, and whenever the kid feels lost, he has a history of running to her."

Fortini let out a long sigh. "Sounds like a conflict of interest to me."

"Or an insight to the case we might not have any other way," Roger said.

CHAPTER 37

Geneva, Switzerland

Annie resisted slapping the bureaucrat standing behind the chest-high barrier. She wasn't sure if he was in his early fifties or if years of saying no through his pursed-up little mouth had aged him physically: it didn't matter. He was blocking her ability to continue her research into the artist who had drawn Mireille's folio. She wanted so much to prove who the artist was, to help secure Mireille's future.

Discovering and authenticating a new artist would give Mireille write-ups in all the important academic journals and maybe more, which would increase her chances for a full professorship.

Mireille would be on her own and would learn to survive like other single mums did. It wouldn't be easy for her, Annie knew, but she also knew how capable Mireille was. Annie turned her attention back to the man blocking her way.

"We can't let just anyone rummage through those old documents," the man was saying. Annie looked over to the desk which he had occupied when she arrived. The nameplate read Fritz Schumacher. Although his French was without accent, she suspected he was Swiss German, not that it was bad to be Swiss German, but the stereotype that they were less apt to bend the rules held true more often than not.

"Who can get into the archives?"

"People with legitimate academic credentials."

"Like a *uni* professor?"

"Maybe."

Never piss off anyone who might otherwise help you, Annie thought. "I really appreciate your consideration. It must be hard saying no to people." She believed he enjoyed it.

"My job can be difficult," he admitted.

I bet, she thought, and you make it more so with your attitude.

The walk to the university from the archive office was not that far. She had to go to the top of the old city wall then down a steep cobblestoned road, through a gold-topped iron-bar fence leading into the university park from the Place Neuve and past two men playing chess, a game that Annie detested. Waiting a long time for someone to move bored her.

"You have no patience," Roger once said to her.

When she answered, "I want patience and I want it now," he'd laughed.

It wasn't true. In some cases she was very patient, but in others she did want whatever, then and now. Maybe that was why she could delve into a historical mystery for hour after hour, day after day, month after month because she wanted the answer and she wanted it now, but the *now* took time.

This time she didn't have hours, days or months. Her job here was almost finished, although the boys had asked her to hang around for odds and ends, like proofing the catalog when it came back from the printers. They also gave her a few more pieces to research for a general auction they were preparing.

Between finishing the catalog for the boys and helping Mireille, she was feeling strained for time. The boys had implied they might have more work for her in December or January, but she wasn't sure how Roger would feel about her staying on. He knew she had already met her expenses for well into the spring of next year.

Being back in the university halls seemed a bit strange. The students looked like her friends in their jeans with scarves wrapped around their necks. The girls still wore their hair to mid back and the boys looked scruffy. In reality they were ten or more years younger than she was.

It was after lunch and the small cafeteria, which served sandwiches, fruit, tea, coffee and soft drinks, was closing. The woman cleaning up the tables, who doubled as a cashier, had not been there when Annie was a student. Having not eaten since early that morning, Annie bought an apple. Accepting Annie's money with a sigh, the woman went back to cleaning tables.

Professor Alice Renaud was a woman in her sixties with the figure and muscle tone of someone in their twenties. She rode her bicycle to the university every day from Carouge, ran half marathons and gave lectures in medieval English history that made students want to live in the time and probably could have wrestled an angry tiger to the floor and have him love her afterwards. Her classes were more exciting than video games or blockbuster movies. Had Annie not already been enamored of history when she started at the school, the tough-talking, highly amusing Professor Renaud would have made her so.

Although it was Friday afternoon, Annie knew that the professor often stayed late on that day so she could finish all her work and have her weekends free: the work-hard-so-you-could-play-hard model was something else that Professor Renaud had taught her along with the idea that you do not do things that you are not passionate about.

Although she wasn't sure the professor had the same office after all these years, Annie took a chance. At least someone might tell her where to find her old teacher, but as soon as she knocked she recognized the voice.

"Annie Young, is that you?" The professor had been working at her computer, but she jumped up to hug Annie the second she recognized her. "One of my best students."

"I'm surprised you recognize me. It's been about ten years."

"With that mass of red curls, who could forget you, even if you hadn't been brilliant in my classes? What the hell are you doing?"

Annie filled her in briefly on own her research, how she financed her projects with her tech writing and her current problem with Mireille.

After commenting on Mireille taking so long to finish her doctorate and the reason for her visit, the professor asked, "Did you run into that asshole Schumacher at the archives?"

Annie nodded.

"Well, he has to let *me* in. We can go together. How's your schedule Monday?"

CHAPTER 38

Geneva, Switzerland
May 26, 1559

"We will go to the service for that poor baby, tomorrow," Uncle Jacques decreed. "Sometimes I think I made a mistake in not letting Elizabeth get engaged to him. That boy will be very successful." He sat at the kitchen table, the remains of the evening's meal still on the table, although Elizabeth had started to clear. A pot of water for washing hung over the fire making the room too hot. Her uncle had the top ties of his shirt open.

Aunt Mathilde bustled around the kitchen, putting things away. "I've lost more babies than she has. A woman needs to get used to it."

"It's God's will, I know," Uncle Jacques said. "But the first time is the hardest."

For a minute Elizabeth thought her uncle sounded almost caring.

The younger children had gone to bed, claiming it was much too hot to sleep, but the quiet upstairs indicated that they were wrong. The older children had gone to the lake, to catch whatever breezes they could. Summer was pushing spring away.

Aunt Mathilde looked up from the bench where she sat mending an apron. "Must we? Go, that is?" She did not often argue with her husband.

"I want him as a client."

"But most of your business is with watchmakers," Aunt

Mathilde said.

"Young Guillaume is branching out. I'm glad I took him on."

"That will be a waste of time. As soon as he is fully trained he will open his own office." She squinted as tried to thread the needle. "Elizabeth, leave the water in the pan and maybe, just maybe some of the burned onions will come lose. I do not see how you manage to burn so much."

"May I come too?" Elizabeth asked.

"I don't see . . . ," Aunt Mathilde said.

"Yes," Uncle Jacques said.

Jean-Michel and Françoise Jacquier filed into the church, followed by her mother and father, her sisters and brothers-in-law. Jean-Michel was an orphan, although a twenty-three-year-old man without parents was not thought of as an orphan any more than Elizabeth was. Still, both of them were parentless, which had been just one part of the bond between them.

Her aunt had stopped to speak to a neighbor then slid in beside her husband with Elizabeth on his other side. Sarah sat next to Elizabeth. The boys would not have come even if they had not had school.

A small wooden box, not much larger than a trunk to keep a few items of clothing, was on the altar.

About forty people attended—some who had apprenticed with Jean-Michel. The rest were friends and business associates of Françoise's parents who were sitting near the altar, leaving most of the church empty. Unlike the heat outside, the church was cold. It was always cold. A little light filtered in through the small windows over the dismal gray walls.

The service was performed by Pastor Calvin himself, who said much about the will of God. His appearance had more to do with the influence of Françoise's father who sat on *Le Grand Conseil,* than with the status of Jean-Michel. Calvin had climbed

the stairs to his pulpit that overlooked the entire church and
that allowed his voice to float down on the parishioners as if
God were speaking.

He told the mourners that there was no way of knowing if
the baby was one of the chosen or not, but his life had been so
short that the baby did not have time to sin, a cause for rejoicing.

That the death had anything remotely related to a cause for
rejoicing left Elizabeth angry, but she was not about to stand up
and yell at Pastor Calvin for being cruel in his choice of words.
Françoise was lost in a spasm of sobs.

Nor did Calvin's word decrease Elizabeth's discomfort with
the idea that people could do nothing to change what God
willed. If God was so merciful why did he not love everyone
and why was success a sign of being chosen? These thoughts
would never be uttered or at least not until she reached England.

The service wound down and ended with yet another prayer.
Françoise stood and slowly walked to the coffin. She put her
hand on it and sobbed until Jean-Michel came up to lead her
back to her seat. She cried into his shoulder as her parents
stood by. At one point her father put his hand on his daughter's
head, but she continued to cry.

The coffin was small enough for one person to lift, but two of
Françoise's brothers-in-law held it on a small stretcher to carry
it to the graveyard. They started down the aisle, followed by
Françoise's parents and sisters and Jean-Michel with his arms
around his weeping wife.

At the row where Elizabeth was sitting, his steps faltered and
their eyes met.

"I am so sorry," she mouthed.

Although death of a child was commonplace, the knowledge
that it was part of life did not lessen parents' grief, Elizabeth
thought. Despite her jealousy when Jean-Michel had married,

her words were sincere. Never would she have wished such pain on either Jean-Michel or Françoise.

Françoise wrenched herself away from her husband. Raising her hands she pushed her husband away and began beating Elizabeth, who rather than hit back put her hands up to ward off the blows.

"You killed him. You killed my son. You cursed him, you witch."

CHAPTER 39

Geneva, Switzerland

"How dare you." Maria-Elena Stoller almost hissed. She had walked into the Renatus Pharmaceuticals reception area where the three policemen awaited her. She wore a white lab coat over a matching navy-blue sweater and slacks. Her eyes were red from crying, not over Urs's death, but that Garth had given her so much trouble about their coming weekend away. At the end he had given in, but his behavior was so contrary to her expectations that she had locked herself in her office and given into tears. "You've no right to bother me at work."

"Is there someplace we can go to talk? Someplace private." Roger ignored Fortini's grimace.

"You can come to my house tonight."

"Now," Fortini said. His tone was anything by conciliatory.

"I am due in a meeting."

"We can ask you to come to the station now, we can talk right here or you might want to find a place . . ." Fortini nodded toward the receptionist, a young woman, who obviously read the latest fashion magazines, based on her trendy hair and clothes.

Although the receptionist was pretending not to listen, Maria-Elena knew that word of the police's visit would be all over the company before the afternoon coffee break.

"Hélène, is the conference room behind here free?"

The disappointment that she would not hear the rest of the

conversation was visible on the young woman's face as she brought up the computer program showing which rooms were free. "No, but 103A is. Do you want me to order coffee?"

"Thank you, but that certainly won't be necessary."

The three policemen almost had to run to keep up with Maria-Elena as she bolted toward the conference room after they stepped off the elevator. This level was mainly administration, they guessed by the secretaries sitting outside closed office doors.

Once in the conference room, Maria-Elena shut the door and folded her arms over her chest. "Talk."

"No invitation to sit?" Fortini asked. His tone was mocking.

"I have only a few minutes."

"We did a complete search of your husband's boat. It was clean," Fortini said.

"Urs always kept it pristine."

"More than pristine. There were no fingerprints, no blood, nothing out of place. There were only a few of his personal possessions, like a hairbrush but without hairs," Christian Morat said. "There was one exception." He mentioned the napkins.

"And . . . ," Maria-Elena said.

"We think that he was given an overdose, maybe on the boat, then taken out, and his body dumped somewhere in the lake," Morat said.

Fortini cleared his throat. "What we want to know is why you never told us about the boat."

"There's nothing to tell. I went out on it once, the first week Urs bought it four years ago . . . or maybe five. I haven't set foot on it since. I don't like boats and he bought it against my wishes. I would have preferred we kept our chalet in the mountains."

Although not fully up to speed on Swiss prices, Roger assumed that a boat such as the one they had just left was considerably less expensive than a chalet. He did not think the Stollers were hurting for money between his full professorship and her management post. "Did your husband have any life insurance?"

"Only the normal policies anyone would carry. I haven't found any new ones if he had any others."

"How hard have you looked?" Fortini asked.

"Not very. You know how much paperwork there is just to unfreeze a bank account? I am in the middle of a very important project. My son is giving me trouble. I try and get through one day at a time."

"I called you several times over the weekend," Morat said.

"I don't always answer the phone." She was not about to say she had been in Garth's flat in Ferney-Voltaire. She had been careful to arrive at two A.M. Saturday morning and leave at the same time Monday morning to not risk discovery by any of his neighbors. The risk made the weekend more exciting, at least until Garth had tried to wiggle out of next weekend away.

"I came by, too," Morat said.

Maria-Elena hesitated a moment. Roger caught the quick look to the side.

"I am really, really busy. This is my place of work."

Fortini opened his mouth to speak, but before he could Roger stepped in. "I know this isn't very gallant, Madame Stoller, but your eyes are red."

Her mouth almost snarled. "I lost my husband. Not just any old way, but you have told me he overdosed." She fumbled in her lab-coat pocket and pulled out a crushed tissue which she blew into.

The men stared at her.

"Now, if you'll excuse me, I'll go."

As she reached the door, Roger asked, "Did your husband have any medical conditions?"

She used all her willpower not to turn around and left her fingers resting on the handle. "I would think that the autopsy would have shown any problems that he might have had."

"What type of drugs are you working on now, Madame Stoller?" Morat asked.

"Our work is confidential." Using every inch of strength that she had she walked out without looking back.

The three men watched her leave without saying anything. They could go no place but through the lobby. The entrance to the main part of the building had a guard standing with his arms crossed.

They drove to a coffee shop in the center of town. There were mirrors along both walls, red-leather-lined benches below the mirrors, tiny round tables and then ten round stools with red round leather cushions attached. Roger and Fortini sat with their backs to the wall as Morat straddled one of the stools. At one end of the room was a small counter with the cash register. Several newspapers each had bamboo poles holding them like curtains.

A waitress appeared and before anyone could say anything Fortini ordered three ristrettos. Roger would have preferred a hot chocolate. Annie had brought him here the first time he had come to Geneva, telling him it was the best hot chocolate in the world. He swallowed his idea that it was a woman's or kid's drink along with the hot chocolate. However, in front of Fortini, he swallowed the bitter coffee without adding the sugar he would have liked.

Morat put in three brown sugar cubes. Morat ignored Fortini's sneer. "So what do you think?"

"Think? You think?" Fortini said. "Or think about anything but that girl of yours?"

Morat looked at Roger who winked. Morat had told him that

205

he was no longer in a relationship, because his work took up too much of his time.

"I think. I wonder if the drugs in Stoller were ones developed by Renatus Pharmaceuticals and if so, could she have given them to her husband."

"They were not a happy couple, according to my girlfriend," Roger said. "And I wondered what a widow lady with her kid out of the house might do with her free time."

"So you think she's guilty?" Fortini asked.

"Maybe, maybe not." Morat got up to get the *Tribune de Genève*. The three tiny cups almost covered the table so he had to turn sideways to ruffle through the pages. "Nothing more on the Stoller murder."

"Give the press time, they'll come hunting for us, writing about how bad we are," Fortini said. "I hate the press."

Roger wanted to say, "You seem to hate everything," but instead asked, "So what have we got?"

"One body, probably deliberately overdosed then dropped in the lake," Morat said.

"The people at *uni* certainly were not that crazy about Stoller. They admired his ability, perhaps were jealous of his international attention, but I got the impression they thought in many ways he was a *vrai con*," Roger said, thinking Annie would use the term scumbag.

"And something is off with the wife," Fortini said.

"Let's see if we can look at his financial records," Roger said. "How do you get ahold of them in Switzerland?"

"I'll get on it," Morat said.

"Not until I tell you," Fortini said.

Both Roger and Morat looked at him.

"So do it." He gave a grin as if he were kidding about Morat waiting for the order, but Roger thought he was trying to make sure he seemed in control.

CHAPTER 40

Môtiers, Switzerland

The moon streaming in the window outlined the Jura Mountains. Maria-Elena could not sleep, but it was not the light that was keeping her awake. She and Garth had left the shutters of the château/hotel open on purpose. He said he liked to look at the moon as he fell asleep, although he hadn't stayed awake long to see it after they had made love.

He wasn't a snorer, but breathed heavily. She touched his chest, which was muscular for a man who spent as much time as he did in an office. His chest hair was as soft as his muscles were hard. God, how she loved him.

How different it was to be on equal footing with a lover. With Urs, from the time he was a guest lecturer, the Big World-Famous Art Expert, coming to Uruguay, and she a little chemistry student, the big-man-little-woman was not just a cliché but the power structure of their relationship. Her university had none of the Anglo prohibitions against students and professors sleeping together, although her Catholic upbringing had given her many that were swept away by the confessional booth. After admitting her sins to her priest and saying her penance she should have gone forth and not sinned anymore. She was back in Urs's bed within an hour.

When he proposed, her family was beside itself. She was marrying a Protestant, a Swiss and she would go far away. What about her education?

Urs had insisted that she finish her studies and he was proud that his wife had earned a PhD, albeit in something like science, which was far inferior to his work in art. When she got her job with the pharmaceutical company, he would brag outwardly, but in bed at night he would put down her "little research." It was his needs, his work, his ideas, his decisions that must rule.

Once Marc was born it did not matter that Urs had no classes when the baby was sick. He was working on this or that book or article, and it was Maria-Elena who must take time off. No matter where she was in her work, she was expected to be home on time to cook dinner. Migros ready-cooked chickens were a temporary godsend, until Urs started complaining that she must be trying to roast every chicken in the Canton of Geneva. An au pair, one that also cooked, solved the meal problem.

Urs wanted a son, preferably two. He never knew that she did not become pregnant again because she had had her tubes tied. He was happy when she made a show of throwing away the birth-control pills, not resisting niggling her about how dangerous birth-control pills in particular and pharmaceutical companies in general could be.

Getting away this weekend with Garth had been the best thing she could have done. She did not have to pretend to be a grieving widow. As always she and Garth did not leave Geneva together. She had taken the train to Neuchâtel where he met her, not at the train station, but at a small restaurant in the village of Peseux where they knew no one.

This was not the first time they had booked into this tiny hotel/château in a tiny Swiss village with its six hundred citizens, six thousand cows and, in good weather, six million flowers. An old monastery that had been converted into a wine *cave* that made reasonably good champagne, although by European law, they could not call it that. Still it made for a nice stop to wander into the old stone tasting room to sample the various offerings.

On their first trip, they had bought a bottle and had a picnic near a waterfall where Jean-Jacques Rousseau was said to have pondered upon his philosophical thoughts during the eighteenth century. Garth had found this more interesting than Maria-Elena, but she had feigned attention until Garth's desire for her took over and they had made love as cows looked on from a nearby pasture.

Each time they could sneak away, which was not often enough for Maria-Elena, they stayed in the village château, which was more like a large stone house where the owners, no longer related to royalty of any kind, had opened a three-star restaurant and rented out four luxurious bedroom suites.

With this stay, they had slept in all four. Although each was a bit different, they all had a canopy bed, Persian carpets that made walking to the bathroom a treat and a fireplace, where the coals gave off a last red glow.

Garth and she were perfectly suited. He said so.

Often!

Why wouldn't he leave his recalcitrant wife? The bitch deserved to lose him, since she refused to move from her tiny village in Cornwall. She was afraid of cities, Garth had told her. She hadn't even gone to London with him when he had a job there. He had to commute weekends back to the coast. She didn't want to live where she couldn't speak the language. "She wants me to come home," but then he had added that he had no intention of doing so. He was happier in Geneva than he had ever been, he told her.

With Marc refusing to come home, Maria-Elena was relishing the time alone. Before Urs's death, she imagined how nice it would be to come home and not worry about anyone else's needs. The reality had been even better. It made her wonder—if Garth were free, would she really want him under her roof?

Garth rolled over from his back and threw his arm around

her. His hair was mussed making him look a bit like a little boy except for his needing a shave. She loved the look that men who sported seven-o'clock shadows deliberately had. Urs was a chronic shaver, removing facial hair at least twice a day.

As for the scratching when they made love—that added to the pleasure. The only problem was when it irritated her face, she needed makeup to cover it. She claimed an allergy to kiwis, thinking the detail made it more believable, when anyone was rude enough to mention her red face, always adding that she loved kiwis so much, every now and then she gave into the temptation. In reality she hated kiwis, except as an excuse.

A cloud covered the full moon, creating an eerie light. She shut her eyes and slept.

The breakfast room was in an alcove, not the main dining room. A table was laden with sausages and other cold meats, hard boiled and scrambled eggs, fresh rolls and bread, jams, honey— all produced from the region.

Maria-Elena smiled at the waitress who poured her hot coffee. The smell of Garth's hot chocolate was appealing, but not without coffee first. They were planning to hike one of the trails in the Juras starting at their waterfall. She remembered another time they had made love there. Garth had put his back to the cold stone. Maria-Elena suspected that she would not have enjoyed the moment as much if he had been pushing her into the rock. Some things are more romantic in theory: the famous beach love-making scene in some movie or other did not take into reality the discomfort of sand seeping into certain crevices of the body.

Garth was the romantic. Although they were more than discreet at work, he would offer her his chocolate that came with their coffee even when it was the black chocolate that he adored. He had met her with a flower, a huge yellow chrysanthemum at the station this time. She didn't have the heart to tell him that in many places it was considered the flower of the dead, one to be left on tombstones November 1. His little-boy smile and eagerness to please had made her tingle.

The trail was marked by little yellow arrows with the estimated times to various nearby destinations. Some of it was uphill. All the leaves were off the trees, but the number of pines made the walk seem green. At one point they walked to the edge of the path where they could look down into the valley with its three tiny villages.

"It reminds me of my model train set villages," Garth said.

The sound of cowbells carried up the mountain.

"I have something to tell you," he said.

Maybe his wife will agree to a divorce. The thought both thrilled and delighted her. She had just won her freedom, but, then again, this was the man she adored.

"My wife has decided to move to Geneva after all."

CHAPTER 41

Geneva, Switzerland
September 12, 1559

Elizabeth could not stop worrying. More and more she observed people crossing the street to avoid her. No one met her eyes. Her aunt no longer sent her to the *boucherie, boulangerie* or *crémerie* for meat, bread or dairy products. Most of the time, Elizabeth was forbidden to leave the house.

She was allowed to go to church, however, and her uncle insisted that she go each day. "Pray for your soul," he kept saying. In church the seats beside, behind and in front of her were always empty. If she sat down near someone they moved.

As much as she wanted to visit Antoine to see if there was word from her grandfather, she didn't dare ask.

On the night of September 12, Elizabeth had settled on the mattress that she was allowed by the kitchen fire. The boys were divided into two rooms now, their old room and the one Elizabeth and Sarah had once occupied, to stop their squabbles. Sarah was now living with her husband. Jeanne had been moved into the bedroom with her parents. Elizabeth guessed that was why that her aunt had not been pregnant since.

The kitchen was far warmer in cold weather than the upstairs bedroom. In the heat of summer when they ate mainly cold food and did not light the fire, Elizabeth's bed was far cooler than the upstairs—rooms that denied any breeze entry and were even more stifling because to open the shutters at night was considered dangerous. She was sure if she told her aunt that the arrangement pleased her, her aunt would insist she sleep someplace else.

The house had settled for the night. Elizabeth herself could not calm her thoughts enough to drift off. Her life was getting worse, but she couldn't understand why. Had she any tears left for her earlier life, she would have shed them, but the happy days on the farm seemed to belong to another person who had only told Elizabeth about them.

A piece of straw from the mattress stuck through the ticking and scratched her leg. As she twisted to a find a more comfortable spot, she saw a flicker of light come down the stairs. Sarah appeared carrying a candle which she sat on the table above the mattress where Elizabeth had stretched out. Her cousin was staying with the family while her husband had taken his children to visit his dead wife's family near Lausanne.

"Can I join you?"

Elizabeth held up the blanket, and Sarah lay down. "I have to tell you what is going on."

"What?"

"The town is saying you're a witch. You killed Françoise's and Jean-Michel's baby because you were jealous of Françoise. You want Jean-Michel for yourself."

Elizabeth sat up. "That's ridiculous."

"I know you're not a witch."

Elizabeth squeezed her cousin's hand. Being accused of witchcraft was serious. A few years ago, twelve witches had been burned, accused of causing the plague, but that had been the last outbreak of witchburning.

Two days later, Elizabeth was arrested as a witch. The magistrate's men came to the house, put her in chains and took her away, not to the jail, but to a special place outside the city walls.

She was told it was because of her uncle's position that she was not going to the regular jail and that her uncle had generously offered to pay for food for her until her trial.

The two men brought her to a small cottage, really more like a hut with bars at the single window, itself more of a slit, and a solid wooden door with iron reinforcements. Inside there was nothing, no fireplace, no furniture, not even a pot for her needs—just a dirt floor.

Both of the men were larger than the average Genevois male. Her hands were chained behind her back and her feet were shackled together. One guard was on each side of her holding her arms so tightly that she was sure she would have bruises. How did they think she could run away from them immobilized as she was?

"Are you going to leave me here alone?"

"There will be a guard outside at all times," the older of the two answered. When he spoke, his accent was unidentifiable.

"What if I need to go to relieve myself or . . ."

The younger man pointed to the corner. "Dig a hole." He had the same accent as the other man.

"With what?"

"That's your problem," said the older.

"You have hands," the younger said. He undid the chains around her hands.

They left. She heard a key click in the lock. Turning around, she realized what a terrible situation she was in. Had she been in the real jail, she wasn't sure she would be much better off, not that she had ever seen the inside of a jail, but she had heard stories. In a real jail there would probably be people around.

The room was five giant steps in one direction and seven in the other. But Elizabeth could not take giant steps. She could only shuffle.

★ ★ ★ ★ ★

Three days later, Elizabeth gave in to tears. The temperature dropped and she was cold. She wore only her dress for she had not been allowed to take her cape.

Although she had tried to relieve herself in only one spot, the accumulation stank.

Her body hurt from sleeping on the cold ground.

At least she wasn't hungry. Twice a day, she was given bread and water. And, yesterday, the younger guard had slipped her some cheese.

What she found hardest was having absolutely nothing to do. She tried making up stories in her mind about her grandfather coming and the two of them riding off to England. She brought out the memories of stories her father had told her of crossing the English Channel and looking at the White Cliffs of Dover.

Other times she tried to remember her brother and herself picking apples in September and the basket she wore on her back when they'd harvested grapes. She thought of her mother roasting chestnuts over the fire, and how the whole family would laugh their way through dinner.

The lock clicked and the door opened slowly because of its great weight. Dinner was still far away, she thought.

Guillaume Dumont, the lawyer from her uncle's office, walked in. He was dressed rather smartly, although he was not particularly good-looking. He had the type of face her mother would have called kind. He surveyed the room. "Is this it?"

She nodded.

"Your uncle did all he could not to have you put in the regular jail. He used the argument that if you were a witch you would be a real danger and needed to be watched closely."

If her uncle was planting doubts like that, what were ordinary people thinking?

"I will see if I can get you a mattress and a pot for your . . ."

He looked at the corner.

She noticed he was breathing through his mouth. "I'm sorry about the smell."

His face gave the response that he understood. "Your uncle wants me to represent you when you go before the magistrates. There was some talk of you being tried by the *Le Grand Conseil*."

"They don't usually do trials."

"I think your uncle didn't want anyone to think he used his influence to let a dangerous witch loose on the good citizens of Geneva."

Elizabeth wondered if there was more than a tinge of sarcasm in what he said.

"Since he's on the *Le Petit Conseil* and the magistrates are under their jurisdiction that would look badly for him if they acquit you."

"They have to acquit me. I'm not a witch."

"How can you prove it?"

Elizabeth did not know how to answer the question. Granted, she thought differently than other people she knew about religious matters, but she had never gone around casting spells or threatening people.

Guillaume shifted his weight from one foot to the other. Finally he leaned against the wall. "That isn't enough. There is a debate going on about witchcraft. There is a Dr. Johannes Weyer in Germany who believes that most of those accused of witchcraft were really crazy old women and harmless."

"The last witches burned were mainly old women. I'm young."

"But there's a new book out by a French judge, Jean Bodin, called *De la Demonomanie des Sorciers*. He believes that anyone who denies that they are a witch *is* a witch. So in reality if you deny it, you could be considered guilty."

"But if I say I am a witch then . . ."

"Exactly."

"I haven't confessed to anything."

"I suppose that is good. But you do face the possibility of interrogation and there can be physical pressure applied."

"What if I promise to leave Geneva and never come back?"

"You have no means. It would be useless."

CHAPTER 42

Geneva, Switzerland

Roger looked at his watch, shifted his weight from foot to foot, looked at his watch again.

"She's okay, she'll be out." Annie stayed as passengers from France streamed by them coming from *quai* eight, at the Cornavin train station.

He looked at his watch again.

"She probably stopped at the toilet or something. Don't be such a worry wart."

"She's not your kid," but as soon as he said it, added, "I'm sorry. I know you love her too. It's just I think fourteen is too young to be traveling alone. Especially at night."

"But she wanted to come to spend the *Toussaint* holiday week with us, and how many teenagers would spend time with their father and his girlfriend over their friends," she said.

"It may have more to do with your parents than us."

Before Annie could agree, she was nearly knocked off her feet by a teenager who grabbed her and was hugging her saying, "I'm here! I'm here!" For once Gaëlle's hair was its normal color: not blue, not purple. The spikes had been tamed into waves, and the length was rapidly approaching her new desire, shoulder-length hair that she could flip.

"Hello," Roger said.

"Don't be miffed, Papa. I saw Annie first." She looked around. "Where are Susan and Dave?"

"At the house. What did I tell you about your parents, Annie?"

"About what?" Gaëlle asked.

The Youngs' kitchen table could comfortably seat four, not six, so they ate in the living room around an oversized coffee table next to the fire in the corner fireplace.

"Every Saturday night?" Marc asked as he took a second serving of Boston baked beans.

"Both of our families, every Saturday night, had Boston baked beans and hot dogs," Susan said. "These were cooked in the pot I used tonight which is the same pot my great-grandmother, grandmother and mother used, which must mean my family has been using it since somewhere in the 1880s."

"Don't worry, it's been washed," Dave said.

The telephone rang. Susan left the room to answer it, but was back quickly. "It's your mom, Marc."

He got up and went to the hall. "Tell her I'm not here." He headed for the hall and grabbed his coat. The door slammed behind him.

"I'll go after him," Gaëlle said.

Gaëlle put her coat on as she rushed to the end of the driveway. When she looked right to the main road and bus stop, she didn't see anyone. Looking left, she caught a glimpse of him heading down the path toward the lake. She followed until he noticed her and turned.

"I really want to be alone."

"No, you don't. You need a friend to talk with. Maybe we could sit on the dock."

"You don't want to do that."

"Yes, I do."

"No, I mean you really don't want to do that." As they approached the dock where the big lake cruisers stopped during the summer, she saw birds lined up on the metal rails and sleeping. "We'd be sitting on bird shit."

"You're right. That gives you a fifty-percent-right score."

Along the *quai* were benches, but Marc led Gaëlle over the rocks to a small beach no more than six feet wide. A duck, disturbed by the intrusion, waddled into the water to find a new place to sleep. Marc pointed to a large rock where they both could perch.

"I know you mean well, but you have no idea what I am going through."

"You mean that your father was killed."

The moonlight shone on his face. He nodded.

"Yes, I do. I came home from school when I was eight. I found police tape outside our flat and Papa almost crazy. My mama had been shot to death, so *oui*, I know."

Marc was silent then said, "I'm sorry. I didn't know. Annie never said anything. Did they catch the guy?"

"It was someone Papa had arrested. When he got out of prison, it was his way of getting back at Papa. But he got back at me too. That's why Papa wanted to be transferred to Argelès. He wanted me out of the city and safe and . . ."

". . . and a new start."

She nodded. "Papa and Mama really loved each other. Their only problem was that Mama thought Papa worked too many hours. She was right."

"I think my parents hated each other. We never sat around a dinner table like Dave and Susan do. We usually ate in our own rooms."

"Did they fight?" she asked.

"They would have had to warm up to fight." He let out a long sigh. "I think my mother was having an affair. How can you improve a marriage if you've a lover?"

"I don't know," Gaëlle said. As soon as she could, she wanted to tell her father. It might help him with the case.

CHAPTER 43

Although it was Sunday, Roger entered the part of the police station where Morat sat at a desk covered with stacks of paper. "Thanks for coming in. I wanted to make sure you understood everything before we presented this to Fortini."

"You found something?" Roger took off his leather jacket and hung it on the door hook. Then he pulled up a chair next to Morat. He could see the papers on the desk were marked with the UBS and Raiffeisen bank logos.

"The Stollers were in good shape financially. Together they made close to 350,000 CHF, had no debt except for the mortgage on their apartment. They owned two other rental properties, which were handled by the *Régies.*"

Roger was not surprised, from what he knew about Herr Professor Dr. Stoller, that he would turn any rental problems over to a management company. He just could not picture the professor being disturbed in the middle of the night with someone's plumbing problem.

Morat turned to his computer. "This is a spreadsheet for the couple's joint account. Both their paychecks went in. Each had a debit card used for ordinary stuff: restaurants, groceries, clothes, etc."

"Who paid the bills?"

"He used e-banking." Morat got up and poured two cups of coffee from the coffeemaker on top of the filing cabinet. "Look at this." He handed Roger the Raiffeisen statement. It was in Urs Stoller's name only.

"Interesting."

"Isn't it?" Morat said. "Each month on the fifteenth he takes out 4,500 CHF from the UBS family account and that matches a deposit of 4,500 CHF into the Raiffeisen account. But he doesn't do a transfer. He uses cash. Then each month on the sixteenth unless it is a weekend he pulls out 2,000 CHF, but with a separate debit card. That's a lot of cash when everything else is electronic."

Roger looked closer. "There are a number of ATM withdrawals, mostly from the UBS office on the rue du Rhone. Isn't that near the university?"

Morat nodded. "The rest are on rue Vermont near where Madame Stoller works. From time to time they are made from Petit Saconnex or the train-station branches."

"I think we need to talk to Madame Stoller again. I bet she knows nothing about this Raiffeisen account," Roger said. "Should we wait until tomorrow when Fortini is here or go now?"

"He'll be pissed if we do it without him. I'm working off the clock, which will make him look bad."

"On the other hand . . ."

"For him there is no other hand." Morat picked up a pencil and began tapping on the desk. "I guess if I want to make myself look good and him bad, we should go over there now. But if I want to get in good with my direct report I should wait until tomorrow."

"What if we say I ran into you downtown and you started talking about the bank statements, and I insisted we come in."

"It would work unless he checks with other people and finds out that I was here alone before you came."

"We could say I had a few things to do before I could join

you? Then I insisted we go over to the Stollers."

Morat smiled. "Do you want to drive to the Stollers or should I?"

As they headed for the door, Morat added, "The report on the tablet they found. It was the same drug that was in Stoller's system, but they still can't come up with the company that manufactured it."

CHAPTER 44

Paris, France
October 1559

James Smythe's horse splashed through the puddles and mud of the Parisian streets. The Seine lay to his right. He never remembered being as wet in his life. The rain had soaked him through to the skin. Every house he passed was shuttered, but considering how late it was, he wasn't surprised.

He wondered if Paris had a curfew, although he knew he should have thought of that earlier, much earlier. If no one was out to enforce it, did it matter? The directions his grandfather had given him were explicit, complete with landmarks, but it had been decades since his grandfather had been in Paris.

One, two, three, four doors from the corner of the street after the church. He dismounted. His horse shook its head as he led it to the door. God's blood, what would the professor think being woken in the middle of night? It didn't matter. James needed to be out of the rain and wind.

The knocker was a heavy piece of metal shaped like a hand holding a cross. He brought it against the corresponding metal plate sharply three times. The rap echoed in the street. Hopefully only the professor would be woken.

He waited and waited. Then he knocked twice more. God, he had never been so cold in his life, not even during any English winter that he could remember. And it wasn't winter, it was only October. When he had set out on his journey many days ago, it had been a beautiful fall day with the smell of the first leaves dropping on the ground.

The crossing had been smooth, almost so calm that the sails barely unfurled enough to move the boat. However, his ride from La Havre to Paris, which had taken more days than planned, had caused delays. His horse had gone lame, and he had had to find another whilst arranging for the care of Redmond. He would pick him up on the way back, having paid for his keep with a farmer that appeared honest enough. The man had let him stay with his family, his wife, two daughters and three sons, and the conversation about crops and people that James did not know made the man seem like a person who believed in giving and keeping his word. At least James hoped that was the case, for he would hate to lose Redmond after all these years.

The farmer had taken him to another man to arrange for the rental of a horse at the price of a purchase. The farmer had taken over the bargaining, getting a much lower price than James would have agreed to. As he left his horse, he patted her on the nose, hoping that she would not be mistreated until he could return. "I cannot give you a date, because I do not know how long my trip will take," he'd said.

"Where are you going?" the farmer asked.

"Geneva."

The farmer snorted. "Full of heretics."

Realizing he had said too much, James said, "If it weren't for family business, I would never go among them."

Thus, as he waited for someone to answer the door, he felt foolish. He was an Oxford student studying religion, not someone to be sent to other countries on a mission that he had no idea how to fulfill. But his father was a jeweler, so he could fake whatever needed to be faked, having listened to talk of gold weights, watches and precious stones at the dinner table.

The door where he waited had a peekaboo door no bigger than a quarter of an adult's face. It opened.

James could see the flicker of light which he assumed was a candle and a man's mouth. He knew it was a man from the stubble on his face even before he spoke.

"Who the hell are you at this time of night?"

"I have a letter from my grandfather." He held up a piece of paper.

"I can't read it from here." The man's voice was gruff and sounded sleepy, which made sense considering the hour. "Put it through the hole."

James worried that he might not get it back. "Are you Professor Edouard Barbier?" He should have asked that first.

"I am."

Should he ask him to prove it? No, that made no sense, since he was the one who had awakened the man.

"And you are a scholar?"

"If you don't know who I am and what I am, how dare you wake me in the middle of the night?"

"I've ridden from England. I'm wet and cold. My grandfather told me that you would give me shelter, if you're Edouard Barbier who teaches Latin at the University of Paris. I'm Tobais Smythe's grandson."

"Let me see the paper."

Still feeling totally incompetent, James shoved the crumbled paper into the house. The peephole stayed open and the little bit of light disappeared then reappeared. James heard the lock click and he was grabbed by the arm and pulled into the house. The door was slammed and locked behind him.

"You must be John. I met you and your baby brother James when I was at Oxford years and years ago. I stayed with your grandfather on my way there and back."

James wanted to say he knew the story, about the French

student who was so brilliant. How his grandfather had befriended him when he had become lost and how after that, the boy had stopped and stayed with his grandfather.

"I'm James. John has gone into our father's jewelry business. However, I'm following my grandfather's path of becoming a scholar."

"How is your grandfather? What are you doing here? Why did you come in the middle of the night?" The man, who was wrapped in a blanket against the cold, held a candle in the hand not clutching the blanket around him. The barrage of questions stopped as suddenly as they started. "Forgive me. You're freezing. Thérèse. Thérèse!" The second "Thérèse" was bellowed.

Within minutes, a woman, also wrapped in a blanket, appeared at the top of the stairs holding a taper that gave little light. "What's going on?"

"We have a guest who is wet and cold. Get dressed and come help him."

Barbier used his candle to light two other candles shedding enough light for James to see his surroundings. The room he was in had a table and straw on the floor. He guessed this was where the professor gave classes. His grandfather had told him about the French university system where the professors had to attract students to their homes and were paid directly by the student. A doorway showed another room, probably the kitchen, where a fireplace had a few coals glowing, banked for the night and ready for the morning meal.

The woman reappeared. She was what his grandfather would call comely with a long dark braid down her back. She had thrown on a dress and shawl. "You're dripping wet." She disappeared and came back with a blanket. "Get out of those clothes, before you catch your death. Edouard, bring up the fire. We need to get something warm into him quickly."

James noticed she did not question who he was or what he

was doing there. By now his teeth were chattering so hard that he could barely speak.

By the time the cock in the yard behind the house crowed, he'd been tucked into bed, but he could not stop shivering despite the warming pan shoved into bed with him.

CHAPTER 45

Geneva, Switzerland

Maria-Elena had washed all six picture windows that ran the length of the living room, dining room, two bedrooms, office and kitchen as well as the two glass doors leading to the balconies. She had packed up Urs's clothes to be given to the *Armée du Salut.* Although the cleaning woman had been cut back to one day a week, there was no real need to clean, because now she was the only one occupying the house. She did assume that Marc would be back someday, but overall he had always kept his mess in his own room.

Had her company been open, she would have gone in, but unless you had clearance as a lab attendant to feed the animals or were in a crucial position in an experiment, going in on a Sunday was forbidden.

Throughout it all she couldn't stop crying. A whole waste-paper basket was filled with her used tissues. Normally, when troubled, working cancelled her worries or sadness. She should have been crying for her husband, but she was crying for Garth. How had she let herself be convinced that he would divorce his wife, she would divorce Urs and they would be together? It only hurt more that he had called her cell phone and left a message saying that even though his wife and children were moving to Geneva on Friday it didn't change anything between them. Yes, it did.

The doorbell rang. Maria-Elena blew her nose once more as

she went to answer it hoping it wasn't anyone important because her clothes were those that she wore when she had painting or heavy-duty dirty work to do.

Glancing through the peephole she saw two of the three *flics* that had questioned her at the office. For a second she debated not answering, but her footsteps walking to the door had been too heavy and they would know she was inside. Anyway, better here than in the office.

"May we talk to you for a few minutes?" said the older one with the Parisian, not Swiss accent.

She stood back and after they entered she pointed to the living room. "I was just about to get myself a cup of coffee? Would you like one?"

Morat glanced at Roger. *"Volontiers,"* Roger said as Morat nodded.

Good, she thought as she went into the kitchen and poured espresso into the machine and prepared a tray. I can think a bit. She knew her face was blotched from crying, a grieving widow—no matter that she was grieving for a lost dream. What was wrong with her that she couldn't find a man who loved her? This was not a question for *flics*.

Morat and Roger did not say anything until they all had taken a sip of coffee. Morat looked at Roger who began. "I'm sorry to disturb you on a Sunday, but we thought it better than another office interruption."

"Thank you."

"We've been going over your husband's and your financial records."

Maria-Elena stiffened. She wanted to say that they had no right to do so, but this was a murder investigation, and personal privacy of family members who might be suspect, would not stop the police. "I would have tried to find statements for you, had you asked. Urs handled all the money for the family." That had been the way in her family, too: she hated dealing with money matters and stupidly, perhaps, she had assumed he would do what was in their best interests.

"We went over both the UBS and Raiffeisen accounts." The older *flic* was staring at her. Why, she wondered.

"And . . ."

"You know about both?" Morat said.

"I have a UBS debit and ATM card, nothing for Raiffeisen."

"Did you know about that account?"

"Not really."

Roger ran his hand through his hair. "I am going to ask you if you could check your husband's desk for statements. We could get a search warrant . . ."

Better to cooperate. She wished now she had paid more attention to what he had been doing. "No problem; do you want to watch?"

Urs's office was exactly as he left it with his folders on different articles he had written or was working on, lectures, notes all in color-coordinated folders lined up with military precision on shelves over his desk. Maria-Elena noticed the men exchanged glances when they saw the laptop. Why hadn't they taken it as part of their investigation? She bet they were thinking the same thing.

"This is his office. I use the small desk in the dining room. Urs did a lot of work at home, but because of Marc, I've tried to keep my home and work life separate."

"We want to take all this with us," Roger said.

I have to act like I care, Maria-Elena thought. They can clean this place out for me, then I will have my own workspace. Finally. "I've been packing up his clothes, but I couldn't bring myself to come in the office." She thought of Garth and forced a few tears to fall.

When she went to open the largest drawer, she found it

locked. "You can force it if you want." She stood by the door as Morat used a Swiss Army Knife to break open the drawers. They pulled out bank statements, more professorial-type documents, tickets and some receipts.

"I'll go to the car and get the receipt pad for all this," Morat said.

"I see UBS statements, but nothing from the other bank," Roger said. There was a hardbound portfolio. When Roger opened it, he found several sketches like the ones Annie had been researching. "Do you know anything about these?"

"I don't know anything about anything, it seems. I wish I could help you, but I can't." Maria-Elena sank into the office chair as if standing was too much for her.

"Are you all right?"

"Yes. No. I will be." She refastened the combs that kept her hair from falling into her eyes. "I just can't make sense of any of this."

Back in the car, Roger and Morat said nothing until they were halfway back to the police station. Roger wanted to say how sloppy Fortini had been in his investigation, but as a chief himself, he didn't want to undermine him in front of Morat. He wished the detective offices were not separate from the rest of the police department, because he would have loved to be able to pick up gossip about Fortini's work and what the other *flics* thought of him. He had to remind himself that he was here only temporarily. He had always heard about how good the Genevan police were, so he had to assume, although he hated making assumptions, that Fortini was an exception.

"So what do you think?" Roger was the first to speak.

"Fortini should have taken all this stuff." Morat stopped at a traffic light.

"About the widow?"

"She seemed upset enough, but during the funeral she was the original ice lady," Morat said, "although, she might have been being brave for her son."

Roger shrugged. He had noticed the insurance policy in the locked drawer. "He had enough insurance on him to make her well off, but not fantastically rich. Yet she seemed totally in the dark about their financial condition."

"Lots of women are. And she does make a good salary herself."

"Family members are usually the most likely murderers," Roger said and Morat nodded in agreement.

CHAPTER 46

Geneva, Switzerland

As Annie awoke in her teenage bedroom, she reached for Roger. Strange to have him here. But he had already left, leaving his side of the bed with the duvet crumpled. The sun streaming inside the window had replaced the fog of the night before. As she turned away from the window she saw that the sun had replicated the pattern of the sheer curtain on her armoire.

She looked at the clock: 9:22. Although she was not supposed to be at the archives until after lunch, she had not wanted to sleep in. Padding downstairs toward the kitchen, her first stop was to check the family message board.

"Gone to the office," her work-adverse father had written. The project that he'd come back to handle had been turned over to an underling, so she guessed he wanted to put in an appearance just to remind the staff now and again that he was a boss.

"Not sure when I'll be back," Roger had written. Nothing new there. Even in Argelès his working hours were uncertain.

"Gone to school with Marc," Gaëlle had written. Now, that was unusual. The two of them had seemed to have bonded from the night they had gone to the lake. Roger must be wondering if his daughter had a crush on Marc and if Marc were too old for her and all the other things that concern fathers when think about their daughters, especially one as overprotective as he was.

Annie had guessed the teenagers' bond was more of shared experience than hormonal, but since Gaëlle would be going home on Sunday, she didn't worry.

No message from her mother. After pouring two cups of coffee from the pot sitting on the black countertop, she headed upstairs to the third floor, the place her mother was most likely to be.

Susan was there under the sloping wooden roof with its large skylights that let in enough light for even the most finicky artist to work.

"I wasn't about to let today's light escape." She took the cup of coffee her daughter handed her. "Thank you."

Susan's work was a portrait of Gaëlle, sitting cross-legged on a bed with earphones in her ears and a kitten curled up next to her. A snapshot of the girl and kitten in the pose was tacked to the upper-right-hand corner of the canvas. "Don't tell Roger. It's his Christmas present from Gaëlle and me. She commissioned me."

"Where did you get the kitten?"

"I borrowed it from next door."

"Roger will love it. How are you holding up with the house so full?" Annie knew her parents always made their home open to her friends for as long as they needed if they were feuding with their parents. And it had been the general meeting place for her gang throughout all her school and university days. If other adults asked how the Youngs could stand it, they would laugh and say, "We know where our daughter is when she and the kids are here." Still, over the last few years the Youngs had been on their own with only short visits from Annie.

When Susan turned to look at her daughter, Annie saw there was a streak of pink paint on her chin. "Now, what are you up to today?"

★ ★ ★ ★ ★

Annie paced outside the Genevan archives, the holy of holies, waiting for her former prof who would get her inside. Alice was late, but she was always late, telling people it was because she was French, not Swiss.

Annie decided not to worry until she had been kept waiting twenty minutes, but Alice showed up eighteen minutes after the agreed time, her hair messed and breathing heavily from running up the hill. "I parked at Saint Antoine's," Alice said. "It would have been better to bike, but they are predicting sleet later on, and I'm getting delicate in my old age. Besides, I can't resist the Roman ruins in the garage." Her specialty was Roman history, although she also taught one course of medieval history every other year, and the fact that the ruins had been discovered when the garage was being built and had been incorporated into the structure had been the subject of one of the first lectures Annie had ever taken with her. It did not convert Annie from concentrating on medieval history, but Alice's enthusiasm was contagious enough for Annie to take two more courses with her.

The two women entered the five-century-old building with its cobbled walkways and tiny windows. However, the lighting was modern. Alice flashed her pass at the guard at the entrance. He was in his early thirties and was reading *20 Minutes,* the local free paper handed out at bus stops. Annie guessed his interest in the archives was limited to his paycheck. "Welcome Dr. Renaud," he said.

"Annie Young is helping me today."

"You know the drill."

Inside there were two long tables that could seat a dozen people with small green reading lamps. It was reminiscent of the English university libraries that Annie had seen. On the desks were boxes of rubber gloves, not the dishwashing kind, but the kind a surgeon would wear.

Alice took out a slip of paper. "We need birth records from?"

Annie gave her the dates. Alice filled out the request form and put it in a tube that shot it upstairs, like in newspaper offices before everything was done online. "Now we wait." Since they were alone in the room, there was no need to whisper. "I suppose you won't consider going for your doctorate?"

"No."

"You would make a brilliant historian, but you need credentials."

This was not the first time Annie had had this discussion with her or her other professors.

"I think I'm too old to change."

Alice let out what could only be described as a guffaw. "Not with what you've done on your own. We would take you back in an instant."

"But I've a life. I don't work more than part-time. I travel. I have a wonderful man."

"Men can be replaced," Alice said, "and they should be, periodically, or at least let them think they could be."

"But the way I work has no politics. I go into a company, do my job and can almost always ignore all the stupid corporate battles. And don't tell me that universities don't have politics."

"Hell, we could write tons of sociological dissertations on them, but they can be fun, too." Before Alice could say more, a man appeared with several wooden-bound books tied with rawhide. He carried them as delicately as if they were precious glass and sat them down on the table gently. Although he couldn't have been much more than forty, he had the air of a man who had suffered much and had been prematurely aged by responsibilities too great to bear.

"Gloves?" he said forgoing the almost obligatory *"bonjour"* practiced by everyone—even cashiers and store clerks. Had he held his nose, she would not have been surprised.

Annie wanted to say, "I did put on deodorant," but resisted. She did not want to do anything to jeopardize Alice's access to the archives.

Both women held up their already-gloved hands.

"Some of the papers are really delicate. There are magnifying glasses in the drawers under the table. Do not turn up the lights. I don't have to tell you not to write on them."

Alice sighed, "You go through this routine every time I come here. Do you really think I would *not* remember?"

The man removed his glasses to clean them. Not a smile flickered across his face. "We can't be too careful."

Alice said nothing until the man had left, shutting the door with softest of clicks. "I think he takes bad-humor pills every day before he comes to work. And he's OCD. Notice how he straightened the books so they are exactly side-by-side."

Annie hadn't noticed.

Between the handwriting, the age and the faded ink, reading the records was extremely difficult. "I suppose if I used the flashlight on my phone, I would be severely punished."

"Burned at the stake, if he had his way." She tilted her head toward the door that the curator had left by. "Fascinating study of a man with a stick up his ass. Now let's get to work."

Annie quickly discovered that the records were not in order: someone born in 1535 might come before his or her parent's marriage in 1525 and other siblings born between the date of the marriage and their own birth.

"Why aren't they in order?"

"Many reasons: records were only kept by law after 1550. Many of the ones before were lost."

That made Annie sigh. "I suppose it reduces our chances of finding what I'm looking for."

"Maybe, maybe not. Many records were discovered in the

last century when they made some repairs on the church. Then others had been kept in City Hall. People put them together in these binders without any order. And although there has been talk over the years of cataloging, photocopying and putting them online, there was never a budget. Now, that could be your doctoral dissertation."

"Nice try."

The curator reappeared. "The archives are closing for lunch."

"We'll be back," Alice said as they walked past the curator's door. "He probably took it as a threat."

CHAPTER 47

Geneva, Switzerland
October 1559

When the man slapped Elizabeth, her head snapped back. Had she not been chained to the wall she would have slapped back, although with the three guards watching, the attempt would be futile, but she would have had the satisfaction of knowing that . . . knowing that . . . knowing what?

She was in more trouble that she could ever have imagined. She had been dragged, blindfolded, her hands chained again. Then she was put into a cart that bumped its way to wherever they were going. She felt sunlight on her face for the first time since she'd been locked in the hut. Had she not been so afraid of where she was being taken, she would have enjoyed it.

The cart stopped. She smelled fresh horse shit and guessed that the beast pulling the cart had let go because the odor disappeared. If it had been farmland, the odor would have stayed longer. Arms pulled her out of the cart and half dragged and half forced her to walk up stairs that scraped her legs. Only when she entered a dreary room with stone walls, no windows and just a few candles creating shadows that were enough to cause even the strongest man to tremble, did they remove the blindfold. From here on she would lose all sense of the little time she knew.

Her inquisitor wore the long black robe of a pastor. His hair was under a square hat, his beard neatly trimmed. If she were to describe his eyes, she would have said he was possessed by the devil, not the spirit of the Lord. She thought she had met most of the churchmen her uncle associated with, but she had never seen this man. He did not give his name: his accent had overtones of German.

"You've talked with Satan. Admit it!" her inquisitor almost spat at her.

"I have never talked with Satan."

"You are a witch. You have the power to make your curses come true."

The questioning went on and on and on. Elizabeth could not remember the last time she had eaten. She wanted to pee, but she used all her willpower to hold it in, not wanting to appear weak.

"Hit her." The pastor used the same tone as if he were saying, "Pass me some bread."

One of guards hesitated. "What if she curses me?"

"Then we'll have the proof we need to burn her."

The guard punched her hard in the stomach. Elizabeth vomited, but only bile projected out of her mouth. There was nothing left in her stomach.

At some point she lost consciousness. When she came to, she was back in her hut.

CHAPTER 48

Geneva, Switzerland

Roger was alone in the office. Once again Fortini and Morat had taken off without him. Although he should have been thinking about work, his mind was back on his daughter.

Marc and Gaëlle had headed for his school. Marc was too old for his daughter, who seemed to have a big crush on the boy. Annie said not to worry. Gaëlle would be heading home on Sunday, but a lot could happen between now and then. What was wrong with being a worrywart father, he had asked Annie, who'd ruffled his hair. It drove him crazy when she humored him like that.

If he had not been a teenage boy himself once, years before the birth of God, he wouldn't worry about his daughter. He wished she would go back to crushes on singers like Patrick Fiori or whatever new boy band was popping up, not real boys that wanted to do to her what he had wanted to do to teenage girls when he was Marc's age.

He was content to let Annie sleep. For once he knew where she was and what she was doing. If only his fiancée would be content to work out of the house like her mother did with her art. *Aucune chance*. No chance of that. Annie's brain contained a built-in suitcase.

What a difference between his future in-laws and his first set, whom he had not seen since his wife was killed. They had never liked him, but he couldn't understand their not wanting to spend time with Gaëlle. Good thing Dave and Susan were fill-ing the grandparent role with vigor. Maybe they would want Annie to produce a grandchild someday. Although he wasn't against it, this was where the fifteen-year difference in their ages became important. If he could only get Gaëlle to independent adulthood, then he could relax.

He wasn't sure what Annie's plans were for the day. She might have said something about the auction house, but, then again, he remembered something about some archives or maybe it was in reverse order or both. He had not been listening all that closely to her. At least she wasn't the type of woman who sulked when that happened—she merely considered it one of his foibles.

He settled back at his desk. He wondered when Fortini would be back from the medical examiner and Morat from the scene of a robbery. Unlike television when an entire police depart-ment work on just one case because only one comes in at a time, Geneva, and probably every other police department in any city anywhere in the world, did not have the luxury. Cases didn't arrive in an orderly fashion.

As much as he hoped they would find the murderer of Herr Professor Dr. Urs Stoller before his exchange was up, he was not optimistic. The phone interrupted his thoughts.

"Inspector Perret, this is Dr. Galy. You talked to me the other day at the university."

He had to think a moment. Was she the young one—thin, athletic but pretty. Or the older woman with the gray hair held up in chignon. No, she was the young one. She had been late for class, but took the card he handed her with the department telephone and e-mail and his name handwritten over Morat's.

"I don't know if the information I have will be of much help. Can we meet someplace?"

"Of course."

"Not near the university, perhaps somewhere downtown. Manora's restaurant?"

The cafeteria-style restaurant was on the top floor of the department store. Large windows overlooked rooftops of nearby stores and apartment buildings. A few shoppers sat with cups in front of them. It was still early enough so that the hot-food stations had not opened, but the performance chefs were busy putting mushrooms, onions, herbs and other such things on trays where they could get at them easily when the diners ordered whatever the day's specials were.

He chose a table in the far corner after the toilets where they would not be observed by most of the people who might come through.

Dr. Galy arrived in the same rush as she had when he had seen her before. He guessed she was one of those women who considered walking slowly an anathema.

"Can I get you something?"

"A ristretto."

Because there were no lines at the cash register, he was back quickly with two small cups on a small wooden tray.

"What can I do for you?" he asked.

"Maybe I can do something for you, but I can't guarantee the information will be useful."

Roger waited while she held the cup in both hands and blew on the liquid. "I suppose you picked up that Urs was not the best-liked faculty member?" she asked.

"That seemed to be the prevailing feeling."

"The man was brilliant. He was a bastard."

"Do you know that from first-hand experience?"

"Almost."

He raised an eyebrow.

"I was dating Dr. Gilles Moutinot."

Roger remembered talking to him briefly and his memory was that Moutinot had the same message: brilliant and a bastard.

"He and Stoller were both avid boatmen. They took turns going out on each other's boats."

"How did they get along professionally?"

"About as well as NATO and the Taliban, although they were more diplomatic. Gilles knew better than to discuss anything with Urs, because it would turn up in one of Urs's articles the next year."

"But they still went boating together?"

"Urs was powerful. It was better to pretend to be his friend. Urs used to say he knew he could count on Gilles. It wasn't the other way around."

"And . . ."

"Gilles was up for a promotion and the rumor mill was saying that Urs was doing everything he could to block it."

"Was he?"

"I don't know for sure, but I suspect that Urs had considered Gilles a threat ever since Gilles upstaged him at a symposium."

Roger took a closer look at her. She was probably in her late thirties or early forties. Despite being a *flic,* he was terrible at guessing women's ages. Her wiriness and good health could have taken years off.

"I was often on their boats when we all went out together."

"Was Madame Stoller with you?"

"She hated boating. And she preferred to stay in her lab. The four of us did go to the theater from time to time. Then there were the routine formal dinners."

"And your relationship with Professor Moutinot now?"

"We are no longer an item. Before you think this is revenge, it is the reverse. When I heard that Urs had been murdered, I knew that Gilles was angry enough at him to kill him. He threatened to right before we broke up. I didn't say anything earlier out of a loyalty to him."

Roger speculated: had she been dumped perhaps for a younger woman?

"In case you're wondering, I broke off with Gilles. The relationship wasn't going anywhere. He was content with what we had. Then I met Luc. After I leave you, we are going wedding-ring shopping." She glanced at her watch just as her cell phone rang, or rather croaked. "I'm running late, *mon cher,*" she said with no other preliminaries to the person on the phone.

As she stood up, she added, "I'm not saying that Gilles killed him, and as much as I disliked Urs, I didn't want him dead. His going to another university would have been fine, but unlikely. I don't like the idea that a murderer might get away with it. But, please remember that Gilles is not his only enemy. I imagine there isn't a person on the faculty that he didn't screw literally or figuratively. Probably a number of students too."

When she left, Roger debated getting another coffee and decided his caffeine level had probably replaced his white blood cell count. Fortini was convinced that the murderer couldn't be a professional colleague. He was focusing in on the wife and cited that, in every murder case he had solved, the murderer had always been a member of the victim's family.

And was the good doctor as content with Moutinot being her ex-lover as she claimed? If it were his case alone, he would follow up on that, but he wasn't sure Fortini would take kindly to it. And worse he was running out of time before he would have to head home.

CHAPTER 49

Geneva, Switzerland

"Coffee?"

Maria-Elena sat in the conference with eight men: Jason Wright, the CEO of Renatus Pharmaceutical; Gunther Schwarz, the COO; Nigel Hancock, head of testing, who'd been brought over from the UK; Garth, vice president of sales and marketing; Jean-Michel Phillipe, assistant vice president of sales and marketing. The other men were representatives of Medical Development, Inc., a multinational firm that did drug trials for pharmaceutical companies throughout the world. She did not know any of them by name, just where they came from. No one introduced themselves.

All of them wore tailor-made suits. The CEO of Medical Development had one of those Swiss watches, the kind that when you went into the store to buy one, they take your order then make your watch for you by hand. It probably cost more than her annual or maybe even two annual salaries, and she was more than well-paid.

She wished she had worn her own expensive suit, instead of leaving on her lab coat. Garth looked tired after the weekend. Half of her hoped he had strained his back with the move. His family had found a flat in the same complex she lived in, which wasn't that surprising. The complex was so close to all the alphabet UN agencies that locals called it the international ghetto, if a ghetto could be inhabited by people earning six-figure salaries, many tax free. The parking was occupied by more diplomatic plates than normal ones. And Renatus Pharmaceuticals was just down the street from them all.

At least he could have had the consideration not to live where she would run into him and his wife in the local Migros when she was doing her Saturday grocery shopping. And she didn't even want to think about how long he must have known his wife was coming, to be able to set her up so quickly. She hated being made a fool of and that was what he'd done. Like Urs had with his various lovers. The difference was Garth didn't have contempt for anything that wasn't him.

"Coffee?"

She looked up at Jason Wright's personal assistant who stood next to her with the pot in her hand.

"Yes, please."

She had been told about the meeting yesterday afternoon and it did not take any conspiracy theory for her to believe that the meeting that brought all these people together had been planned long in advance. The Medical Development people had flown in from the US and Africa. It still took X hours to get on a plane in San Francisco and get off in Geneva, get on in Durban and off in Geneva. It was not a decision that had been made at five in the afternoon when Garth's secretary had told her about the meeting.

In the past Garth had fought to have her included in meetings on the blood-thinner pill under development, which was the reason they were all in the room. Since the new CEO had come on board to help boost profits, Maria-Elena had found herself sidelined.

At least Garth did not take their break-up as a reason to exclude her. Then again, maybe he thought that if he changed his position on her, it might arouse suspicions about their relationship, or that he was hoping to win her back.

She didn't need to think of these things. She needed to concentrate.

The conference room had a large window overlooking the *Jardin Botanique*. Its trees were stripped of leaves. Branches bounced back and forth in the *Bise*. Maria-Elena took a long look to become centered.

The men were chatting about why the US wasn't crazy about European football, and the CEO was being teased that the reason was that Americans had given the sport the sissy name of soccer. So much testosterone all in one place.

She tried a trick she sometimes used when she felt uncomfortable, especially with a group of high-powered executives. In her mind, she imagined them all naked, with hairy chests and limp pricks. The American CEO was overweight, and she thought of him spilling his coffee on his rolls of fat. Although it worked, she still hated herself for feeling inferior, a little girl from Uruguay, playing with the big boys.

The personal assistant handed her a thick folder. "Here's the report they are going to be talking about." She was turned out in a perfectly tailored woolen suit more in line with Maria-Elena's clothing budget. The woman was efficient and kept to herself. "Will there be anything else?" she asked the CEO.

"No, thank you." He waved her out of the room with his hand. It was clear there would be no note taking, no minutes of this meeting.

The meeting would be in English. The COO, an Austrian, spoke five languages fluently. Maria-Elena had seen him use his language skills to his advantage more than once. Garth, the CEO and the head of testing spoke only one. Maria-Elena would have wagered the people from Medical Development, all of whom were American, were also monolingual.

Resentment bubbled up. She spoke four languages, had as many degrees as any two of the men in the room, yet she was being treated as the least important. She could ignore it or call attention to it.

"I notice that all of you had the information before I did. Why wasn't I given it at the same time?"

"We were still fine-tuning it," Garth said.

Right, she thought. "Give me five minutes to review it?"

The CEO didn't quite roll his eyes. "There's an executive summary."

Maria-Elena was a speed reader. The executive summary listed the number of trials that had been run by several American hospitals. A second series of tests, triple the number, had been conducted in South Africa.

The report was as far from complete as possible. Too many of the criteria were not listed, the parameters were not given. The individual case studies, especially from Africa, lacked vital information. Looking at the report, she knew she had been right in fighting to have those tests done by her department, research and development, not by sales and marketing, who had hired the firms to do the clinical trials.

She'd lost that battle long ago.

Everything had gone to hell since Urs died. Why had she thought it would go smoothly if he were no longer around? Urs had not smothered her. If she were to find any good in her marriage it was that he had encouraged her to study and reveled in her passion for her work.

Reveled from a distance, that is.

"Ouch." Coffee had splashed onto her hand and the report. She dabbed the pages with the napkin that the personal assistant had left under the coffee cup. The words "unexpected overdoses," caught her eye. She delved deeper, and it seemed a second pill taken too soon afterwards caused men, more than women, to hemorrhage. Five deaths had been reported. Why would a person reach for a second pill? If they were sleeping pills, someone might take a second if sleep wasn't forthcoming. But a blood thinner? It did not make much sense to her. If it were more women than men, it could be lesser body weight, but there were no tables on weight.

"What about the autopsy reports on those that died?" she asked. This drug was nowhere near ready to go to market. And the costs if later the drug was found to be dangerous and the company knew about it: the resulting lawsuits could put Renatus Pharmaceuticals out of business. How many times had she read about companies who did nothing, all the while *knowing* their product would harm people. She'd wondered at the time how executives who made those decisions could sleep at night.

"We have them in San Diego," said the CEO of Medical Development. He sounded like John Kennedy, from those old tapes that Marc played. She didn't understand why her son was so fascinated with a long-dead American president. Maybe Annie had introduced him to the man.

"Can you have them sent through?" she asked. "I have some doubts and . . ."

"Which is why we've put Sales and Marketing in charge of the clinical trials," Garth said. His look pleaded with her: *don't make a big thing of this*. "We should have FDA approval by March, once we submit the data and a little grease. The marketing campaign is ready to roll out: adverts in magazines in the States, letters to doctors in other countries."

"That isn't why we are here," her CEO said. "We are here to go ahead based on the clinical trials. Do not put any of this in writing. If you have anything in writing, destroy it." Maria-Elena guessed he was from the southern part of the US because she had trouble understanding him. Nine times out of ten when she couldn't understand an American it was because he was from the south.

"We just need you to sign off, Maria-Elena," the CEO said.

"You like your job. You sign off. Adjourned." He bolted from the conference room.

Although Maria-Elena tried to follow him, he disappeared so fast it was like someone had waved a wand and transported him elsewhere.

She went back into the conference room. The rustle of papers being shoved into folders, the shuffling of chairs moving backward on the polished hardwood floors and footsteps echoed as one by one each of the participants walked out of the conference room.

Maria-Elena began separating the memos and reports to destroy from the ones to keep. She would have to clean her laptop and tell her secretary to do the same. Why? If she did that she would be just as guilty of negligence as she thought the others had been.

Maybe she could become a whistle-blower and contact the medical journals on the problems with the testing. Or the FDA? And if there were reports of problems how long would it take them to figure out that she was the one responsible? She was a single parent, and now the sole support of herself and her son. Her chances of ever working in her field at any pharmaceutical company once she was found out, and she *would be* found out, were nil.

She thumbed through the report. The way it was written, it was impossible to say conclusively that the drug was dangerous. She would be a good little girl and shut up, but she had no intention of not keeping a record of what had transpired today.

She looked up to see Garth almost hovering. "What do you want?"

"I think we should talk."

She wanted to ask what they should do about the new drug that she thought was unsafe or at best its safety unknown based on the clinical tests. "If it is about business, call my secretary

253

for an appointment."

"It's about us."

"There is no us."

CHAPTER 50

Geneva, Switzerland

Roger was putting on his coat to head back to the Youngs for dinner and hopefully a good evening with Gaëlle and Annie, although his daughter had been spending most of her time with Marc. The youngsters would deign to join them to eat but then would disappear into the attic where Marc slept and hung out under the eaves. Roger's "leave the door open" had earned him a stare, that had his daughter been a witch, might have caused ill health at least.

Morat was at his desk looking at lists.

"What are you working on?" Roger asked him.

"Phone calls that Maria-Elena Stoller made and received on her cell. Interestingly enough there's a Garth Chase that she talked to frequently. He just happens to work with her so it could be innocent enough. He never called on her landline."

"Hmm. What do we know about him?"

"Only that he works with her. He's high up on the food chain. I'm wondering about an affair."

"Did you mention it to Fortini?"

"I did as he left to investigate the latest of a series of robberies in and around Champel. *'Cherchez la femme,'* is what he said. He always looks to the spouse."

Roger put down his overcoat. "What about the husband's cell? Did we find one?"

"His wife said he didn't have one."

Throughout his career Roger had had *feelings* that turned into facts more often than not. "Let me make a few calls."

No one in the Young household was surprised when Roger said he would be delayed. In fact Annie had said, "Ho hum." In the past this had often almost started a fight when she accused him of feeling his work was more important than hers. What prevented the fight this time was her saying, "I'm teasing." Her laugh told him that she was speaking the truth—not that she ever lied to him if you didn't include the fact that sometimes she didn't mention things he thought he should have been told.

One by one he called the people he had talked to at the university. All of them confirmed that they had seen Stoller with a cell at one time or another—or at least they thought they had. Roger dialed Madame Stoller's line.

"I'm sorry to disturb you, but did your husband have a cell phone?" he asked after he introduced himself. Her sigh made him think she might be annoyed.

"I told Inspector Fortini he did not. He hated them, he always said. He wasn't a technophobe or anything like that. He just didn't want to be interrupted."

Morat looked at Roger. "I will see if I can find a cell phone registered to the professor. But I can't do it tonight. Everything is closed."

CHAPTER 51

Paris, France
October 1559

Had it not been for Thérèse Barbier, James was sure he would have died. His chest had filled with fluid. He was alternately so cold and so hot, he thought he traveled from the tip of Northern Scotland to hell several times within the same day.

Thérèse spooned soup into his mouth, held his body over a pot so he could relieve himself. Days turned into nights and into even longer days. He had no idea how long he had been in bed. Mostly he slept.

Then slowly, the extreme heat and cold racking his body became less extreme. It no longer hurt to swallow and the coughing bouts that left him exhausted were shorter in time, although every muscle in his chest and shoulders still ached.

The professor came in each evening to ask how he was. Thérèse would always say, "He'll be fine," although James doubted it.

The sun shone through the small crack in the wooden shutters covering the window to keep out the cold.

Thérèse arrived with new straw and a clean sheet. "Lean on me," she said and guided him to a stool while she remade the bed.

He wondered if he would survive long enough to ever lie down again, but he did and the clean bedding and fresh straw smelled wonderful. "Thank you," he whispered and fell back asleep.

In the evening the professor came with a bowl, more broth, but this had a few pieces of meat and onion in it. "Try and eat this." He spooned the nourishment into James's mouth but not with the same gentle touch his wife did. James found he had the strength to wipe his own mouth for the first time.

Over the next few days, James found himself being forced to stand and take a few steps until he was able to descend the stairs and take the evening meal with the couple. He wondered why there were no children, but it was not a question he would ask. Because he had been raised by his grandfather and grandmother while his father was busy in the jewelry shop, the importance of making people comfortable had been stressed along with how to survive in a changing religious climate where the wrong words could lead to the gallows.

As James gained strength, the Protestant–Catholic flip-flopping in England became a debate topic. The heretics who had flown Catholic France were another. "As long as we talk behind closed doors, we're safe, unless you're a spy," the professor said, "who came to my door and pretended to be deathly ill." Unlike many Frenchmen, he spoke slowly so that James could follow.

James had learned by this point that the man was a tease. He had listened from his bed to how the professor had handled his students, making fun with them not at them. He wished that some of his teachers had been as good. He wished he were back at Oxford instead of here.

"You will be well enough to travel soon." Thérèse put her hand over James's.

"Then maybe my wife will pay more attention to me," the professor said.

"I've wasted enough time."

"What will you do when you get to Geneva?" Thérèse asked.

"Find my cousin and take her to Grandfather in England." And as much as he dreaded the rest of the trip, as much as he worried about how he would find his cousin, he knew he had to start soon. He also knew Thérèse was right. If he traveled too soon he would fall sick again.

CHAPTER 52

Geneva, Switzerland

"Annie, look!" Conrad tossed the printed catalog for the prince's auction at Annie as soon as she walked through the door of the auction house. "Your writing is brilliant."

Annie almost missed it but she managed to grab it. She put it down long enough to take off her mittens, unbutton her coat and unwrap her scarf. Picking it up, she began to thumb through the pages.

The photos of each item were first class. Reading the descriptions in French, German and English was like reading tiny news stories. She assumed the other languages read as well. The catalog was grouped by sections such as furniture, dishes, jewelry. But Annie had also put together a ballroom section and created an imaginary ball complete with some of the costumes which would come under the hammer.

"The catalog is a collector's piece in itself," Conrad said.

Thomas, who was standing behind Conrad, nodded. "I wish you'd work for us full-time. It has to be more fun than dreary old technical manuals telling you which button to push."

"There I have to agree with you, but my place is with Roger." She was surprised that she'd said that herself. Maybe she was beginning to really have a place in the world where she truly belonged, not because her parents were assigned there, but because she'd made it for herself. Not that Geneva didn't have a homelike feel for her. It was where she'd finished high school and university. If it had taken her into her thirties to put down her own roots, she wasn't going to start sawing them off. The strangest part of her roots was that she no longer resented being a Third Culture Kid. She'd witnessed the good side too: the ability to go into a strange place and make connections. With Roger, for the first time since she and her family had left Massachusetts when she was eight, she felt as if she belonged someplace.

"I'll be happy to do more projects, especially if we talk auction percentages and my doing some work from France."

"Using telecommuting to write about antiques—how twenty-first century," Thomas said. "I can live with it."

Conrad nodded.

And I can live with not working more than six months a year, Annie thought, but she knew that for her whenever she had a history project it never felt like work. When she got paid for doing something historical, that was definitely a win-win.

"Where's Mireille?"

"In her office."

Annie poured herself a cup of coffee and stood at the door of Mireille's office. The young woman was standing in front of a mirror framed with gold leafed curlicues and holding her dress tight. When she noticed Annie, she smiled. "I am beginning to have a real bump."

Annie cocked her head. "Right now it looks like you might need to do a few more sit-ups. Have you felt the baby move yet?"

"I'm not sure if it was baby or gas. Did you see the catalog yet?"

"Annie, telephone." Conrad's voice filtered up the stairs. "I'll put it through to Mireille's."

Annie picked up the French porcelain antique phone with the thin handgrip.

"Annie, it's Alice."

Annie put her hand over the receiver as she whispered, "Alice Renaud."

"Give her my best."

"Mireille is here and she sends good wishes. When can we go back to the archives?"

"That's why I'm calling. *We* can't. The Grump raised unholy hell that unqualified people were going through the documents."

"Merde."

Mireille frowned and cocked her head.

Annie was annoyed when Alice laughed. "*We* can't, *I* can. In fact, I'll be spending the afternoon there. If there is a way to find out anything about that girl, I will."

As soon as Annie hung up, Mireille asked, "What?"

Annie filled her in. "I'm disappointed. I loved going through those old papers. Wanta go to the Spaghetti Factory for lunch?"

"I'd love to, but money's really tight these days. I gotta pay the rent, you know."

Annie smiled. "You sure do."

Although it was not part of her job, she helped Conrad and Thomas get ready for the auction. Ads had been placed in the newspapers that there would be a viewing of the items on sale all day Saturday. News releases were not only in the Swiss papers, but also had been sent to London, Frankfurt, Paris, Milan, New York, Washington, Rome and Moscow, where the nouveau riche relished owning things which once had belonged to royalty.

Unlike many other auction houses, Conrad and Thomas had made special arrangements with the Beau Rivage hotel for suites of rooms for those flying in and they had limos pick up distinguished buyers at the airport and ferry them to the hotel and to the auction.

Phones were set up for those who wanted to bid from the comfort of their wherevers or to remain anonymous. And Carsonwell also accepted Internet bids.

The prince himself appeared. Annie, who was closest to the door when the bell tinkled, led him into Conrad's office. She knew Conrad well enough to read when his smile was sincere, and when it was not. She also knew his little ticks when he was hiding unhappiness by the way he ran his hand through his hair. He did it several times as he smiled at the prince.

"I didn't expect you."

The prince leaned on an ebony cane. "I sprained my ankle stepping off the curb the wrong way." He settled himself in one of the gold-leafed chairs. "It's almost all better."

Annie started to leave but the prince motioned her to stay.

"I was going to ask if you wanted coffee."

"Excellent," the prince said. "And where is that handsome Thomas today?"

"I believe he's at the printers," Annie said, hoping Thomas would not appear.

She found Thomas in the auction room arranging the items in the order in which they would be brought to the block. Each tag was a work of art in itself: printed with the logo of the auction house and a brief description of the item on the back with its lot number, a minimum bid expected which matched the catalog's lowest estimate. The description was taken from Annie's catalog entries. Thomas had picked one or two sentences for each.

"The prince is here. I gave the excuse that I thought you were at the printers if you want to slip out the back.' "

"Dirty old man. I may be queer, but I have strict standards."

"I know you do." Annie thought about the man who had once been his partner for four years. Thomas had been heartbroken when he had discovered not that he was unfaithful, but that he had lied about it. Her longtime friend had entered a period of celibacy and his description of it could have made him a hit in any stand-up comedy club. That he seemed happy with his current partner really pleased Annie.

"Thomas, you make a lousy queer. You want to settle down just like a straight person."

"I can't help it. I prefer a quiet night at home to cruising the bars. I like having someone who will be happy to stay in and watch DVDs and sip champagne and who, if we don't have any champagne, will be as happy with a cup of tea. And that prince definitely ain't it. He's creepy."

"And then there's Damien."

"And then there's Damien. I know when I have it good, because I've had it bad."

"Well, you can run for it, or you can bring us all espresso."

"I'll ask Mireille to do it and I'm outta here."

After the prince had finished his espresso in his delicate Limoges nineteenth-century cup, Conrad asked, "Would you like to see the display?"

"I'm not sure I am up to it. When I think of how all my family for generations and generations touched and loved everything . . . I . . . I . . . am not sure I can go through with it."

Conrad sat immobile in his seat, his eyes looking at Annie's. He must be ready to kill the prince. She wasn't sure if she should speak or not, but Conrad seemed speechless. He had spent a great deal of money already between publicity and printing of the catalog, not to mention the time.

Still, the silence hung.

For a second, Annie wondered if the prince were playing a game to reduce the commission he must pay. She wished she could communicate that idea to Conrad.

The prince let a tear escape his eye, and his sigh resembled a sob.

Annie reached for his hand, ignoring Conrad's eyes widening. "I'm sure it must be very, very difficult."

"I did not keep my family's trust. I betrayed them."

Of course you did, you asshole, she thought. "I can see how badly you feel," she said as the prince let out another sigh. Her mind was racing, wondering what to say next.

"I know you have a lot invested in the auction, but . . ." The prince let out a deeper sigh if that were possible.

Conrad was getting paler.

"It is not just about money. I've known Conrad for years and years." She had to be careful or she would make herself sound too old. "Of course, he needs to make a profit, but he's one of the lucky few who works for love. And because he loves his work, he treats every item with the love and respect that it deserves. I'm sure every one of your ancestors would approve of his care and handling."

She kept her eyes boring into the prince's. She wanted to look at Conrad, but didn't dare.

"Just look at this." She held out her hand, and Conrad placed the catalog in it. She found a figurine and read the copy to the prince. "Imagine someone reading this. They would have, they would have . . ." Her pause was combined with a hand wave as if it would help her find the right phrase. Then she finished with "the same love of the item that your family had. And instead of your things being hidden away in one place, people from all over will be enjoying them. What a tribute to your family . . . to you."

The Prince took out his handkerchief and blew his nose. "But what if I don't get the money I need?"

Annie was sure money was the reason behind the regrets.

"Remember you have reserves on all the items to make sure

you get your price, but considering the calls we are getting, I'm sure that the auction will bring you what you want. Will you be with us tomorrow? Or do you want us to call you when it is all over?" Control his choice.

"I don't know yet. It would be hard to watch everything go, but on the other hand it would be exciting."

"Do let us know, so we can set up a place of honor for you," Annie said.

"Annie was brilliant," Conrad said as they sat with Thomas and Mireille in the room where the auction would take place before they did a dress rehearsal for each item. Although Conrad auctioned the items off from a lectern that looked as if some medieval professor at Oxford or Cambridge would have used it to lecture from, there was a screen in the table, giving him information he could choose to mention or not.

"You think the old bastard was about to try and hold us up for more money?" Thomas asked.

Conrad nodded. "Annie kinda backed him into a corner. He certainly is a good example of rich and dumb."

"Well, not so rich considering how much of the family fortune he has squandered," Mireille said. "Do we want to run through everything one more time to make sure it is all in place?"

"I'm too tired, but I think everything is fine," Conrad said.

Annie's cell phone rang.

"Annie, it's Alice. I found your artist. Or at least I found an Elizabeth who was born of a couple with the names you brought me. It is enough to make a case."

Annie put her thumbs up to Mireille. When she hung up, she said, "I think we can assign an artist's real name to your sketches."

CHAPTER 53

Geneva, Switzerland
November 1559

"Sometimes I think you *are* a witch." Guillaume Dumont, Elizabeth's lawyer, sat on the floor next to her.

He opened his cloak and brought out a baguette of bread, a large slice of ham, cheese and apples hidden in a sack.

Elizabeth eyed the food trying not to grab it. The rations provided by her uncle had been minimal and grew stingier with each passing day. "You could get in trouble if you get caught bringing me food."

He reached out and pushed a piece of hair away from her face. "I could say it is a matter of justice. You don't deserve this treatment."

Elizabeth liked this handsome young man with the brown wavy hair and deep brown eyes shining with intelligence. Because she had so much time alone, she tried to conjure up the times she needed to take something to her uncle's offices. At the time she'd thought how she would love to capture those features on paper. And she remembered his meeting her by accident on the street and would have liked to talk longer to him but propriety ruled. "I doubt if anything can save me. My uncle wants my land. To get it he needs me dead."

The first time she had said this to him, he denied it, but over the past two weeks, he'd begun to take her seriously.

Guillaume put his hand to her lips. "The guards might hear."

"Can't you bring that up in court?"

He shook his head. "Accuse my employer who allegedly wants to free you from these horrible charges. Of course he is giving me all sorts of reasons you might be a witch. He wants to make sure that Françoise testifies about her baby's death, the owner of the *crémerie* about how often you had to return rancid butter although it did not happen to his other clients."

She had to put her ear almost to his mouth to hear what he was saying. How could she tell him she'd given up, that it would take more than a miracle to prove her innocence? Several weeks in this room—with not enough to eat, not enough to keep her warm, nothing to wash with including during her monthly periods—had left her little hope. That Guillaume could touch her as filthy as she was, was more than she could understand. When she came to trial she knew she would look like the witches in drawings: haggard and filthy.

"I don't know what I can do for you, and I hate that. I mean really hate it. You're innocent, I know, and I'll do everything I can to stop this . . . this . . . travesty of justice."

Elizabeth hugged herself as if she could make herself warm. "But you just said you believed I was a witch."

"You've bewitched *me*. If things were different, I would ask your uncle if I could marry you."

"My uncle, he would say no. He said no to . . ."

"The printer, I know." Guillaume kept his voice at a whisper. "I believe your uncle is evil despite his position with the *Conseil*, despite his friendship with Calvin. Our only hope is to arrange your escape."

"I only wish I could get word to my grandfather in time."

Guillaume leaned next to her. His words were spoken so softly she thought she'd almost imagined them. "I sent him a message, your grandfather, that is. I went to the French countryside, through the forest where there are no borders. I found a man who said he would take the message to England."

Elizabeth had to stop herself from crying at this unexpected news. "When?"

"When you first asked me. After you were first arrested. I didn't say anything before because I didn't want to get your hopes up. But after your questioning, I think you need a bit of hope. Maybe there are diplomatic channels that your grandfather could use?"

"Maybe during the reign of Henry, but certainly not now. Queen Mary's return to Catholicism changed all that. Elizabeth is too new on the throne to trouble with a state as little as Geneva, even if we're all Protestants, even if my grandfather has any influence." She let out a very long sigh. "He taught my mother not so much to believe in God, but to show a public face so we could live in peace. That's all I want to do."

He gathered her to him. His warmth penetrated the cold.

"Guillaume?" She spoke into his chest.

He lifted her chin with his hand and stared into her eyes. "Hmm?"

"I'm afraid. I'm so afraid and even if word does come from the powerful in England, Calvin won't listen to English Protestants. Uncle Jacques says Calvin thinks they are just Catholics using another name."

"You can't give up."

As much as she wanted to share his hope, she couldn't. "Any word from England will take too long."

"I paid the rider extra to have him ride straight through."

Elizabeth wondered if the messenger would have taken the money and not gone anywhere, much less England at top speed.

As if he could read her mind, he said, "He's trustworthy. He's my cousin."

She didn't know he had a cousin. There was so much she didn't know about him. She watched his face break into a grin that was more like a mischievous young boy.

"He's back and said that he did deliver the message and that your grandfather said he would send your cousin, but what worries me is that he has had plenty of time to get here."

There was a sharp rap on the door. "How much longer?"

"I need more time with my client."

"Well, hurry up before she casts a spell on you," the guard said.

"You already have, cast a spell, that is. If we can get you out of here, I'm going to marry you. We can both go to England. With your cousin, when he gets here."

If he gets here, Elizabeth wanted to add, but the expression on Guillaume's face said that he thought it was possible, maybe even probable. She wanted to ask him how he planned to free her. Had something happened to her cousin on the way? Questions, questions and so few answers.

She wished Guillaume had told her earlier, but she was not going to do anything to upset him. He wanted to marry her. He wanted to go to England with her. Although she believed none of it would happen, for the first time she saw the tiniest glimmer that it might be possible.

CHAPTER 54

Geneva, Switzerland

Maria-Elena could have taken the bus home, but she decided to walk up the hill, which only took about twenty minutes. She needed to clear her head. Most of the traffic along the Route de Ferney had gone. The remaining cars' headlights were muted by the fog, the cold of which picked at her cheeks. She shoved her hands deep into her pockets and wished she had remembered her lined mittens which kept her hands toasty.

Nothing waited for her at home. Marc was not returning her phone calls. She wished she could be sorry that Urs was dead, but sometimes coming home to nothing was better than coming home to his lack of welcome, which was colder than this late-autumn evening. So many times she had imagined what it would be like to have him gone, and now he was. It made her happy.

No, happy was the wrong word. What she wanted wasn't so much Urs dead because he made her life unpleasant with his demands and his one-way attitude for anything. She just wanted him gone as if by the wave of some magic wand. Her home had never been a real home at least not like the movies showed. There were no weekend walks with their son in the woods near Geneva where they would pick mushrooms; no sledding or ski trips to nearby Saint Cergue on a Sunday afternoon, much less going on a one-week trip to any Swiss ski resorts. Even their chalet had seldom been used, just rented to others before they sold it because the hassle was too much work.

Urs had held most activities as time stolen from "HIS WORK" spoken as it were some kind of deity. "Her work" was always lower case, secondary. That she had spent years developing a new blood-thinning tablet that could have been a major accomplishment was nothing compared to her not-so-dear late husband's achievements.

Now even that might come to nothing. All those years in the lab. The problems with the clinical tests bothered her, but what worried her more was that the company—in its rush to bring the drug to market—was ignoring the clinical test results. She thought, yet again, of all the pharmaceutical firms who went through years of lawsuits when they knowingly released some pill that had problems.

Being known as the head chemist that created a pill that killed would do nothing for her career. She wondered if it were time to change companies while her reputation remained in good shape. It might mean a move to Basel where more of the pharmaceutical companies were, or even going back to Uruguay.

There was nothing for her here. She had been so tied up in her work that she had never bothered to make friends, close or otherwise. She had only colleagues.

Marc could stay with the Youngs. He was about to go to university anyway.

What if Garth's last attempt to save his marriage failed? Maybe he would come back to her. If she bailed too quickly . . . no, she had to believe that part of her life was over.

By the time she reached the traffic light where she crossed the street, she was nearly frozen. She could see the lights on in the apartment of Mireille, the Bitch. She had never been a hundred percent certain that Mireille had had an affair with her husband, but 98.99 percent was fine. Not that Urs ever did anything obvious to give himself away; it was the way Mireille acted when they all ended up in the elevator together. When the building had its annual Christmas get-together in the lobby, the fact that they didn't speak at all was another reason she thought they might be sleeping together. The avoidance had been like magnets with their opposing ends forcing themselves away from each other, and that was not natural when he was overseeing the woman's thesis.

Well, neither of them had to deal with Urs now. So many times Maria-Elena had thought of ways to kill her husband. About a year ago, when Garth and she were at their most passionate, she went so far as to put scallops in a meat pie she had baked, thinking his allergies would do what she didn't want to do with a gun or a knife. He had vomited and vomited, but still went to his lectures the next morning.

And about two years ago, when Urs had been particularly nasty for an extremely long time, she had cruised the *Pâquis* area looking for one of the Eastern-bloc refugees who might think a good amount of money was worth murdering someone. All she found in the Pâquis that night were the prostitutes standing around in short skirts and high heels waiting for their next customer.

Was thinking of ways to kill her husband all that different from letting her company release a drug that might kill people?

Yes.

The people that took the drug would be nicer than Urs. Or some of them would be. She had to decide how to stop the drug from going to market, but without losing her job.

CHAPTER 55

Geneva, Switzerland

"Look! Look!" Thomas was prancing and waving the *Tribune de Genève* in his hands as Annie entered the auction house, quickly closing the door behind her to keep out the snow flurries.

She took the paper that Thomas had left open to the business section. The headline read, "Auction house scores $7.3 million hit." It went on to describe some of the prince's key items, and the prices for which they sold.

"And we made the *IHT,* the *Guardian* and even a squib in the *Financial Times.* Conrad wants us all to meet in his office as soon as we are all in and since you are the last one . . ."

Annie hung up her coat and climbed the stairs to Conrad's office. She found Mireille, the secretary and Thomas all around his Louis XVI gold-leaf table. On it was a bottle of champagne and five glasses.

Conrad had one of the devices that made anyone opening champagne look like a professional sommelier. The pop made just the right sound. He filled up four of the glasses and in the fifth he poured no more than a swallow and handed that one to Mireille. "We have to let little Zoë get a smattering of the good life."

"Do you know it is a girl?" Annie asked.

"Had the sonogram yesterday and I was just showing the men the first photos of my daughter, who they've named Zoë. Don't take it as official."

"We have to celebrate the biggest auction we've held," Conrad said.

"And the publicity," Thomas said. "Not to mention that we did it without my sleeping with that awful old prince."

The others groaned.

"Well, I didn't."

"With the percentages the buyers and prince pay, we can sleep nights. I don't have to tell you all how close we've come to failing over the past few years; sometimes we have to squeak in stupid estate auction just to cover the basics."

They all nodded. Annie seldom came to Geneva for more than a week without meeting with both men to see how they were doing. They exchanged e-mails on a regular basis as well.

"And since you've all been wonderful during the thin, and we're now in the thick, let me present you with a thank-you." Conrad opened his desk drawer and pulled out three A4 envelopes with the secretary's, Mireille's and Annie's name on them in calligraphy and fastened with sealing wax into which the company's logo had been pressed.

"Classy, say what?" Thomas said.

"He's out-smiling the Cheshire cat," the secretary said as she took her envelope.

Annie broke the seal as gently as possible and pulled out a piece of parchment. Written in more calligraphy and green ink was a thank-you, along with a note that 100,000 CHF had been deposited into her bank account, 45,000 more than she had agreed on for the project. Before she could ask if it were correct, Mireille, having read hers, started not just to cry but to sob.

"My God, my God. This means my immediate money worries are over," Mireille repeated over and over until Thomas burst in, "Good God, girl, if you think of all the times you donated your time to us, I suspect we still owe you money."

"Don't get carried away, Thomas," Conrad said. "She might ask for more. Seriously, without all of you, we could never have pulled this auction off. Annie, your catalog was a brilliant piece of work. The publicity you wrote for us got bidders in we might never have found otherwise."

Annie had learned, not all that long ago, to not protest when someone paid her a compliment or gave her an unexpected gift. "Thank you." Going into the new year, working would now be her choice so she could accept only the good assignments. Or none. Roger would be happy if she were home with him more often.

The guys did what guys often do with a crying female. They looked uncomfortable.

Annie dug into her pocketbook for some toilet tissue to hand to Mireille.

"We give you an elegant thank-you, one of you has a nervous breakdown and the other one only has tacky toilet paper instead of tissue," Conrad said.

Mireille fought for control. "If only . . . I mean . . . I wondered how I was going to take care of the baby, and . . . and"—a shudder in place of a sob—"and . . . and I know I could work for you . . . part-time . . . but I want to finish . . . my doctorate . . . and . . . maternity leave for part . . ."

"Knock it off, Mireille," Conrad said. "Or we'll take it back."

Annie, without meaning to, got a peek at Mireille's letter. The figure of 180,000 CHF jumped out at her. She was incapable of being jealous, knowing that in the beginning of the business, Mireille had put in many, many unpaid hours, no matter that it was against the law. She looked at them all and realized that friendship comes in many forms and theirs had continued for well over a decade. The blessings she was feeling were made up only in a small part of the Swiss Francs that were about to grace her bank account.

CHAPTER 56

Geneva, Switzerland
November 13, 1559

James shifted in the saddle as he approached Geneva. He could see the gray-brown stone walls of the city as his horse meandered through the fields where sheep huddled against the wind blowing off the lake. In the failing light of day he could see a huge stone mountain and behind it a white-capped mountain.

Both he and his horse were tired. His grandfather would not be happy that he had wasted a complete month, but first he had been too ill then too weak to travel. His host and hostess had forbidden him to leave until most of his strength had returned and even then they outfitted him with warmer clothing. When he offered them money, they refused, saying that his grandfather had shared with Edouard more than enough hospitality, years back in Oxford.

"I'm grateful I finally have the chance to repay your grandfather's past kindnesses," Edouard had said. "Now go rescue your cousin from those fanatics."

Now that he was at his destination, he was not sure of his next step. He knew that his cousin was in trouble, but what he could do about it was unclear. He wished that his older brother had come in his place—but his sister-in-law ad been about to give birth. She probably had by now. His brother would have known what to do. That he was missing classes at Oxford did not bother him. James was a good student and knew he could catch up later.

Concentrate: how do I get into the bloody city? He saw a hay-filled cart pulled by a donkey that did not seem in any rush, ignoring the urgings of the farmer pulling the beast's bridle.

"You going into the city?" James asked in French.

The farmer responded in something that resembled French but sounded as if some of the hay had been stuffed in his mouth and he was choking on it.

After several failed attempts to communicate with words, James pointed at the cart then at the wall.

The farmer nodded.

James moved his fingers as if walking, stopping and trying to go forward, being blocked then continuing. He did this several times. The farmer frowned then understood. He took a stick and kicked the dirt clear of leaves, before sketching a rough outline of the city, and pointing where the different entry points were.

"Merci." The farmer understood that.

James took off not at a gallop, but a trot, leaving the farmer to continue pulling his donkey. He realized that in the entire communication the farmer never did anything but frown or look serious. James would have found his hand gestures amusing.

At La Tour Maîtresse he found the gate opened and a guard resting on a stool. The man barely looked at him as he waved him through. Rather than ride in, he dismounted. First he needed to find a hotel and a place to board the horse. He hoped his own horse was doing well back in France.

The city streets, although not as busy as Paris, were full of activity. A wagon, full of planks, was being urged up a hill, despite the reluctance of the horse pulling it. The owner was cajoling the animal with apples. James passed at least five houses where extensions were being added on top of their existing two to three stories.

Along the rue Molard there were several places that had signs offering rooms and food. James really wanted to do nothing but sleep, but he couldn't afford the time.

One of the hotels looked rather dilapidated, but two others seemed in a bit better condition. The first one was full, or at least he thought that was what the man sitting in the main room at a table had said. Strange, strange French these people mumbled.

In the second hotel, a woman dressed in gray, her head fully covered, greeted him, not with a smile, but at least without a frown. Her French was at least understandable as she said, "I've a bed in a room with four others. How long will you be staying?"

"I don't know. I have to see a relative. After that I'll be leaving." Stupid, he thought. His brother would never make the mistake of giving any extra information to a stranger.

"You can eat here for less than you might some other place. Our bread is fresh."

"Do you know where I can board my horse?" He had left the door open so he could keep his eye on the animal.

"We've a stable out back. We also have boxes where you can lock up your things."

"Let me settle the horse first, then I can settle myself in the room."

The stables were clean with fresh hay in each stall. A man was rubbing down a roan stallion.

"It is only fifteen percent more, if I polish your horse," the man said. "Look at the ones I've done. They're almost smiling."

More than any human that I've met in the last three hours, James thought. Thank God, his grandfather had given him more than enough money—sewn into his clothes.

He had heard that Geneva was a wealthy city and that the residents attributed their richness to God smiling on them more than on the heathen Catholics. He believed his grandfather's caution to never even mention he was Catholic and to never cross himself. It was his mother who insisted that they stay Catholic rather than flip-flop between religions, although like the rest of his family his street religion was whichever the current ruler said it was.

None of his family, with the exception of his mother, ever mentioned religion anyway or even considered it all that important except as a means of family survival. His family was always active in the church to keep the neighbors at bay, so to speak. Intellectual or business accomplishments were the gods of his childhood household. His grandfather acting as a church historian in their little village as well as teacher in the church school was enough.

He had never met his aunt, who had left for Geneva before he was born, but he'd heard stories of the handsome lawyer from Geneva who did business with the wealthiest of the wealthy, signing contracts for jewelry and clocks, even baby clocks to be pinned to clothes.

It was part of the family lore, just like the story about how his father had opened a small shop in the village. At the time everyone told him it would be a failure. The village was too small, the doubters predicted, but his father carried his products into London, which was where he had come across Yves Huguette and they had struck a deal on the exclusive importation of watches for the wealthy burghers in London whether by direct sale or through jewelry shops in the heart of the city. The contract did not cover the aristocracy or other major English cities, but it had made his father a wealthy man.

Yves had taken the beautiful Anne Smythe back to Geneva.

She never returned to England. His grandfather, who had missed his only daughter, eagerly awaited any messages brought by his son-in-law on his trips.

Yves Huguette had not come to England for—what was it?—three or four years? James wasn't sure because he had been away at school. There was talk of sending someone to Geneva to restock the shop with watches, but the different changes of monarchs had postponed any buying missions.

Then a letter had been delivered by a new representative from his daughter's brother-in-law saying that his daughter, son-in-law and grandson had all perished with The Sickness. Young Elizabeth had been taken under Jacques Huguette's wing, and Grandfather had no cause for worry. The girl was as well as could be expected under the circumstances.

Grandfather had sent letters with each person he found heading for Geneva, but he heard nothing more until Elizabeth herself had written. Her letter had been dispatched nine months before he received it. The rider had been killed on the way back, according to a man who frequently made the London–Geneva route and had retrieved the letter and delivered it when he found himself near Beckenham.

Elizabeth told of her mistreatment and gave him an address where he could reach her. Under no circumstances was he to try and write her at her uncle's address.

More and more the old man faltered in his speech and his indecision about how to help his granddaughter. James had long noted that businessmen and scholars act and react differently. He saw scholars dither over decisions the same way they argued over a theory, while businessmen rushed into undertaking whatever action was needed. James did not limit this theory just to his grandfather. His teachers were often the same way.

Then the latest messenger arrived with a letter from a lawyer, a Guillaume Dumont, saying that Elizabeth had been accused of being a witch and that he had been hired by her uncle to defend her, but that he did not think he could save her. If anyone could get to Geneva quickly, there might be a sliver of hope that they could help her escape.

And just as his grandfather was planning to leave he fell off his horse, hurting his leg and making riding any great distance next to impossible. His son, James's father, voiced his concern, telling the old man he was far too aged to go running across the channel and over the French countryside to rescue his grand-daughter.

All that led to James wandering up the hill in search of Antoine, the shoemaker, who grandfather had said was the go-between. About a quarter of the way up the hill was a shop with an iron boot hanging above the door.

James entered the shop.

Surrounded by candles, an old man sat, cutting a sole around a last. The smell of leather was almost suffocating. *"Bonjour."*

"Bonjour. I am looking for a shoemaker."

"Well, I'm either a candle maker making a shoe or a shoemaker trying to see by candlelight."

At least I can understand his French, James thought. He had pictured the shoemaker as someone young and vibrant. "Are you Antoine?"

The old man spit. "His work is not half as good as mine. Damned immigrants—think they can just move and take all our work away."

"Oh, I don't want him for shoes, it is something personal. A friend gave me a message for him."

"Hmph."

"No, really." He held up his foot. "See, my boots are in good condition. I won't need a pair for a long time."

The man peered at James's outstretched foot. Then he took his foot in his hand. "Not made around here."

James did not want to reveal anything else. "Do you know where I could find Antoine?"

"Go up the hill to the end of the street to the Place du Bourg-de-Four. Then go left and take your first right. He is about five doors down, same side of the street as I am here. It's parallel."

"*Merci.*"

"Hmph."

The door did not shut completely and James heard the man shout, "Come back and shut the door." He did.

Although he didn't know what the Place du Bourg-de-Four was, he walked to the end of the street and turned left as told. He had to push through a flock of sheep. Another man was selling chickens in cages from his cart. A cow, not quite fully grown, nuzzled him as he tried to get his bearings.

"She'll be a great milk cow," a man said. "I can give you a good price."

James shook his head and found the parallel street as the grouchy old shoemaker had said. Leaves swirled up the street as if attacking his feet.

He saw the shop, which also had an iron boot over the door, but this one was not rusted. When he entered, a fire burned in the fireplace making the area warm. Because of the cold, the closed shutters made the shop a bit darker than the other one, but instead of a confusion of materials, three pairs of boots sat on top of a shelf. Although utilitarian, James could see that the stitches were perfectly aligned. A low bench had various tools lined up in order.

A man, probably ten years James's senior, sat astride a bench with a last in the middle. He was rubbing a cloth across the toe of a lady's shoe. "May I help you?" The accent was different than the other mumbled ones he had heard since he entered the city and understandable more or less.

"Are you Antoine?"

The shoemaker nodded.

"Do you know Elizabeth Huguette?"

Antoine moved back. "May I ask why you are asking?"

"I'm her cousin. I've ridden from London to . . ."

Antoine jumped up and grabbed James and hugged him. "Thank God you've come. It's almost too late."

CHAPTER 57

Geneva, Switzerland

Roger sat in the office of the inspectors' wing of the police station, a cold coffee between his hands. His notes were spread out on his desk as he tried to piece together that which was missing on Professor Stoller's murder. He had been in a village too long, certainly nothing like when he had been at his peak in Paris. But, then again, he had time for a life in a small town. He had enough: interesting work, a great kid and a woman whom he loved, even when she drove him slightly mad.

With only a few more days left before he had to go back to Argelès, he doubted that he would see the end of the case. The program had worked in that he had had a chance to sharpen his skills a bit, but not enough to solve the murder. In Fortini, he got a valuable lesson on how not to be a boss along with the gratitude that mostly he was his own boss, although he did have higher-ups. Fortunately they more or less ignored him as long as nothing went radically wrong. Sleepy little villages except during summers had major advantages.

And although it looked good professionally for him to have come here, he knew that his main reason was to have more time with Annie.

The phone rang. "A Colette Bauer to see you," the receptionist said. "She says it has something to do with Professor Stoller's death."

"Send her up."

Madame Bauer was in her early thirties, her hair shoulder length, loose and expensively highlighted, which she swept out of her eyes. He could see her hand shake.

Once seated, he offered her coffee. She again brushed the hair from her face. "Yes, please."

As Roger poured her a demitasse, he asked, "What can I do for you?" Since she seemed nervous, he thought she might prefer the question if he wasn't looking directly at her. Although he could have taken a position behind his desk, he felt she might be more at ease if he sat next to her. She swiveled in the chair so they were facing but she didn't meet his eyes. Nervousness, he decided.

"I'm not sure I was right to come, because I don't know anything for certain, but something didn't seem right."

Roger cocked his head.

"Why don't you start by telling me who you are."

"Colette Bauer. I work for Renatus Pharmaceuticals and I'm the department secretary. The department that Madame Stoller heads up."

"And . . ."

"It's about my boss, Madame Stoller. I know she was supposed to be grief stricken and all, but I walked into her office when she was talking to our vice president, and it sounded like they were finishing an affair, a love affair." She went into detail on what she had overheard. "There had been a couple of rumors, but I never gave them any credence. I mean, she never talked to her husband on the phone, like some wives do, but she is also deep into her work. We've developed this new blood thinner and it is in the testing stage and everyone is on pins and needles."

"Blood thinner?"

"Yes, it is both in a liquid and tablet form. It has no real taste and is supposed to really help with a number of medical conditions. I've been told, there may be some testing problems. Everyone in the lab is unhappy."

"If it is no good . . ."

"Companies like ours spend a fortune on developing drugs, but more don't work out than do. When it comes to the clinical tests, well, if they fail, people could have wasted a good part of their careers developing something no good."

Everything was lining up, the cause of death and the origin of the drug that had killed Stoller.

Before he could ask another question, Fortini and Morat walked in. As usual Fortini could have been a Columbo stand-in, and Morat was spiffy, as Susan Young would have described him.

Roger summarized what Madame Bauer had told him.

"Can you get us a sample of the medicine? Does it have a name yet?"

"The marketing people are still working on it. Focus groups haven't been able to agree on anything and it is beyond regional differences. They wanted to release it as soon as approvals come in, which we expected in the spring, but with the testing problems and all . . ."

"But can you get us a sample?"

She nodded.

"Now?"

"Maybe."

"Morat, go with her and then take it to the lab *tout de suite* or faster if possible," Fortini said.

As soon as they left, Fortini said, "If that sample matches the one we got from the boat and the one in Stoller's body, we should have enough for an arrest."

"Motive?"

"The wife wasn't faithful. They were anything but a devoted couple." Fortini frowned. "What do you want—a videotape of her doing him in?"

"I like playing devil's advocate."

"Well, stop it."

CHAPTER 58

Corsier Port, Switzerland

When Roger opened the door of the Young house, the first thing he heard was laughter. He popped his head into the kitchen, just right of the entry and the source of the laughter, to see Dave, Annie, Marc and Susan all in various stages of dinner preparation. Marc was peeling carrots, Dave was setting the table, Susan was stirring something that smelled good. And Annie?

Well, Annie was standing to one side. Seeing Roger she went over to put her arms around him. "I'm the slave master here, telling people what to do."

He stiffened.

"What's the matter?" Annie asked.

He didn't want to spoil this happy moment. "Just work." He would get her and Susan alone later to try and work out a strategy.

"Gaëlle called," said Susan. "She loves her exchange family in Austria." She added, "She's looking forward to both of you being home in a couple of weeks."

"What do you think if I spend almost all my time *chez toi?*" Annie asked.

"I don't suppose this means you want to set a wedding date?" he said.

"Don't be silly. I want to offer Mireille my place for a couple of months so she can finish her thesis without interruption."

Roger knew how conducive for work Annie's nest, as she called it, was by the way she hibernated when she had a work-from-home project. She would hole up, venturing out only to buy food. He had learned to leave her alone during those periods.

"Not so silly. Any chance we can get her and you to make the arrangement permanent?"

"No."

"Haven't you learned by now, Roger, how stubborn my daughter is?" Susan asked.

"I'm still having trouble believing that I can't crack it," he said.

He excused himself to wash up and change. As he took off his trousers and shirt to exchange for jeans and a sweater, there was a knock on the bedroom door.

Annie entered. "What's wrong?" When he didn't answer, she continued, "I can tell by your tightness. Give."

That she could read him so well was one of the things that he loved about her, maddening though she could be. "Marc's mother was arrested this afternoon for the murder of Stoller."

Annie sank onto the bed, which was rumpled. She had lain down to read mid-afternoon and had dozed off. "Holy shit!"

"The drug that killed him came from her company."

"We have to tell Marc, but breaking it to him . . ." Annie left the bedroom for the top of the stairs. "Mom, can you come up here?"

As soon as Susan arrived, they told her the problem.

"We have to tell him now," Susan said. "Roger, since you were there . . . you were there when they arrested her?"

He nodded.

"Then you have to be the one to tell him. He'll want to know how she is and where she is," Susan said. "That poor, poor boy."

Marc looked confused that Susan, Annie and Roger had called him into the living room. He looked at Dave who signaled he had no idea what had stopped supper preparations and why the threesome looked so serious. Tonight, there was no fire in the fireplace.

"Roger has some bad news for you," Annie went over and sat next to him. Susan flanked him on the other side.

"We arrested your mother today," Roger said.

"Why?" Before Roger could respond, Marc said, "Not for the murder of my father?"

Roger nodded.

"She couldn't have. I know they didn't get along, but . . ." He jumped up, stepping on Susan as he rushed by her. He did not even stop to put on his coat. Or his shoes, which family members automatically exchanged for house slippers kept by the door for that purpose when they entered.

Roger and Annie were right behind him, only they grabbed coats from the rack, including Marc's. Roger, because he could run faster than Annie, caught up with the boy on the dock. Annie came panting up behind him.

"Leave me alone." Marc pushed Roger's hands off his shoulders where the older man had grabbed him.

In the moonlight, Annie could see him fighting not to cry. "We will, but back at the house. Roger, how much can you tell him?"

"Please tell me everything you know." Marc's voice reminded Annie of a whimpering puppy.

"The drug that killed your father was a test drug made by your mother's company." Roger handed Marc his coat and buttoned his own.

"But why would she?"

"The police found out she had been having an affair. They see opportunity and motive."

Marc broke down. Instead of a seventeen-year-old-man-to-be, he cried like a little boy. Annie put her arm around his waist and led him to one of the benches at the end of the dock. Although she was much smaller than Marc, she tried to encircle him. He fell into her.

A man walking a German shepherd slowed as he walked by. Roger used his hand to indicate he should move on. The man did.

Annie had no idea how long they sat there. She knew she was cold. Finally, Marc sat up, then shuddered with a few remaining sobs.

Annie fumbled in her coat pocket for the toilet paper she usually stuffed in because she never remembered to get tissues.

"You must think I'm an awful baby."

"Not at all," Roger said. "You've lost your father and now your mother has been arrested for his murder. She's all right, by the way. She's worried about you and she sent her love."

"Did she admit it?"

Roger told him how she claimed innocence all the way through the questioning and the booking. Because there was no way they could pinpoint the time of death, Maria-Elena could not establish an alibi. Trying to verify her whereabouts from the time Stoller had last been seen until his body was found would be impossible. Even if Marc could have said she was at the house every night, she could have gone out when he was not there or even left in the middle of the night while he slept.

Marc took in the barrage of unknowns. "She couldn't have done it."

"I know it is hard to accept," Roger said.

"No, I mean she couldn't have done it," Marc said. "The

person dumped my father's body in the lake. My mother doesn't know how to run the boat. She would never have been able to get him out on the lake to put him in the water."

"She could have had an accomplice. Maybe the lover," Fortini said.

Roger had called him as soon as they had gotten back into the house and Marc was calm.

"And I don't appreciate being interrupted at home. It's been a long day."

"I know, but if Madame Stoller can't operate the boat how did she . . ."

"She could have learned without the kid knowing. I can get Morat to check that out. And we do want to talk to her lover, but so far we haven't figured out who he is, and she won't talk."

"Try Garth Chase," Roger said. "And it's only a guess by the number of calls from his phone to her mobile."

CHAPTER 59

Geneva, Switzerland
November 3, 1559

"I snore like a pig," Antoine warned as he dropped James's saddlebag next to the fireplace where a few coals did little to dispel the chill, "but it is better here than in the hotel."

"He does snore," said Marie, the shoemaker's wife.

James looked around the room. The shutters were closed. He could hear the wind outside. A single candle did little to dispel the darkness.

"Your cousin spent a lot of time here after her father disappeared and her mother and brother died. Or at least she did when she could escape her aunt and uncle."

Antoine got some bedding from a trunk and tossed it on the floor. "I won't give up my bed, but I'll bring in some straw."

"No need. I'm just grateful for what you're sharing with me." And he was. He realized that his clothing and accent made him stand out.

As if he could read his mind Antoine said, "It is better people not see you."

The door in the shop downstairs sounded. "Anyone here?"

"Upstairs," Antoine said.

The sound of footsteps was followed by a well-dressed young man walking through the doorway. "You must be James, Elizabeth's cousin. I'm Guillaume Dumont, her alleged lawyer."

James took in the word "alleged." Until Guillaume responded, he did not realize that he had spoken it aloud.

"Her uncle is pretending he wants me to defend her, to save her from the fire. But he never gives me time to work on her case. He stops me from bringing her food, by claiming that he will bring it, but then he doesn't bring it. I've always believed in actions, not words."

Antoine went to a cupboard and brought out a loaf of bread and some cheese. He sliced off thick hunks which he put on the table for them to select their own. "Guillaume has fallen in love with Elizabeth. But, if anyone finds out, it will be worse for her."

"They will think she's bewitched me, and in a manner, I think she has, but not by using supernatural powers."

"Your cousin is a charming, bright young woman, who just does not fit in with the Calvinists."

"But you are one, Antoine, and you, too, Guillaume."

The two men looked at each other. "Protestants, believers, not Papists. But that does not mean we are as strict as the city fathers want us to be. If God gave us beauty, why is it a sin to enjoy it?" Antoine asked. "In France, I would have been killed for my Huguenot beliefs: here I could be punished for being too liberal, but nevertheless I fit in better."

"We need a plan to free Elizabeth, get her first to France and then back to England," Guillaume said. "And I will be coming with you. I want to marry her."

CHAPTER 60

Geneva, Switzerland

Fortini hovered over Roger while Morat sat at his own desk. Roger thought if the younger man could make himself disappear he would. Better men than Fortini had tried to intimidate Roger without success. Roger, a good five inches taller than Fortini, rose. "I tell you we have the wrong person. Maria-Elena did not kill her husband."

"And I'm telling you, the case is closed." Fortini could have been heard out on the alley behind the police building and through the closed window. "You know, your exchange only has a couple of more days to run. I suggest you make this your last day. No, make this your last minute."

"No problem," Roger said.

"I'm going out to lunch. When I'm back, I want you gone." Fortini slammed the door.

Roger sat down in his chair.

"You really think she's innocent?" Morat asked.

"Yes. She couldn't have dumped him in the lake."

Morat picked up a copy of *20 Minutes,* the daily free paper. The headline read, "Police arrest wife of murdered prof."

"The big boss doesn't like to admit her team made a mistake. Going to her won't solve anything, if that's what you're thinking."

That had been what Roger was thinking. He didn't care if it did any good or not. Well, he did care, but he did have to tell someone higher than Fortini because he couldn't live with himself if he had let an innocent woman go to jail.

Of course, he could have been wrong.

So many people hated Stoller, but it was only his wife that had access to the drugs. But Maria-Elena was too small to lift her husband's body into the lake on her own, even if she could have taken the boat out. It could have been her lover: he had access to the same drugs.

For that matter of fact it could have been Marc if you looked at access. The kid knew a lot about sailing. But although Marc was angry at his father, Roger did not think Marc was capable of pulling off a complicated murder. He lacked deviousness and was more like a puppy that had grown too fast and was not used to its body. Roger was not ready to close out the case, but he was not in charge.

"I'm going to try."

"Fortini will probably put out a contract on you for going over his head," Morat said.

"What do you think?" Roger asked.

"I think there's a sixty-percent chance we've got the right person, but I would like to eliminate the forty percent."

Gathering up his things Roger went over to the head of the Geneva Police Crimes Investigation office. He had to wait a half hour.

The Big Boss was an attractive woman, he thought, when he was invited in, and she looked intelligent. "How have you enjoyed your exchange?"

"It was interesting to be back in a city again."

"You were where?"

"I was in charge of the murder division in Paris. At 36."

She whistled at his mention of the 36, the French equivalent of Scotland Yard headquartered at 36 quai des Orfèvres in Paris, and the best-known crime unit in Europe after Interpol. "Big job. Doesn't being in a village bother you? No excitement? Not many murders?"

"As a single father of a teenage girl, the quieter work doesn't bother me at all. She has priority. But at the same time it was good to be back where more is happening. In Argelès I'm more family counselor and social worker than a detective, although all the same skills are necessary."

"How much longer will you be here?"

"Fortini suggested I make today my last day."

She raised one eyebrow. "I sense tension there."

"We disagreed." A copy of the *Tribune de Genève* was on her desk. It carried a headline that was visible about the arrest of Maria-Elena Stoller, to which he pointed.

"I don't think she did it." He went on to explain about Marc staying with his future in-laws, Maria-Elena not being able to pilot the boat.

"And it is in your gut, too."

"It's in my gut, but I'm not that long out of Paris, that I know my gut isn't enough."

"So who do you think could have done it?" She leaned back in her chair.

"If you want a motive of those who didn't like Stoller we would have at least twenty-five people, but murder doesn't necessarily follow dislike. A secretary from the wife's firm who came to see me told me it could be the vice president of marketing. Madame Stoller was alleged to have been sleeping with him."

She got up and went to her file cabinet. A box with folders was on top. She took it down and riffled through until she found what she was looking for. "When he was questioned his wife had just moved over from England. Religion came up, and he appeared to be a strong Catholic."

Roger's phone rang. He took a look and saw it was Morat

before sticking it back into his pocket.

"Catholics commit adultery," Roger said.

"But it could stop him from murdering someone."

Roger had been there during Garth's questioning. At the time they did not know about the possibility of an affair between him and the wife. He had no strong feelings that it was the boyfriend who might have done it, but he considered the boyfriend as likely a suspect as Maria-Elena.

Roger leaned forward in his chair. "I just don't think we have enough proof to close the case."

"I can't go against my team on this. It'll be up to the courts." She stood and stuck out her hand. "I'm sorry it turned out this way, both the case and your early departure."

Roger hated it when he couldn't convince others he was right. He stuck out his hand.

As soon as he was outside, he returned Morat's call.

"So how did it go?"

"It didn't."

"*Merde.* I'm not surprised. And if it helps I do agree with you but I can't do anything either. *Double merde.* Fortini's coming." The phone clicked off.

CHAPTER 61

Geneva, Switzerland

Annie sat on the bed as Roger packed. "Isn't there anything you can do?"

He stopped folding his shirt. She marveled at his packing. Everything was folded with precision. Once she had looked at two shirts that he had taken out of the suitcase to notice the creases were in exactly the same place. Her method of packing was to throw everything into whatever she was using for a suitcase or backpack.

"*Chérie,* there's nothing I can do." He looked at her face. "There isn't." When she still didn't respond, he said, "I am a guest officer in an exchange program. Since that is ended, I'm due back in Argelès."

"But you could find the real killer."

"I've a job."

"Take some vacation days."

He put down the shirt, sat on the bed and pulled her toward him. Taking both her hands in his, he angled her so she was standing in front of him. He looked up. "*Chérie,* you know most of my vacation time goes to following you on your different assignments."

She couldn't say anything to that. It was part of the compromises they had both made to satisfy her. "I want to say that is unfair, but you're right."

"Where's the tape recorder, I want to get that down."

She pulled one of her hands free and punched his arm with her fist.

"Ow!"

"Don't overact," she said.

"What's happening with Marc?"

"Dad talked with the social-service agency that would take him into custody. Someone is coming out to talk to them next week, but since he'll be eighteen next month and out of their jurisdiction they'll probably leave him with my folks."

"He can stay with your folks how long?"

"I suspect my folks will stay here until the end of the school year for him—at least that is what they were saying. He can go to university next year, although he isn't sure what he wants to do."

"Would they take him to the States when they go for the summer?" Before she could answer, he said, "I bet they've discussed that already."

How well he knew her parents. They had already decided to be available to Marc directly or indirectly. The subject of university in the States came up, but was put aside quickly because of cost. Why spend tens of thousands when Marc could go for hundreds here? And in the States he would lose the allowance every student got in Switzerland for the loss of a parent.

Although she would never say it out loud, Marc's misfortune had been a godsend to her. If her parents were providing a home for him, they would only spend summers in the States, where her father had inherited her aunt's house and her mother was involved in a co-op art gallery. Summer was tourist season.

Annie had no desire to live with her parents, but she did like sharing a continent.

"And you, of course, would be miserable, if your parents spent more time here."

"We're getting off the subject." She ignored his nodding head that signaled he knew he was right.

Roger resumed packing. "If it is any help, Morat is going to continue poking around on his own time."

"Not much." She went to the door. "I'll get the car keys so I can drive you to the station. I have to get over to Mireille's anyway."

CHAPTER 62

Geneva, Switzerland
November 14, 1559

Antoine, James and Guillaume sat around the table in the room above the shoe shop. A bottle of wine was half drunk, and the carcass of a chicken was in the middle of the table. The bread they used in place of plates had been soaked with the fowl's juices, and periodically one of the three men would break off a piece and eat it.

Antoine's wife sat in the corner near the fireplace, knitting.

"We cannot wait any longer. She'll come to trial in two weeks," Guillaume said. "I do have some ideas."

The other two men looked at him.

"Since she is kept just outside the city walls, I will—well, we will, James and I, be outside them at curfew. There is a copse of woods not that far from the hut where she is. James, can you check it out tomorrow, so you are familiar with it?" He took a piece of charcoal, one of Elizabeth's old drawing sticks, and sketched the layout of the area onto the wooden tabletop.

James lifted the candle to see better. A bit of wax dripped onto the skin between his thumb and forefinger.

"Ouch!" He put the candle down and sucked the burnt area. "Of course, I can go look. Will anyone think it strange that I am wandering around near the hut?"

"Antoine, can you loan him some clothes, when he is out and about the city? Then he will look like one of us."

"Of course. We're about the same size."

"Make sure he wears your cape," Marie said from the corner of the room.

"The path by the hut is not all that well traveled. You don't want to say anything or people will know you are a stranger. But, then again, if you gallop by you will get a feel of what we are up against."

"And then what?" Antoine asked.

"I will stay out after the gates are locked, hiding in the woods. James, you will be with me."

"I'll get my horse from the stable ahead of curfew," James said. "But what are you and Elizabeth going to ride?" Guillaume had told him earlier he had no horse. "Can you afford to buy two horses?"

Guillaume shook his head. "And it would look strange for a young lawyer being paid miserly wages to be able to afford two when he couldn't afford one."

"When is the next animal market at the Place du Bourg-de-Four?"

"Tomorrow," Antoine said. "I can't buy one either. People know I have no need, and if I become too fancy they will think my prices are too high to pay for my fancy life."

"And they might tie you into Elizabeth's escape, which would be very dangerous for us," Marie said.

"A cart?" Antoine asked.

"Too slow. Too noisy. Even outside the city, the guards would hear us approaching," Guillaume said. "A cart is harder to hide. The woods aren't that dense."

"And three horses will be invisible?" Marie said.

Antoine stood up from the table and walked over to his wife. "She always looks for the holes in anything I want to do."

"And a good thing too. It makes you think things through." She attached another piece of yarn to the last of the ball.

"If we can get her out of the house, she could run to the trees then pick up the horses," James said.

"Maybe. Maybe not. She is not in good condition. Not having enough food, and living as she is made to live, has sapped a lot of her strength."

"We don't have money for two horses." Guillaume's frown looked almost sinister in the flickering candlelight.

"Yes, we do," James said. "I have more than enough to buy two horses."

"My cousin is a farmer living on the French side. He could come into the city and buy the horses for you, then take them to the forest and wait for you," Marie said.

For a minute James wondered if the cousin was trustworthy. He could run off with their money. However, they did not have many other choices. "So we have the horses. What else?"

Antoine poured everyone more wine. "It's almost curfew, Guillaume. I can't put one more person up."

"And my landlady would think I was doing terrible things if I didn't come home," Guillaume said. "Two nights from now, the moon is at its smallest. We will be outside the city walls and hiding in those woods. I suspect the guards fall asleep."

"How many?"

"There were two in the beginning, but now there is usually only one at night."

"I can distract him, and you knock him out. Then we grab Elizabeth and by morning when the new guard arrives, we'll be well on our way to Paris."

"Do you think they will follow us?" James said.

"Probably," Marie said from the corner. "That snake of an uncle won't like it that his niece has gotten away from him."

James knew she was right, but he wasn't sure how far they would be pursued.

CHAPTER 63

Geneva and Saint Cergue, Switzerland

"You aren't going to have to tell them if you keep your coat on," Annie said to Mireille. "And if you take it off you still won't have to tell them. They'll see it." Her friend had blossomed in the last couple of weeks of pregnancy. They were standing in the foyer of Mireille's apartment. Annie, having dropped off Roger at the train station, was now going with Mireille to her parents' house using her parents' car.

"I'll change." Mireille disappeared into her bedroom and came out wearing a floor-length skirt, an oversized sweater, boots and a shawl. "How's this?"

"You look chubby, but not necessarily pregnant."

"I still want you with me."

Annie wasn't sure what she could do to help Mireille, although her friend had sworn that if Annie were there they would be calmer.

"I can do the bad news, good news thingie."

"If you tell them the bad first, you'll never get to the good news about the artwork." Annie had not bothered to take off her coat but was simply waiting for her friend to gather up her pocketbook, copies of the drawings and the flowers that she had bought for her mother. "Hurry, you know how your mother is if she has to hold lunch."

The drive into the village where Mireille had grown up—and where her father ran a bottling plant for water brought down from the Alps as well as for a local apple juice company—was less than an hour. The village up in the Jura Mountains had the typical postcard Swiss look: a small center with a Migros and Co-op, one or two locally run stores, a fountain and view of Lac Léman with the Alps beyond.

The Bosset family lived just outside the center in an eight-room, two-story yellow stucco building. The forest-green shutters were closed where rooms were not in use.

"Maybe we should drive around a while," Mireille said.

Annie parked. "Get out of the car."

Mireille's mother did the three-cheek kiss greeting to both young women and ushered them into the living room. "Really, Mireille, your clothes do lack style."

"I go for comfort, Maman."

Madame Bosset shook her head and seated the girls around a small marble table. An *apéro* had been set out with white wine and a few thin, twisted bread sticks.

"May I have some juice since I'm driving?" Annie asked.

"I'm not driving, but juice sounds good." Mireille's eyes thanked Annie.

Madame Bosset disappeared into the kitchen as her husband entered. He was dressed in full work regalia with a handkerchief matching his tie in his chest pocket. He too bestowed the three-kiss greeting on the young women.

They barely had time to finish their juice before the meal moved to the table which was set to impress the clients of any five-star restaurant.

"What is new with you, Annie?" she asked.

Annie told her about the catalog, adding, "It is still up on the Internet."

"My wife doesn't go on the Internet," Monsieur Bosset said. "As for myself, I let my staff deal with the technology." He turned to his daughter. "So tell me, Mireille, what have you been doing?"

"The first draft of my thesis is finished."

"And have you found a new advisor?" This was asked as her mother jumped up to get the bread she'd forgotten. She could not have heard the answer because the door between the kitchen and the dining room swung shut behind her.

Mireille waited until her mother returned. "Yes."

"I will never understand why you decided on an art degree. By now you should be married. Did I tell you that I saw Pamela the other day? She was pushing the twins into Migros."

"Pamela was one of my friends when I was in school. She lived two doors down," Mireille said to Annie.

"Karl is doing well at the UBS," Monsieur Bosset said. "He is being sent to Zurich to train for some high position with the bank."

"Karl always was ambitious," Mireille said. "He's Pamela's husband and was two years ahead of us in school."

"Did you see the article in *Le Temps* on how well the auction did?" Annie asked Mireille's parents. "Mireille was incredible in her part between what she put on the Internet, the photos she took and the publicity she brought."

"The one with the prince's affairs? I didn't realize that you were working on that," Monsieur Bosset said.

"That one. And the boys, the owners, have helped me evaluate some artwork I found, which goes back to the time of Calvin," Mireille said.

"We are having the Savarys for dinner next week, along with the Favres," Madame Bosset said.

"Annie went to England and then did some research here as well and we found out who the artist was."

"Interesting," Monsieur Bosset said although his tone implied otherwise.

"Daniel, the Favre son is back from Dubai. Do you remember

him?" Madame Bosset said.

"Vaguely. He was too far ahead of me in school for me to have much to do with him."

"He's joining us. Why don't you come too?" Madame Bosset asked. "I know the Favres would love to see you again . . . how long has it been now . . . two . . . three years."

"Are you matchmaking, Maman?"

"It wouldn't hurt for you to find someone like Daniel," Madame Bosset said.

"And settle down," Monsieur Bosset said.

No one had been doing much eating. Mostly shredded carrots and lettuce were being pushed around the plates.

"I think you should tell them, Mireille," Annie said.

"Tell us what?" Madame Bosset asked.

"I'm having a baby."

Both parents put down their forks. Annie thought the cliché "the silence was deafening" would have worked to describe the moment.

"Who is the father?" Monsieur Bosset asked.

"When is the wedding?" Madame Bosset asked.

Mireille was staring at her plate. "The father is dead."

Monsieur Bosset put down his napkin and stood up. "Mademoiselle Young, will you excuse us please. Mireille, *Chérie,* in my office. Now!"

Annie wondered what to do next. She pushed back her chair and looked out the window. She heard the sound of raised voices then silence then raised voices, but she couldn't make out the words. A door slammed.

Mireille appeared with her coat on and Annie's over her arm.

"We should go," she said.

Chapter 64

Geneva, Switzerland

The wind was cold as Annie jumped off the Number Three trolley and walked the half block to the four-hundred-year-old Café du Soleil. The blanket, hanging in the alcove between the door and entrance to the brasserie, helped keep out the cold. Annie was hit by the warm air, half from the heating and half from all the clients crowded around every table.

She hoped Mireille had remembered to make a reservation. This was a place where artists, musicians, and writers, locals, workers in the international community and all the UN agencies met. If she'd forgotten, they would have to find someplace else.

Then Annie saw Mireille wave from the corner. She pushed through the crowd maneuvering around the mismatched wooden chairs until she reached the one free chair in the restaurant opposite her friend. Taking off her coat she draped it over the back of her chair.

The waiter arrived with the menus.

"We know what we want," Mireille said. "*Viande séchée,* a fondue for one, five deciliters of Fendant and a cup of black tea." When Annie frowned, Mireille said, "A little wine won't hurt the baby all that much. Besides we're celebrating."

"Celebrating what?"

"My thesis. I went over it with my new advisor." She paused and waited for Annie, who cocked her head as if saying,

"And . . . ?"

"He approved what I've done so far. If I can continue at the same pace, the baby and the thesis should arrive one after another, although I'm not sure in which order."

"Fantastic!"

"I really wanted to order champagne, but I can sip a couple of swallows of wine, whereas having to drink *only* a sip of champagne—well, that would be torture."

A shadow appeared across the table. When the women looked up, they saw an acquaintance, the brother of one of their classmates. "It's impossible to be here without seeing at least one person you know," the man said.

"No place for a *rendez-vous*," Annie answered.

"Or a perfect place, because no one would believe anyone having an affair would be stupid enough to come to such a well-known spot," Mireille said.

The waiter appeared with a plate of the dried meat accompanied by pickles and cocktail onions as well as a pitcher of white wine. The man, giving the women the required three-cheek kiss, wended his way back to his own table.

"What about you, Annie? When are you heading back to Argelès?"

Annie shrugged. Roger had been unhappy, although he said he understood that she did not want to leave Marc, despite her parents' open-arms policy toward him. "Dad convinced him to go back to school, reminding him about university next year. He needs to prepare for *la matu* and he has to keep his grades up if he wants to get into EPFL next year."

"Surely they would understand that having your mother arrested for murder is a slight destabilizer." Mireille ground some pepper onto the almost transparent slices of meat before winding it around a pickle and taking a bite. "He had so many problems with his parents, and what is a damned shame is that he was proud of what they did. He thought that his mom was great for developing medicines and now that one was used to kill his father, it must be terrible for him to cope."

The waiter removed the empty meat plate and sat down the flaming hot fondue and a basket of thick slices of white bread with thick crunchy crusts. Each woman put a piece of bread onto her fork and swirled it. They ate silently.

Mireille's piece came off her fork, and she moved the melted cheese back and forth trying to locate it. When she couldn't she speared another piece of bread and dipped it into the pot. "Or maybe it would be better for him to drop out and go back in the fall for his last year."

Annie had no idea what would be best for the boy. Last night, just as she was about to turn off her light to go to sleep, he had knocked on her door.

"Can I talk with you?"

"Of course."

He was already in his pajamas or at least the bottoms. He wore a white T-shirt for the top and one of her father's old bathrobes that had a ratty belt, which he fiddled with, once he sat on the bottom corner of the bed. He didn't say anything for a long time.

"So you want that we look at each other?" Annie had asked.

He almost smiled. "Maybe?"

She pushed herself up and moved her head so she was staring at him without blinking as long as she could.

They used to have blinking contests when he was little.

He lost. "I guess I don't have the concentration I used to."

"You do have a few things on your mind." The room was chilly, her parents already having turned down the heat for the night. "So talk."

He fiddled some more with the belt. Despite his slight beard, his posture was that of an unsure little boy, afraid to tell his parents something he had done wrong.

"Spill," she said as she had so often when he was in grade school.

"Do you have to go back right away?"

"You want me to stay?"

His eyes filled with tears and he turned his head away.

Annie got out of bed and turned his head.

"I'm too old to cry."

They'd been through this before. "No, you're not. There is no age limit on tears when you've been through the stuff you've been through. And it's scary."

"I'm too old to be scared."

"You're never too old to be scared either. Grown-ups just get better at hiding it."

"It's not that your parents aren't wonderful or anything." Annie knew that. Her father had helped Marc find a top lawyer for his mother. He had gone with him to the place where Maria-Elena worked to pick up her personal items. The company hadn't fired her, but they had put her on indefinite leave without pay until she was cleared. At a moment when Marc couldn't hear, Dave Young had told his wife and daughter about Renatus Pharmaceutical's belief that Maria-Elena wasn't coming back.

"I hate to have them stay in Geneva because of me. I know they want to get back to Caleb's Landing."

My parents don't do things they don't want to do." Annie knew he was right, but they had said to her they felt Marc's needs were greater than theirs.

"They will go back after the school year ends and of course you can go with them."

"Not if that is when the trial is."

"I suspect the trial won't begin until fall. At least, that's what the lawyers think." Also not a good time for Marc if he were starting university. Time out for him seemed like a better and better idea.

"It's just that since I was little . . . and we could . . . you know . . . I mean, I could tell . . ."

"You could tell me anything, and it's harder for you to talk to my parents."

He'd nodded.

"I'll stay for a little while," she'd told him. "Or at least come back and forth."

This time he had smiled, and Annie realized she had not seen him smile since they told him about his mother's arrest. "Really."

None of this would she share with Mireille.

Annie said to Mireille, "So tell me more on the thesis."

"Once he saw my tables of repeated colors, types of clothing, themes, I had my new advisor fascinated. I am beginning to think the thesis is going to run at least a thousand pages excluding the tables. I suppose I should be grateful to Urs for being such a hard taskmaster."

"He certainly didn't let his relationship with you make work on your thesis any easier for you."

"That didn't bother me, but on one level I was always wondering if he would take my research. Not in the beginning of course . . . I brought this." She delved into the gigantic multicolored cloth bag which she had placed between her chair and the wall.

Annie thought Mireille might be bringing out part of her thesis, but instead she handed her a small black-and-white photo of a fetus. "Voilà, the latest photo of my daughter. Now tell me she's beautiful."

Annie took the copy of the sonogram. "She's beautiful. Any thoughts on names?"

"Carrie, Miranda, Samantha. I always did love *Sex and the City.*"

Annie extinguished the flame under the fondue pot, and the waiter came over to scrape the burned part of the cheese for them to nibble on. When he left she asked, "Do you think it would help if I tried to talk to your parents?" She tapped the photo, which she had placed on the paper covering of the table. "Maybe even showed them this. It *is* their grandchild."

Mireille shook her head. "Maybe the real thing might work, but I wouldn't give it much more than a ten-percent chance. Flexibility is not their greatest quality."

"If you want me to. I can stay for a while when the baby is born." She could just imagine how Roger would feel about that.

Mireille reached across the table and grabbed both of Annie's hands. "You're a really good friend. Maybe if she's a cutie, we'll try it . . . or not." She dropped the sonogram into her bag.

A man and woman came in and sat next to them seconds after the two men that had been occupying the table had left. The waiter cleaned up around them, and as soon as he had laid a fresh paper covering and left tableware, the woman said in an English accent, "I don't like the smell, Garth."

"It's the cheese, honey."

"Do they have anything else but cheese?" the woman said. Annie couldn't identify which part of England she was from, but it wasn't a North American accent. However, the Café du Soleil was a regular Babel because of its popularity with the internationals.

"There is a good lentil salad."

The woman frowned.

"You know how you tell the children when they make a face, if they aren't careful, their face will freeze . . . ," Garth said.

"You're not funny."

The waiter stopped at their table but Garth sent him away.

"The menu is in French." The woman let out a sigh.

Garth translated several things. "You should sign up for a

language course."

"Not with that stupid school system where the kids come home for lunch. And at different times even."

"There I have to agree with you, but you thought my flat in Ferney was too small. The French schools have a canteen."

"I wish I'd never come here."

Annie and Mireille exchanged looks. Annie took a chance that the man did not understand German, *Ich wettete, dass er wünscht sie nie kommen lassen zu sein.* Annie was positive she was right in the man wishing the wife had not come and Mireille, whose German was weaker than Annie's, understood enough to nod.

"Do you want tea or dessert?" Mireille asked.

Annie shook her head. "I want to get to Rive to catch the E bus."

"You could stay with me tonight."

"Marc." If they could hear what the neighbors were saying, the neighbors could hear what she was saying.

The cold air seemed even colder than when she entered although the big thermometer on the store across the street still registered a couple of degrees above freezing. Before she and Mireille kissed good-bye, Annie said, "I thought of a great name for the baby."

"What?"

"Elizabeth . . . after the artist of the paintings you found."

Mireille stopped to look both ways before they crossed the street to take a left to walk home while Annie was taking a right to wait for the trolley at the Petit Saconnex stop. Although there were no cars at that time of night, she didn't move. "Elizabeth. Elizabeth. Elizabeth. What a great idea."

"You like it?"

"It'll at least be the working name. And now that she has a name, would you consider being her godmother?"

Annie threw her arms around Mireille. "I'd be honored to be Elizabeth's godmother. Not that I'm religious, and if that bothers you . . ."

"I'm not religious either, but she needs a godmother, and, well, we've been friends for so long."

The Number Three trolley rambled its way toward the Petit Saconnex stop and Annie shouted a *"Bonsoir,"* burst across the street and ran half a block to hop on the last car. Only two other people were riding with her. The temperature had been jacked up so she undid her scarf, took off her woolen hat and shoved her mittens in her pocket.

A godmother. She liked that. Annie's biological time clock had never gone off, and she suspected it wouldn't. It was not that she didn't like kids . . . she did . . . other peoples'. She was great for taking friends' kids to parks, movies or even babysitting. She adored Roger's daughter. However, none of that meant she wanted one of her own. If—no, make that *when*—she married Roger, she knew he would make a good father, but now that he was in his forties, and had a teenage daughter, his desire to start over with diapers and midnight feedings was limited, he had told her, but had added that if she really, really wanted a baby, they should begin trying now.

"Not now," she'd said.

She thought of the picture of the fetus, her future goddaughter. She imagined buying pretty little dresses for her, although she had had enough experience with kids to know that it was more likely the baby would throw up on the dress. She imagined spelling Mireille for a couple of nights when the baby was little, and taking Elizabeth to the park when she was older, or just sitting and coloring with her.

As happy as she was for Mireille with the baby, with the thesis, something about the conversation was bothering her, but she couldn't make out what it was. The trolley rattled through the deserted streets. Geneva was not a night town, especially during weekdays.

She changed for the Number Sixteen trolley at the train station and arrived at Rive in time to run madly to catch the E bus for home. And as the bus turned toward Corsier along the lake, she realized what it was. She would have to call Roger as soon as she got home. He was going to be so upset.

CHAPTER 65

Geneva, Switzerland
November 16, 1559

Guillaume had promised to come after midnight and free her. She knew the guard Henri was on duty tonight. Henri curled up in furs and went to sleep as soon as the other guard left, something she had known from listening to his snoring through the wooden door.

Henri never awakened her in the middle of the night as the other guards did, sometimes shining a candle in her face, sometimes using the moon as a light as they prodded her with their feet. Her body bore their bruises as well as that of the beatings during her questionings. Those marks were beginning to heal, for she had not been questioned in the last two weeks. Guillaume had said that was because they had set a trial date, a week from today.

The conclusion of the trial was predetermined. She would be declared a witch. Her spells had killed Jean-Michel's baby.

She had turned butter rancid.

When she visited a neighbor, she spoiled the milk as she did in her aunt's house.

Another neighbor had lost her cat because of something Elizabeth had done, although no one was clear on what that was.

She had been observed dancing in the light of the moon by a farmer's wife after curfew out in the countryside with a figure that looked like Satan. Elizabeth knew she had never been anywhere near the place, but the woman was prepared to give evidence, Guillaume said. The "facts" had mounted and mounted making the trial a formality.

Guillaume's plan was simple. He and James would come after midnight and if Henri awakened one of the men would knock him out. She found it hard to think of gentle Guillaume doing anything as violent as knocking a man out. They were bringing rope to tie up Henri.

Guillaume had promised her that the horses would be ready in the nearby wood. Because Uncle Jacques did not give generous salaries to his young lawyers, saying that poverty forced them to work harder, she had no idea how they could even finance one horse, much less two, but Guillaume had said when her cousin had arrived he had with money with him.

Her grandfather hadn't deserted her after all.

Elizabeth was afraid that the plan would not work, but when she told Guillaume, he reminded her that getting out of Geneva was her only chance of survival and that he was going with her—she allowed herself a dollop of hope.

Guillaume told her to act naturally until he could get there. She had smiled at that. What could she do differently in the small hut? What she wanted to do was make the time go faster, but instead she forced herself to sit quietly as she did all evenings. The hardest part of her captivity had been having nothing to do. Her keepers told her that if they gave her anything to read, anything to sew, anything to keep her hands busy that she could use it to cast spells.

The only thing that had kept her sane was imagining herself creating sketches, dreaming where she would put each line. In her imagination she had colored pencils with which she mentally shaded people, still lifes and nature's beauty. When the guards would ask her what she was doing, she would say she was praying in hopes that word would get back that she really was a

God-fearing woman.

However, the response of the guards were statements like:

"God doesn't listen to witches."

"You'd better."

"It's too late to save your soul."

Her dinner had been an egg and a piece of bread. The guard had brought in a pitcher of scum-covered, mud-smelling water.

She was so sick of being hungry, cold, dirty and exhausted.

Her eyes had grown accustomed to the small shafts of light that filtered through the slits of her prison hut. On a bright day when the door was opened to the outside, the sunshine hurt her eyes. But she hated to look away, because a glimpse of grass and trees, even for less than a minute, had become a gift.

Thus she waited, huddled under her cloak in the dark.

The door opened, banging against the wall.

Elizabeth jumped at the sound of wood hitting stone.

A man wrapped in a cloak so his identity was not readily apparent looked around and, seeing no one, said, "Where could she have . . ."

He didn't have time to say "gone" before Elizabeth shuddered at the voice and stood up. "She couldn't have *gone* anywhere. Your eyes aren't used to the dark, Uncle Jacques. This is a surprise." The fear, as much a part of her being as blood and skin, increased.

Her uncle whirled around and shut the door. "I don't want you to escape, although you would not get far."

"I can't really." Although common sense told her it was smarter to be deferential, at this point she hoped Guillaume would not come while her uncle was here.

"You won't be leaving tonight," Uncle Jacques said.

"I don't understand."

"I think you understand very well. Your little plot with my former employee came to light when he sold his mother's affairs. You bewitched him, my darling niece."

Elizabeth did not say anything. What can one say when a last hope is destroyed? She knew there was no chance for her at a trial.

CHAPTER 66

Corsier Port, Switzerland

"I can't believe you didn't tell me."

Annie's ear felt the ice in his voice through the phone. When she arrived home everyone had been in bed. She had headed to her room, closing the door so her parents sleeping across the hall would not hear her. Marc was one floor up, and she certainly didn't want him to hear what she had to say.

What would be the best way to tell Roger?

Right out.

He hated indirectness from her as she did with him. No matter how she said it he would be furious and mostly she wouldn't have anyone to blame but herself. Although she hoped she was wrong about what she thought, she was equally sure that she was right. And this was one time she hated the idea of her being right.

"*Oui, hallo,* Perret." His voice sounded sleepy.

She imagined him in the king-sized bed that they shared more nights than not when she was in Argelès, although some nights she still went back to her nest, a bit to retain her independence and a bit to get a night's sleep without hearing snoring. "It's Annie."

"Hmmm."

"I need you to wake up."

She could hear a rustle and she imagined he was sitting up in bed and putting on the light. "Is something wrong with you?

Your parents? Marc?"

"We're all fine. I've something to tell you, and I know you'll be angry." She knew better than to ask him not to be angry.

"You're not breaking up with me?"

She has been so off and on about their relationship, she didn't blame him for thinking that first. Maybe this time, he would want to break up with her. How could she explain that she didn't think he needed to know the information because the possibility of what she was about to say had never entered her head. "Marc's mother is innocent."

"You woke me up to tell me something I know."

"Mireille did it."

Silence.

"She was having an affair with Stoller."

"When did you find out?"

"The first night I was back here." She could have lied, but it would be the first time. With all their other differences since they met, dishonesty was too costly to their couple.

"God damn it, Annie, and you didn't tell me that?"

He couldn't see her shake her head. Nor could he know that tears were forming behind her eyes.

"I promised not to tell anyone. It could have jeopardized her thesis."

"You and your ability to keep a secret. Why can't you be like other women and spread gossip?"

In other circumstances that would be funny, but Annie knew he hadn't meant to be funny, so she said nothing.

"I think a murder investigation is a bit more important than a thesis." His voice was cold, the words spit out.

"I just couldn't think of her as a murderer. Especially when she was having his baby?"

"She's having his baby?!"

"Please don't yell."

"I'll yell if I want to!"

"Papa, what's the matter? I heard the phone, and you're yelling!" Annie could hear another voice in the background.

"Gaëlle, go back to bed. Annie and I are having a disagreement."

"You aren't going to break up again, are you?"

"Break her neck, maybe, break up, no. Now go to bed."

"Gaëlle worries about us," Annie said.

"Don't change the subject."

"There's more. Mireille was angry with him about stealing some of her work. And he gave her incorrect information about the value of some drawings that she found that turned out to be worth a lot. He stole a couple of them, although I don't think she knew it at the time she killed him."

"The motive is building, but that's . . ."

"It's true that she didn't find out about how much the art was worth until after he was dead."

"I will call Morat in the morning. I'd call him tonight, but I don't have his home phone number." He chuckled. "It will be good for his career if he can break the case, and it will be good for Fortini to realize that he was wrong."

"But there's more."

"More?

"Mireille and I went out for a fondue tonight. She wanted to share good thesis news, show me the sonar of her daughter, ask me to be the godmother." Oh God, what would happen to the baby now?

"Café du Soleil?"

"Where else do we go for fondue? Anyway we were talking about Marc and she mentioned that it had to be hard for Marc to know his father was killed by his mother with a product that she had developed, one that wasn't on the market yet."

"Did you tell her that? I told you in secret."

"I keep your secrets too. I don't know how she could have known if she hadn't been the one to give him the medicine."

"Annie, I'm not sure how they'll prove that, but I think you just rescued Marc's mother."

"Are you still angry with me?"

"Yes, but not as much as I love you. However, I think I'm going to take a day or two off and come up and help Morat with this one. Be prepared to meet with the police."

CHAPTER 67

Geneva, Switzerland

Annie stood her ground at the *Cornavin* train station as early-morning commuters bustled around the train station. Roger emerged from *quai* eight, his backpack over his shoulder, looking sleepy eyed. His kiss—only on her cheek—half said that he was still annoyed with her, which was definitely an improvement from the beginning of their phone conversation last night.

"We're meeting Morat at Mont Brilliant." Annie glanced at her watch. "In twenty minutes."

The hotel restaurant coffee shop was out the back station door and up a few stairs. As they entered, a breakfast buffet for hotel guests had been set out.

"We're not guests, but we'll be having breakfast," Roger said to the waiter who greeted them. "We'd like an out-of-the-way table."

The waiter led them to the back of the room. The chairs were covered in a dark blue. The table had matching napkins. By the time Christian Morat arrived, they were on their second cups of coffee.

"I didn't expect to see you so soon. In fact, I didn't expect to see you at all." Morat shook Roger's hand.

As they ate, Annie brought Morat up to date. The three decided not to bring Fortini in at this point but that Roger and Morat would go question Mireille.

"I'm coming," Annie said.

"No, you're not," Roger said.

"You guys aren't on official business. It's Morat's day off, and you have no authority." I think I can help in getting her to talk." Annie lifted her coffee cup to her lips but didn't drink. "Jeez, I sound like some TV cop."

"You can't come," Roger said.

"Wait a minute, she may be right," Morat said.

Mireille was still in her pajamas when she answered the door. The computer glowed in the background.

"I have already been working since five," she said. "But a break will be nice."

The four of them sat at the kitchen table. Because the leaves had fallen off the trees they could see across the Route de Ferney to the park with its white *château.*

As they had role-played in Morat's car on the way over, Annie was to start. "Mireille. Did you kill Urs?"

Mireille jumped up so fast she had to catch her chair before it fell. "Are you crazy? Of course not. Why would you say such a crazy thing?"

"Because you knew he was killed with a blood thinner." Annie almost whispered the words. She fought to not cry. She wanted her friend to be innocent, but she knew she wasn't.

"You must have told me."

"I didn't."

"Then I read it in the paper."

"It was never in the paper," Morat said. "The blood thinner was deliberately never mentioned to the press, because that is one of the things that can cause a trial to fail."

"Then Marc . . ."

"Marc didn't know either," Roger said. "He still doesn't."

"Yet you told me at the Café du Soleil that Marc must feel badly knowing his mother killed his father with a drug that she had helped develop."

Mireille stomped into the living room, followed by Roger, Morat and Annie. The two men sat and Annie followed Mireille around as she paced. Annie grabbed her friend, "Tell us."

Mireille sank onto the sofa and put her head in her hands.

Annie motioned for Morat to move over then she put her arms around her friend, who buried herself in Annie's shoulder. "Tell me. Then we can decide what to do next."

"I loved him."

"I know you did." Annie patted Mireille's head.

"He stole my work, he lied about the value of the artwork I found. I saw the evaluation so I called the expert in Paris, only there was no such number."

"Did you confront him?" Morat asked over Annie's shoulder.

"Are you crazy?" Mireille sat straight up and looked at Morat. "He would have ravaged my thesis."

"So you decided to kill him?" Roger said.

"Not right away. It was about two weeks before, but things kept getting worse."

No one said anything.

"I found out he was also sleeping with another student, Fabienne Forestier."

"I don't know her," Annie said.

"No reason you should. She's twenty-two, a law student."

"Did you accuse him of that?"

Mireille shook her head.

"How did you get the blood thinner?" Annie asked.

"From Maria-Elena."

Annie wondered if the two women were involved in the murder together, wife and mistress against one cheating bastard.

"When Urs was on a trip to give a presentation in Göttenburg, she invited me down, which was unusual, because I know she suspected we were having an affair. I thought maybe she was going to accuse me outright, so I didn't want to go, but not going would have been impolite and maybe it would confirm her suspicions about Urs and me."

"So how did you find about the blood thinner?" Morat asked.

"There were six lab bottles with pills in them on the coffee table. The conversation started out politely. I asked her about her work. She told me they were working on a blood thinner. Maria-Elena was in the habit of keeping, at home, samples of different batches of whatever she was working on."

"Strange," Roger said.

"Not really. Urs had said his wife was superstitious. She thought having six samples were like good luck charms. Six was her lucky number."

"Lucky charms are out of character for a scientist," Roger said.

"Urs blamed it on her Latin American childhood," Mireille said.

"And how could you take them without being noticed?" Annie asked.

"When Maria-Elena went into the kitchen to make coffee, I opened all of the bottles and put three pills from each into my bag. I didn't think she would notice a few gone from each, and I was right."

"And then . . . ," Roger prompted.

"She came back. The real reason she invited me was to ask if I was having an affair with Urs."

"And you denied it."

"Of course. She told me she'd found a woman's lipstick in his pocket, which is how I found out he wasn't faithful to me. She showed it to me, and it was a color I'd never wear. I told her that having an affair with a thesis advisor was a really stupid thing for anyone to do, and I wasn't stupid. She said Urs never went after stupid women. But I don't think she believed me.

And I think letting me know that I wasn't his only lover made her happy."

There was silence before anyone said anything. Annie reached over and put her hand over Mireille's. "How upset you must have been."

Tears spilled over onto Mireille's cheeks. She didn't brush them away but took a long sniff. "That was the same day I took the pregnancy test."

"Did you tell Urs?"

"Not that night. Two days later, I had him over for a romantic dinner. Marc was away on some overnight school trip and Maria-Elena was staying in Basel. That was the mess you found when you arrived, Annie. We had sex, because I no longer could call it making love. The man screwed me."

"In more ways than one." Annie ignored Roger's frown. "But where did you do it?"

"I suggested since it was such a beautiful fall night that we take the boat out. Urs loved being on the lake at night. It was still early, about twenty-one hours. He took the car and I took the bus to rue Vermont where he picked me up. I suggested we spend the night on the boat since neither of us had anything to do first thing in the morning. At first he wasn't too keen on it, but I reminded him we could make love again. I used the words make love. Urs may have been in his fifties, but he was as strong as a twenty-year-old. Viagra would go broke if all men were like him."

Again there was silence as Roger and Morat waited for her to say more. This time Annie said nothing, but just squeezed Mireille's hand.

"Once on the boat I made him a decaf coffee. I put the pills in that. We were about halfway to Yvoire when he dropped anchor and said he didn't feel all that well, light-headed."

Annie held back the impulse to say, "And then?"

"Two hours later he was gone. I had to struggle to get him up the stairs and over the edge of the boat. I guess adrenaline gave me more strength. I brought the boat back, rowed into shore, left the dinghy where it always is."

"But you weren't here when I came."

"I came back to the flat, took a couple of things and went to my parents' house for a couple of days."

"How did you feel?" Annie couldn't imagine killing Roger and being so matter of fact. But then Roger treated her wonderfully.

"Calm, relieved." Mireille sighed. "A little sad that Urs wasn't what I had thought he was." She pulled her hand out from under Annie's. "I really loved the man I imagined and probably still do, but he doesn't exist."

Annie bit back, "Not now, he's dead."

"What's next?" Mireille asked.

"We need to take you to headquarters," Morat said. "We'll give you time to get dressed."

"May I shower?"

For a second, Annie worried that Mireille might try to kill herself, but she put that aside. She doubted if she would kill the baby. Still she listened attentively as the shower ran and there were various bumps and movement noises. Once she heard the hair dryer, she didn't worry. Mireille was vain enough to want to look good.

From where she was sitting she saw Mireille rush by in her robe, and she heard the opening and closing of closet doors, dresser drawers, and the cabinet where Mireille kept her shoes. She was back and forth through the hall getting different things.

"Are you almost ready?" Annie asked.

"Almost."

The two men said nothing, but all three of them heard the front door of the flat open and shut and the click of a key.

In less than two seconds they were at the door. Mireille had locked them in.

"Annie, do you have a key?"

Annie nodded. "But it's in Corsier."

"Merde," Morat said. "We need to call the station. Fortini will love this."

He dialed the station and asked for the Big Boss and related what had happened. She must have asked, "How do you know?" because he pulled out a small recording device and played some of Mireille's confession back to her. As he talked to her, he paced up and down.

CHAPTER 68

Corsier Port, Switzerland

Marc was in his bedroom under the eaves in the Youngs' house. The mattress had been stripped, and used sheets, pillow cases and a duvet cover were piled on the floor.

Annie sat in a straight-back chair in front of the desk and watched him shove his freshly washed clothing in his backpack. "You're right to go back to your mom's."

He didn't say anything.

"It is just the two of you."

He still didn't say anything.

Annie had talked with Marc's mother the night before. Maria-Elena had been released the preceding week. She had promptly resigned her job and was interviewing with two other companies, she'd said. Annie wasn't sure if it were her choice or the company's. In the *Tribune de Gèneve* that morning there'd been an item about a new Renatus drug failing in its trials. Although she suspected it might be the blood thinner, Annie wasn't sure.

"Do you think they'll ever catch Mireille?" Marc asked.

"I don't know. She's got enough money to last her for a while, but all her other plans are shot." Half of Annie wanted Mireille to escape. The other half didn't like the idea that a murderer would go free. The two points of view battled each other: personal versus theory.

She wondered where Mireille could have gone. French-speaking Canada? One of the French territories? How would she work without papers? What would happen with the baby? Despite the fact that her friend had killed someone, and with premeditation, she wished her well without approving of her actions. She would keep these thoughts to herself. Roger would not understand. Her parents might, for they were seldom judgmental.

If Mireille were to stay in hiding she needed to be careful and not travel with fake documents. Interpol now had lists of stolen passports, and some airlines checked the list against passengers.

Annie could not imagine what her friend's life would be like from now on, living in fear of discovery, trying to raise a child.

Marc interrupted her thoughts. "Your parents said I could still spend the summer with them in Caleb's Landing if I pass my *matu.*"

Annie knew that. Her parents had debated keeping Marc with them until his exam, but they thought he should try and reestablish a relationship with his mother. The two had never been without Urs's influence, and maybe with him gone, things might be better.

"Your mom also said that if it doesn't work out with my mom by April, I can come back," Marc said. "She added it wasn't an excuse to sabotage whatever chance I have of developing a good relationship with my mother."

"Sounds like my mom," Annie said. She had sat in on the what-to-do-with-Marc strategy session, but she wasn't about to share that information with him.

"For the first few days you're back with your mom, I'll be down the hall getting my flat ready to sublet. You can come down anytime."

"Like old times."

"Like old times."

Except that it wasn't like old times at all, but she knew Marc would be fine.

CHAPTER 69

Geneva, Switzerland
December 1, 1559

Elizabeth had been transferred from her hut to inside the wall and to a cell. Her trial had lasted less than a morning. The verdict came down before the last witness left the room. Guillaume was not there and her uncle defended her, if you could call confirming the witnesses' testimony against her a defense.

How strange it was to know that this was the day you were going to die. Would she have felt differently if she were older? If she had done more paintings, loved more, brought forth a child?

She would never see England, run where her mother had run as a girl, talk to her cousins. And what had happened to her cousin James? Asking her uncle or the guards would only call attention to his presence in Geneva and she didn't want to endanger him.

Nor did she know what had happened to Guillaume.

If only she had clean clothes, and could comb her hair. If she must die, she would do it with dignity.

James and Antoine stood on the side of the hill away from the pyre of wood that was close to half a story high. Dried pine branches with dead brown needles filled in the cracks. In the center, a pole stood above it all. In the middle, six stairs had been built and on the top was a chain and lock.

A crowd had already gathered to watch the witch burn.

As a little boy, James had had nightmares almost every night and his mother would awaken him and hold him until he fell back asleep. This was a nightmare from which he never would awaken. Never could. Never! How he would tell his grandfather he had failed at his mission, he did not know.

"I've heard that the city fathers feel that if Guillaume prays enough, and if they pray for him, they will be able to undo the spell Elizabeth cast on him. He won't die, at least," Antoine said.

James pulled Antoine's cloak tighter around him, although this was the first sunny day since the verdict had come down. The snow that had fallen last week was melted, and, for once, no *Bise* blew cold from the lake. Still he was bone cold.

A man walked by them. "The witch has changed the weather for her death day," he said with a smirk.

"Thank you for leaving some of her drawings with me," Antoine said to James. "It will give us memories of her."

The rest of the drawings James had tied to his chest under his shirt. That was all he could give to his grandfather and father in memory of a daughter and sister. Had she not been transferred to the city jail the same day that Guillaume had been arrested, they might have stood a chance of a rescue, but breaking her out of that prison was impossible.

James had wanted to go to the court and offer to take her away, but Antoine warned him that he too might be tried for witchcraft.

Thank God, that after his cousin was dead, he would leave this strange city, never to return. People could not smile at the ordinary pleasures of life, but let some be killed and they would smirk.

The crowd grew restless. Antoine used his elbow to nudge James and his head to point to the left of the woodpile.

A cart, drawn by a brown horse inched its way through the crowd.

"Satan's whore," someone called.

"Hell will take your soul," someone else screamed.

Elizabeth looked ahead, her back straight, her head held high. She did not turn when people screamed insults at her.

She must have been pretty before all this, James thought.

The cart stopped. Because her hands were tied behind her back, it would have been impossible for her to get down from the cart without falling. Two guards, one on each side, lifted her to the ground. She shrugged them off and walked to the pyre.

Six steps had been built in the middle and she mounted them, one by one until she reached the long pole, where she would be tied. Elizabeth turned around and leaned against it, and the guards secured her with chains.

The main judge stood below and asked her something that James could not hear.

She did not acknowledge his presence.

The judge nodded and a man carrying a flaming piece of wood touched the dead pine needles: little flames became bigger, igniting the faggots, then larger and larger pieces of wood until James could only see the fire and not his cousin.

FOREIGN WORDS
USED IN THE TEXT

apéro. Snacks and a cocktail.

ârret demandé. A passenger's request for a bus to stop.

avocat. A lawyer.

bac. The exam French high-school students must pass to graduate.

bande dessinée. A comic book.

boulangerie. A bakery.

Bise. A wind that regularly attacks the Geneva area.

canicule. A heat wave.

cave. A cellar or basement.

con. Impolite slang insult similar to asshole.

coup de foudre. Literally, a thunderbolt, but used to mean love at first sight.

crémerie. A store in which dairy products are sold.

fac. Slang for university.

flic. Slang for police officer, but used much like the American word cop.

Grand Conseil. The ruling body of Calvinistic Geneva.

grippe. Influenza, the flu.

pâtisserie. A store for baked goods, usually made fresh on-site.

Petit Conseil. The lesser governing body in Calvin's Geneva.

plage. A beach.

Régies. Real-estate agents, who oversee most of the property in Geneva.

rösti. A regional food much like hash browns, from the German-speaking section of Switzerland.

Vieille Ville. The old town in Geneva.

vrai. True.

Read ahead for a preview of
the next exciting entry in the
Third-Culture Kid Mystery series featuring
part-time tech writer Annie Young!
Murder in Paris
COMING JUNE 2013

"YOU *FORBID* IT?" Annie Young stared down her fiancé, Roger Perret. The couple was seated at his long oak kitchen table in the French coastal village of Argelès-sur-mer.

"I forbid it." He sat at an angle to her, turning the knife he had just used to peel an apple: blade to handle, handle to blade, blade to handle. Each time he turned, it clicked against the green tile table.

Annie stood up so fast her chair turned over bringing it crashing to the red tile floor. The skin on the back of her legs where they had stuck to the green leather hurt with the suddenness of the movement, but she chose to ignore it. Still, anything more than shorts and a T-shirt would have been too warm to wear. Despite the July heat, the thick walls kept the house cool in comparison to outside and definitely cooler than the temperature of the couple.

"I've a chance to work on a dig in Paris where they've found enough of a fourteenth-century inn to get an impression about it, and *you* forbid me to go?" Annie righted the chair. "I don't believe it." With all their ups and downs, if he didn't realize how important her passion for historical research was, he didn't know anything about her.

"I've gotten used to you going off on this or that *paid* writing assignment. *Mon Dieu.* I never know if you'll be in Zurich, Amsterdam or . . . or . . . Someone invites us somewhere, I can only tell them if Annie is still here blah, blah, blah. I've gotten used to this; that's your work . . . but this is a *freebie*."

Any other time she would have been amused by his use of the word freebie with his French accent. The couple went back and forth between English, French and Franglais. She thought they had worked through the major problems of the earlier stages of their relationship, before she had finally agreed to an engagement. She knew he still hated that she earned her living working part-time as a tech writer taking short-term contracts all over Europe.

She wished he could be proud that she was multi-lingual—English, Dutch, French and German. She wished he could be proud that she earned top money working less than six months a year. The rest of the time she spent indulging her passion: historical research, the same research that he didn't want her to do now.

"It doesn't matter that I'm not getting paid. This is the chance of a lifetime."

"The only reason you were asked is because Luca is your ex-boyfriend. You're not an archeologist."

It was true, she wasn't. But she had taken a course in it, and her translation and research skills on what was found would be valuable to the project. And it was a short-term project. Roger touched on the truth when he said that Luca sought her out because he knew her. Luca was as passionate about his work as she was about her love of history.

When Luca was excited about something, he talked faster and faster.

During his call inviting her to come to Paris for three weeks, the time allotted by the city for the dig, she'd had to keep asking him to slow down so she could understand his Italian-accented French. But she had caught his excitement at the chance to excavate the remains of a building hidden for centuries in Paris's Latin Quarter before a modern building would make it disappear—perhaps forever.

"Luca and I dated six months when he was on an exchange from the University of Rome to the University of Geneva. That was over ten years ago."

"But you've kept in touch with him all this time."

"He's a friend."

"He's Italian."

Annie didn't know how to answer that. Roger was not normally jealous.

ABOUT THE AUTHOR

D-L Nelson is a Swiss writer who grew up in Boston, MA, and the author of six other Five Star novels: *Murder in Argelès, Murder in Caleb's Landing, Running from the Puppet Master, Family Value, The Card* and *Chickpea Lover (Not a Cookbook)*. She lives in Geneva, Switzerland, and Argelès-sur-mer, France. Like Annie, she knows what it is like to be torn between cultures. She only wishes she had as many languages as Annie does. Visit her blog at http://theexpatwriter.blogspot.com.